FATAL FALL

When we emerged from the ladies' room, the hallway was empty. I pushed open the heavy fire door that led to the stairwell and Faith ran on ahead. Quickly she trotted down two flights of stairs with me hurrying to keep up. We had only one flight to go when I heard a door open above us.

The sound of hushed voices echoed through the vertical chamber. More of my fellow contestants, I guessed. I probably wasn't the only one whose dog didn't like elevators.

Quick footsteps tapped a staccato beat on the metal steps above us. Then I heard a sudden scream. It was followed quickly by a series of thumps. Faith and I both froze where we stood.

"Hello?" I called out. No one answered. Only my own word echoed back . . .

Books by Laurien Berenson

A PEDIGREE TO DIE FOR

UNDERDOG

DOG EAT DOG

HAIR OF THE DOG

WATCHDOG

HUSH PUPPY

UNLEASHED

ONCE BITTEN

HOT DOG

BEST IN SHOW

JINGLE BELL BARK

RAINING CATS AND DOGS

CHOW DOWN

HOUNDED TO DEATH

DOGGIE DAY CARE MURDER

GONE WITH THE WOOF

DEATH OF A DOG WHISPERER

THE BARK BEFORE CHRISTMAS

LIVE AND LET GROWL

Published by Kensington Publishing Corporation

CHOW DOWN

A Melanie Travis Mystery

LAURIEN BERENSON

KENSINGTON BOOKS
http://www.kensingtonbooks.com

KENSINGTON BOOKS are published by

Kensington Publishing Corp.
119 West 40th Street
New York, NY 10018

ISBN-13: 978-1-4967-0484-9
ISBN-10: 1-4967-0484-3
First Kensington Hardcover Edition: September 2006
First Kensington Mass Market Edition: August 2007

eISBN-13: 978-1-61773-144-0
eISBN-10: 1-61773-144-7

10 9 8 7 6 5 4 3 2

Printed in the United States of America

1

Champions Dog Food Company
1066 Industrial Avenue
Norwalk, CT 06855

Dear Melanie Travis:
Congratulations!

We are delighted to inform you that your Standard Poodle, Champion Cedar Crest Leap of Faith, has been selected as a finalist in our "All Dogs Are Champions" contest. The winner will be named the official spokesdog for our new dog food, Chow Down, and will be awarded an exclusive advertising contract in the amount of one hundred thousand dollars. The essay and pictures you submitted on your Poodle's behalf were very persuasive; we quite agree that Faith would make a superb representative for our product.

Being chosen from among the thousands of entries we received is both an honor and an achievement. As outlined in the contest rules on the entry form you submitted, each of the five remaining candidates must now make themselves available to compete in the final phases of the selection process. We appreciate your cooperation in this matter, and a representative from Champions Dog Food will be contacting you shortly so that arrangements can be made for a personal interview with Faith at your earliest convenience. Thank you for your interest in Chow Down dog food and, once again, our heartiest congratulations on being chosen as one of our finalists.

Sincerely,

Doug Allen
Vice President of Marketing
Contest Chairman

Huh? I thought.

Not the most scintillating response, but hey, it was early. I'm never at my best before my first cup of coffee.

I stared at the letter in my hands, hoping that a second reading might help my comprehension. It didn't.

Chow Down dog food? I'd never even heard of it. And I certainly hadn't entered Faith in any contests, much less submitted an essay and photos. The Poodle in question was one of five—all big black Standards—currently snoozing on my kitchen floor.

Faith was highly intelligent but I'd never seen her compose a letter or lick a stamp. And why would she have wanted to enter a contest? Fame? Fortune? She already had all the dog biscuits she could eat.

That brief flight of fancy was enough to send me straight to the coffee maker on the counter for what was obviously a much-needed jolt of caffeine. Summer mornings, I grab the chance to sleep late whenever I can. During the other, more productive, nine months of the year I teach at a private school in Greenwich, Connecticut. From the moment my alarm goes off at six-thirty, I'm up and running. So by the time June arrives each year, I'm ready for a break and the unaccustomed luxury of a little laziness.

Sam and Davey, my husband and eight-year-old son, respectively, had risen at least an hour earlier. Over dinner the night before, there'd been talk of building a tree house in the backyard. That had led to plans for an early-morning visit to Home Depot to purchase supplies.

Sam had gotten up, let the dogs out, and started the coffee. Davey had brought in the mail and left it sitting on the counter. By the time I'd made my way downstairs at eight-thirty, both had disappeared. Only the five Poodles—Sam's and my recently blended canine families—remained.

Faith lifted her head as I navigated my way through the obstacle course of Poodle bodies. Her dark eyes watched me with avid interest. We'd been together for four years, and our bond went far beyond that of master and pet. Faith knew my strengths and exploited my weaknesses. She read my thoughts and anticipated my moods.

Right now, she knew I needed coffee. If she'd possessed opposable thumbs, she probably would have already poured me a cup.

As it was, I had to perform that task for myself. I added a splash of milk to the mug, carried it over to the back door, and walked outside onto the deck. We'd been in our new house less than a month and I was still getting used to the unfamiliar surroundings. Having a deck to enjoy was only one positive change of many.

I sat down on a chaise, drew up my legs underneath me, and breathed in deeply. Later the day would be hot, but now the dew had yet to burn off and the morning air was fresh and cool. It smelled of honeysuckle and roses; both bushes grew wild over the fence that enclosed the large expanse of our new backyard.

I had left the screen door open. One by one, the Poodles picked themselves up and followed me outside as I'd known they would.

Faith had been part of my family since she was a puppy. So had her daughter, Eve, born two years earlier in a whelping box next to my bed. Sam and I had gotten married in the spring, and his three Standard Poodles—Raven, Casey, and Tar—had been added to the mix.

All five were show dogs; the three oldest were retired champions. The youngsters, Tar and Eve, were still "in hair," which meant that they sported the highly stylized continental clip that was required for competition. The continental is the trim of pom pons, shaved legs, and big hair; the trim that makes Poodles unique, eye-catching, and sometimes a little goofy-looking; the trim that gives rise to the notion—not without due justification—that Poodles are clowns with a great sense of humor.

Tar was Sam's "specials" dog, a title that identified him as one of the best of the best. He'd finished his championship handily at a young age and now competed against champions in other breeds for the prestigious group and Best in Show wins. Eve, hampered by having me for an owner handler, was nearly finished herself. Only one more major win was needed to put the coveted title of champion before her name. It was a goal I was hoping to accomplish over the summer.

The thought of summer plans reminded me of the letter I'd left sitting on the counter. I wondered if it might be some sort of scam and if a request for money would follow shortly. The letter looked genuine, but how could the contest committee have gotten Faith's name, much less her photograph?

Sam wouldn't have entered one of my Poodles without my consent. Our marriage was new enough that we were still feeling things out and finding our way, but we'd been a couple for several years. I knew him well enough to be quite certain he wouldn't have done something like that without checking with me first.

Without the slightest pause, my thoughts slid directly to the next most likely culprit: my Aunt Peg. Margaret Turnbull was a force of nature; one I alternately embraced or cursed, depending on the circumstances. On good days, Aunt Peg was a blessing. On bad ones, her presence was akin to an itch that I couldn't quite reach, or a pebble lodged inside my shoe.

Peg could be imperious and demanding; living up to her expectations was a constant challenge. Never satisfied with less than anyone's best, she held herself to the same high standard. Aunt Peg had been a mainstay on the dog show scene since before I was born and she'd taught me everything in the world I knew about Poodles. Half the time she drove me crazy, but there were few people in the world that I loved more.

Might she have entered Faith in a contest on a whim? It seemed unlikely, but where Aunt Peg was concerned, I'd learned never to discount any possibility.

I got up, walked inside, and retrieved the letter and a telephone. Aunt Peg's number was first on my speed dial list, a testament to how often we spoke. I didn't even hear a single ring before she picked up. A perfect, drowsy summer morning and Aunt Peg was in a hurry. Somehow I wasn't surprised.

"What?" she barked into the phone as I carried it outside and settled back down on the chaise.

"It's me," I said.

"I know that. I have caller ID. How's the tree house coming?"

Trust Aunt Peg to be up to speed on all current events, even those that had been decided upon only the evening before. I think she has some sort of subliminal radar that keeps her constantly apprised of what we're up to. A network of spies wouldn't surprise me, either. I know for a fact that she has ears like a bat.

Need I mention that she had accepted Sam's proposal before I did?

"It's still in the planning stages. Sam took Davey to Home Depot to buy lumber and nails. If I'm really lucky they'll come home with a general contractor."

"Pish," Peg scoffed. "I can't see any reason why

Sam wouldn't be perfectly capable of constructing a tree house on his own."

"That's because he's never tried to repair your ice-maker or rewire your microwave."

I love Sam dearly, but Mr. Fix-It he isn't. I let him change my oil once. That was a learning experience. Now I've gone back to doing it myself.

"All things considered, lumber seems fairly safe," Peg mused. She'd been at the dog show with me when my engine had seized.

"Yes, but he's not building this structure on the ground. He and Davey are going to be up in the air."

"How high?"

I looked out across the yard. Davey and Sam had chosen a lovely old oak tree with a thick trunk and spreading branches for their project. A fork midway up seemed like a likely choice. "Fifteen feet?"

"I suppose someone could break a neck falling from there."

"Go ahead," I said, "make me feel better."

"That's what I'm here for." Aunt Peg sounded cheerful. "Would you like me to come and supervise?"

Heaven help us all. We'd end up with a Taj Mahal on stilts, or the Petite Trianon in a tree. Deftly I changed the subject.

"Actually I'd rather have you answer a question."

"Excellent," said Peg. "I'm good at that."

"What do you know about Champions Dog Food?"

"They make a perfectly decent product and, I believe, a fairly popular one. Despite their company name, they've targeted their previous marketing mostly toward the pet owning public, though it seems they're currently looking to change their focus."

"How do you know that?"

"I received a couple of flyers in the mail. I might even still have one lying around here someplace."

I heard the sound of papers being shuffled, but Aunt Peg never stopped talking.

"I got the impression that the company had bought some kennel club's mailing list and done a mass mailing to local exhibitors. I'm surprised you didn't get a brochure yourself. There was a promotion for a new product with a perfectly ghastly name . . ."

"Chow Down?"

"That's it," Aunt Peg confirmed. "So you did hear about it."

As of ten minutes earlier, yes. Though I didn't remember receiving any brochures. Which wasn't to say that one might not have been overlooked. My days were generally so busy that anything that arrived looking like junk mail was promptly disposed of unread.

"Apparently they're running a contest . . ." I let the thought dangle for a moment, just in case Aunt Peg might want to jump in and make a full confession.

"Right. That was what the new promotion was about. Although why any self-respecting breeder would want her dogs associated with a kibble with an odious name like Chow Down, I have no idea."

"So you didn't fill out an entry form?"

"Heaven forbid." Peg laughed. "Hope and Zeke are not about to go prancing around on television touting the virtues of anything, much less a dog food that sounds like it fell off the back of a wagon train."

Hope was Faith's litter sister. And Zeke was Eve's brother. Our canine families, like our human one, were indelibly intertwined.

"Why the sudden interest in Champions Dog Food? Are you thinking about switching to a new brand of kibble?"

"Nothing that easy," I admitted. "I got a letter from the company this morning. To my surprise, Faith has been named as one of five finalists in their 'All Dogs Are Champions' contest."

Aunt Peg gasped. Or maybe she was laughing. "*Faith* has?" she sputtered. "Well, why didn't you *start* with that information? I would imagine you must know a great deal more about the company than I do."

"Hardly. This is the first I've heard of them, or their contest."

Aunt Peg moderated her tone. Like she was speaking to a child, or a particularly slow relative. "Then why did you send in an entry?"

"I didn't. I have no idea where they got Faith's name from. Or her picture."

There was a brief pause. Then Aunt Peg said, "Oh."

The single syllable spoke volumes.

"Yes?"

"Maybe it's nothing."

"I doubt it." Years of experience backed up my reply.

"You might remember that I gave Davey a digital camera for his last birthday."

Of course I remembered that. My son adored his present. He'd quickly become adept at capturing all of us in his photographs. We'd printed up the results on Sam's printer and stuck the best ones up on the refrigerator with magnets.

"About a month ago, Davey called and asked how to email someone a picture. I couldn't see the harm in telling him."

Oh, indeed. "And you didn't stop to wonder why he hadn't asked me or Sam for help?"

"I just assumed you were busy."

If Aunt Peg had been a wooden puppet, her nose would have been growing.

"Did you happen to ask where he was planning to email the pictures to?"

"No, I didn't. It seemed to me that an almost nine-year-old boy was entitled to have some secrets."

"Not when he's on the internet he isn't," I said firmly. "Did you help him write the essay, too?"

"I did not!"

As if I would be impressed by a show of outrage *now*. "I thought maybe that was another secret."

"Oh, pish," said Aunt Peg. "Stop being annoyed long enough to think things through. Apparently Davey took photographs and wrote an essay that was polished enough to beat out thousands of other silly, ambitious people who were all trying to turn their beloved pets into the next Morris the Cat."

She had a point. My heart swelled briefly with pride at Davey's achievement. I was still annoyed, though.

"I like my beloved pet just the way she is," I grumbled. "Happily anonymous."

"Perhaps you ought to try explaining that to Davey."

"I suppose I should."

"After that you can simply call the Champions Company and decline the honor. Let the contest committee choose some other, equally deserving dog to serve as finalist."

"Good idea."

"You see?" said Aunt Peg. "Problem solved."

As always, she made things sound so simple.

I'd been in this spot before, though, and I knew there'd be a catch. There was always a catch.

It was only a matter of time until I found out what it was.

2

"We're home!" Davey sang out as he came barreling through the front door.

As if anyone who lived with a crew of large, attentive watchdogs could possibly have been oblivious to that fact. I hadn't heard Sam's SUV come up the driveway, but the Poodles had. Scrambling to their feet, they'd deserted me without hesitation. No doubt Sam and Davey's return seemed more likely to provide biscuits and other forms of excitement than my talking on the phone had.

"In the kitchen," I called back.

I'd left the deck and started to follow the dogs toward the front of the house, but Davey was moving faster than I was. Perennially hungry, he must have come inside and headed straight for food. He raced through the doorway as I was putting the phone back on the counter.

My son had shot up two inches in the last year. Suddenly when I looked at him, I saw only lingering echoes of the little boy he'd been. It was hard to believe that in another year he'd be ready for middle school.

"Hey," said Davey.

His sandy brown hair hadn't seen a comb that morning; his cargo shorts were at least a size too big. A T-shirt from the Norwalk Maritime Center floated, untucked, around his narrow hips. He sketched a wave in my direction, slipped past me, and grabbed an apple from the fruit bowl on the table.

"Hey yourself. How was the shopping trip?"

"Productive," Sam said. He walked into the kitchen, his Poodle escort trailing along behind. "We got everything we needed. Once we get it all unloaded, we'll be ready to start building."

Unlike Davey, Sam didn't sidestep around me. Instead he dropped the plastic bags he was carrying onto the counter and folded me into his arms for a quick kiss.

It was a crime that anyone could look that good first thing in the morning. Then again, Sam had the kind of appeal that wore well at any time of the day: shaggy blond hair, direct blue eyes, and a face that only grew more interesting with age and experience. Amazing, I thought, as I leaned into him, that this man was now my husband.

"Sleep well?" Sam asked.

"Umm . . ."

With Davey in the room, I wasn't about to elaborate. But one look at the expression on Sam's face told me I didn't have to. Married for three months, we were still honeymooners. Both of us had been blissfully worn out by the time we'd dropped off to sleep the night before.

I stepped back out of his arms and said, "You're

not going to kill yourself climbing around in that tree, are you?"

Sam grinned cheerfully. "I hope not."

That was reassuring.

"What about Davey? He's my only son and heir, you know."

Something flickered briefly in Sam's eyes, and I felt a small pang. Both of us were eager for another child. We'd been trying but so far it hadn't happened.

When Sam spoke, however, his tone was light. "Don't worry. Kids his age don't go splat, they bounce."

"Charming." I peered into a bag. I saw two boxes of nails, a new tape measure, and a small hammer, the size that Davey could easily wrap his hands around.

"We aim to please," said Sam.

Davey only giggled. The notion of bouncing—or going splat—apparently held more appeal for him than it did for me.

"I got something interesting in the mail this morning," I said.

"What was it?" Sam had followed Davey to the fruit bowl. He selected a banana and began to peel it. "Coupons for free pizza? An envelope from Publisher's Clearing House? Did we win a million bucks?"

"Not quite. Though apparently one of our Poodles may be on the fast track to fame and fortune."

"Faith?" Davey perked up. "Did she win the contest?"

Well, I guessed that answered my next question.

"What contest?" Sam asked, banana poised in the air midway to his lips.

" 'All Dogs Are Champions.' "

"They are?"

"That's the name of the contest. It's sponsored by the makers of Chow Down dog food."

"I've heard of them. They're headquartered around here somewhere, aren't they?"

"Norwalk," Davey said impatiently. "They're in Norwalk. Did Faith *win*?"

"Not quite. But she's been named one of five finalists—"

"Yippee!" my son shrieked. He began to twirl in circles around the room.

"Not so fast, Lord of the Dance. Did it ever occur to you that it might have been a good idea to check with me before you went ahead and entered Faith in a contest?"

"Umm . . . no."

Davey's exuberant steps never even faltered. I watched him and sighed. I supposed, if nothing else, I had to give him points for honesty.

"Faith is a champion," Sam pointed out. I don't think he had a clue what was going on.

"That's what I told the people at the booth," said Davey.

"What booth?"

"The Chow Down booth. They have one at all the dog shows."

"They do?" I'd never noticed. Then again, when I'm at a show I'm usually busy either exhibiting or getting Eve ready to go in the ring. I seldom spend time browsing the concessions.

"That's where I found out about the contest. The man told me they were trying to get show dogs interested in eating their new kibble."

"Presumably they were trying to attract the dogs' owners," Sam said under his breath.

"No," Davey corrected. "The food is for the dogs. I told the man about Faith and he gave me a brochure and an entry form. There was a web site to go to and I filled everything out online."

"All without mentioning it to me?" I said again.

"I couldn't *tell* you," Davey said earnestly. "It was supposed to be a *surprise*."

"Trust me, it was."

"Is this the letter?" Sam picked up the sheet of paper from the counter. His eyes skimmed down the page. Midway through, he was biting back a smile. "A personal interview with Faith . . . ? I'd like to see that myself. This sounds like quite an undertaking."

"It sounds like *fun*," said Davey. "Faith could be famous. She could make lots of money! She could be on TV, like in commercials and everything. Everyone would know who she was!"

Maybe that seemed like a good thing to an eight-year-old. To me, it sounded like a nightmare. I've never understood the appeal of fame. Fortune, sure. Who doesn't like money? But thanks to a video game Sam had designed years earlier, he and I already had more than enough.

Besides, it was summer. This was supposed to be my time off. I had no desire to shepherd Faith through the final phases of a selection process for a contest I didn't particularly want to win.

"The notification letter was addressed to me," I said.

For the first time, Davey's eyes slipped away.

"Did you sign my name on the entry form?"

Davey developed a sudden interest in his apple. "Not exactly," he mumbled.

"Then what did you do?"

"The form was online, so I just typed your name in."

A small distinction, but at least I didn't have to add forgery to his crimes.

"The owner of the dog was supposed to sign. Faith belongs to me as much as she belongs to you . . ." Davey looked at me for confirmation and I nodded. "Except that . . ." Another pause, then he blurted out the rest. "You had to be over the age of eighteen to enter."

A rule imposed to prevent an occurrence like this one, presumably.

"Please, Mom!" Davey pleaded. "Just give it a try and see what happens."

I glanced at Sam, who merely shrugged. This was going to be my decision.

"I'll tell you what," I proposed. "I'll call the company and find out what the contest is all about, see how much time and effort it would take to continue on with the selection process. But until I have a clearer idea of what's involved, I'm not making any promises—"

"Yippee!" Davey shouted again. "Faith is going to be famous."

Oh joy.

The phone call to Champions Dog Food went just about as well as the conversation with Davey had.

After Sam and Davey had gone outside to unpack the car, I dialed the number on the letterhead and asked to speak with Doug Allen, the contest chairman.

"May I ask what this is in reference to?" the receptionist inquired.

I considered for a moment, then said, "No."

Obviously it wasn't the answer she'd been expecting.

"Is it about the results of the contest we're currently running?" she asked after a pause. "Because if it is, I need to inform you that the decision of the judges is final. We at Champions Dog Food are terribly sorry if your pet wasn't selected, but with so many worthy applicants to choose from . . ."

The woman sounded as though she was reading a prepared speech. I wondered if the company had actually been fielding phone calls from disgruntled losers. And more to the point, since I'd found out only that morning, how did the people whose dogs hadn't been chosen already know the results?

"That isn't the problem," I broke in. "My dog is supposed to be one of the finalists."

"Oh well that's different, then. Congratulations! In that case, you'll be contacted shortly—"

"I've already been contacted." It was an effort not to grind my teeth. "Otherwise how would I know she'd been chosen?"

"The preliminary results were posted on our web site last night," she said helpfully. "And it's been a madhouse around here ever since. Well, frankly, it's been like that ever since the contest started, if you want to know the truth. We hoped the contest would strike a chord but we never expected a response like this. Who would have guessed there were so many people who were dying to get their dogs on television?"

Who indeed? I wondered. Davey was eight. What was everyone else's excuse?

"I'll get Mr. Allen for you right away."

I was put on hold and left to listen to music that my grandmother would have found boring. "Right away" turned out to be ten minutes. I spent the time watching Sam and Davey unload what looked like enough lumber to build a second garage. Or maybe an addition to the house.

Surely they weren't planning to haul all that up into the branches of the old oak? The tree would probably collapse with both of them in it. And if I was really unlucky, the Poodles, all of whom had gone outside to oversee the project, would be under the tree when it came down. That gloomy thought was interrupted by two quick clicks, then I was reconnected to a live person.

"Ms. Travis?" Doug Allen sounded bright, highly motivated, and more enthusiastic than anyone had a right to be about dog food. "Sorry to keep you waiting! How are you and Faith doing this morning?"

"We're fine but—"

"I'm happy to hear that! And congratulations, by the way. I want you to know, getting this far was no small feat. Not only that, but it's going to be one heck of a competition from here on in."

"That's what I wanted to talk to you about—"

"Each of our five finalists would make a very worthy spokesdog for Chow Down dog food. Narrowing the selection process down further is going to involve splitting some very fine hairs, if you'll pardon the pun! Not that all our remaining competitors are long-haired dogs, of course. That would hardly be fair, now would it?"

I assumed the question was rhetorical. Good thing because Doug didn't pause long enough for me to answer.

"Of course you would know that by now. I'm sure you've looked on the web site and scoped out the competition. Let me tell you, though, just between the two of us"—his voice lowered confidentially—"I've always been partial to Poodles. I mean, what's not to like about a breed that combines beauty and brains with such panache?"

At least Doug Allen had good taste.

"Nothing," I said quickly, wedging in the word when he paused for breath. "Poodles are superb, they're wonderful dogs. But they're not pushovers. They have minds of their own. They don't eat just anything that's put in front of them like Labs or Beagles do."

"Oh, we're not worried about that. All dogs like Chow Down."

"How do you know?"

Suddenly I found myself picturing an eat-off among the finalists. Five dogs and five big bowls of Chow Down dog food: a race to see who could gobble down their kibble with the most gusto. Eve liked most foods, but Faith was finicky. She liked to take her time and sample new things slowly.

"We've done taste tests, of course! They were an integral part of the development process. Every dog that saw Chow Down lapped it right up."

"Were they hungry?"

"Pardon me?"

"Were the dogs hungry when you fed them? Had they missed a meal or maybe two?"

Doug seemed surprised by the question. "Well I should think so. That would be the whole point, wouldn't it?"

Or perhaps the point was that a dog that was hungry enough would eat almost anything. Rather than mentioning that, however, I steered the conversation back to the topic I'd meant to discuss.

"What I wanted to ask about is how much of a time commitment I'd be looking at. You know, in terms of Faith continuing on with the selection process."

"Pretty extensive, I'd say. Choosing just the right spokesdog to represent our product and our company isn't something we take lightly. It's important for us to see the dog as it will appear in a variety of challenging situations. First on the agenda will be the personal interviews. And then all of you will be vetted by our PR department and focus groups. We've booked an appearance on the *This Is Your Morning Show*, which will be followed by a press conference . . ."

Doug kept talking, but I was so stunned by the enormity of what he was proposing that his words had stopped registering. Focus groups? Appearance on a morning show? Those didn't sound like the kinds of things I needed to have on *my* agenda. Especially not when I was supposed to be enjoying a lazy summer with my new husband and my darling child who—at that moment—I could cheerfully have strangled.

"Listen, Doug," I said. Amazingly he stopped speaking. "I'm not really sure that any of this is going to work for me."

"What do you mean?"

"I mean I don't think Faith is the dog you're looking for."

"Of course she is! Or at least," he quickly amended, "she might be. You're just feeling overwhelmed by the enormity of the opportunity. Believe me, her chances of being chosen are as good as anyone's. Better than some, though I shouldn't say that—so let's just keep it between us. Several members of our committee loved Faith, adored her, in fact. She was a very, very popular choice."

"Thank you," I said firmly, "but I'm afraid she needs to be unchosen."

There was a long moment of silence. Then Doug said slowly, "That's not possible."

"Sure it is. You're right, this is an honor and a wonderful opportunity. But for somebody else, not us. We respectfully decline. Go get your number six pick and bump them up."

"We can't do that. The announcement's already been made on the web site. The media's already been notified. Faith's picture was included in all the material that went out. Changing things now would undermine the integrity of what we're trying to accomplish and I'm afraid we can't allow that to happen. People who have been following the contest will expect to see a big black Poodle eating Chow Down dog food."

"Maybe I didn't make myself clear," I said. "I'm withdrawing my entry."

"Maybe I was the one who wasn't clear," Doug shot back. "You can't do that."

"I hardly see how you can stop me."

"When you submitted the entry form, you were making certain warranties about the ownership and availability of your pet. You entered into a binding contract. All of that was spelled out on the web site and in the brochure. Didn't you read the fine print before entering the contest?"

I hadn't read *any* print, that was part of the problem. Admitting that, however, would only get Davey in trouble, so I didn't bother.

"Let me read it to you," said Doug. "Wait a minute, I have it right here.

> "I, the undersigned, agree to abide by all rules and conditions of this contest, as spelled out above, including but not limited to permitting my dog's name and likeness to be used in print or television advertising as deemed suitable by the Champions Dog Food Company . . ."

Doug continued reading but once again I'd stopped listening. It was beginning to look like Faith would be remaining a finalist whether I wanted her to or not.

That part was bad enough. Even worse was the fact that, left to her own devices, Faith was a formidable competitor.

If I wasn't lucky, she might just go ahead and win the whole damn thing.

3

"Let me get this straight," said Bertie. She was trying hard not to laugh. And not entirely succeeding, I might add. "Davey entered Faith in a dog chow contest and now you have to spend your summer chauffeuring her around to auditions?"

"Something like that." The prospect didn't sound any more appealing now than it had two days earlier when I'd finished speaking to Doug Allen.

Bertie was a dear friend and my sister-in-law, having married my younger brother, Frank, two years earlier. She was also a professional dog handler and mother to six-month-old Maggie. Like most women I knew, she was habitually overcommitted and overworked, and occasionally underappreciated.

Bertie, however, multitasked with aplomb. Now she was combing out the topknot on a Miniature Poodle, looking over the day's schedule that was taped to the inside of her grooming box, and making fun of me. Simultaneously.

Oh, did I forget to mention that we were at a dog show? Well, we were. It was Saturday and we were gathered at the Mid-Hudson Kennel Club event in Dutchess County, New York, where Bertie had a dozen dogs entered in nearly as many different breeds. As for me, I was hanging out and helping her groom. Though Eve still needed a major to finish her championship, I had elected not to show her.

One of the good things about being an owner-handler is that if you don't approve of a judge's knowledge or credentials, you can decline to enter. Professional handlers don't have that luxury. They show—rain or shine, week in and week out—exhibiting their clients' dogs in front of experts and buffoons alike.

Some days they look like heroes. Other times they go home with almost nothing to show for a long day's hard work. It was a tough way to make a living, but Bertie thrived on the competition. Plus she was very good at what she did.

When Bertie and I met several years earlier, Aunt Peg and I were showing Standard Poodles and Bertie was showing almost anything but. Like many of the terrier breeds, there are exacting requirements for the upkeep and presentation of Poodles' coats. They're a specialized breed, not for those who lack patience or artistic talent.

The previous summer, however, Bertie had attended the Poodle Club of America national specialty, fallen in love with the breed, and decided that Aunt Peg and I were going to teach her everything she needed to know about Poodle hair. Along the way, that had evolved into our current situation, where I was working as Bertie's part-time assistant at the shows, and Aunt Peg was overseeing our efforts with her usual imperious elan. Fortunately, for the sake of our relationship and my sanity, I refused to take my position as underling very seriously.

"So how good is this Chow Down stuff anyway?" Deftly Bertie parted the hair on the Mini's head with a knitting needle and began the process of putting in the tight, show ring topknot. "I've never even heard of it."

"It's a brand new product." I was working on a Standard Poodle that belonged to one of Bertie's clients, scissoring the long hair in his mane coat as he stood atop a rubber matted grooming table. "I don't know if anybody's tried it yet, except the groups they've test-marketed it to."

"Sounds yummy," said a voice from the next setup. "Chow Down. What self-respecting dog wouldn't want to dive right into a bowl of *that*?"

The voice, and the arch delivery, belonged to Terry Denunzio. He was partners with one of the top Poodle handlers in the Northeast, Crawford Langley, and the two of them were frequent competitors of ours.

We often set up next to one another at the shows, as Terry was always entertaining to be around. He'd never seen an occasion he couldn't turn into a party. Even Crawford, who was quite a bit older and supremely dignified, had finally begun to turn a benevolent eye toward his handsome partner's shenanigans.

Bearing that in mind, I wondered what the handler thought about Terry's current outfit. Usually impeccably dressed, today Terry had veered off the straight and narrow and was heading directly toward camp. His muted plaid shirt was crisply ironed, his silk tie a complementary shade of steel blue. But inexplicably he'd wound a lavender feather boa around his neck.

Every few minutes a stray breeze would waft under the grooming tent and the feathers would ripple and lift into his mouth. Unfazed, Terry would spit them out and keep grooming. If he wasn't going to acknowledge the eccentricity of his attire, I certainly wasn't going to bring it up.

"I don't think Faith would actually have to eat the stuff every day," I said. I'd been feeding another brand of kibble for years and wasn't looking to make any changes. "All she'd have to do is look as though she likes it when they're filming."

"So much for truth in advertising," said Terry.

"Is there truth in advertising?" Bertie raised a brow. "I wasn't aware of that."

"Funny," I said. "And don't worry, it's not going to come up. Faith isn't going to win. I didn't even find out about this stupid contest until she was already one of the finalists. The only reason she's still in it is because it's too late for us to back out."

"I can't believe you want out," said Terry. He was running a comb through a small, ice-white Maltese. "I can think of at least a dozen people here today who'd give anything to be in your position."

"Really?" That surprised me. "Here?"

"Why not here? This is a dog show, isn't it? That's the whole point of Champions' new campaign. Chow Down is supposed to be a premium brand, marketed toward breeders and exhibitors."

Aunt Peg had said something about that as well. Was I the only one who was oblivious to the latest developments in dog food? I glanced over at Bertie, who shrugged. Maybe it was a Mom thing. We had other stuff to worry about.

"A couple of our clients entered their dogs in the contest," said Terry. "We had to scramble around to get them just the right kind of pictures. One even sent a professional photographer over to the kennel to do a photo shoot."

"I think Davey emailed a couple of photos he'd snapped of her around the house with his digital camera," I said with a laugh.

"Don't tell that to Allison and Bill Redding. They were promoting their Brittany, Ginger, as a triple threat. You know, conformation and obedience, plus she competes in field trials, too."

"Is that all?" I said, still laughing. "Faith can probably keep up. Let's see . . . She's a champion, she has her CD in obedience, and I'm pretty sure she'll jump through a hoop if you hold a biscuit on the other side."

"There you are, then," said Bertie. "She's a natural."

"Marion Beckwith entered Harry," said Terry.

My scissoring slowed. "Her *husband?*"

"No, Harry the Bernese Mountain Dog."

"Now that you mention it, her husband looks like a Bernese Mountain Dog," Bertie commented.

"Isn't his name Harry?" I was still confused.

"No, he's Harvey," Terry told me.

"Are you sure?"

"Of course I'm sure. Harvey's the one who signs the checks that pay our bills."

"And they have a dog named Harry?"

"And a daughter named Hettie." Terry sighed. "Don't even ask."

I didn't and we all went back to work. Poodles were due in the ring in twenty minutes.

Hardly any time had passed before Terry looked up again. "Speaking of which—"

"Which what?" Bertie had finished putting in the topknot. Now she was looking around in her tack box for hair spray. "Harry or Harvey?"

"Neither."

"Then we weren't speaking of them."

"Don't be so literal," Terry rolled his eyes. He relished the role of drama queen and lived up to the title with gusto. "Is it any wonder I like men better than women? A man would at least let you get an entire thought out before interrupting."

"That's probably because he wouldn't be listening in the first place," I said.

Bertie nodded in agreement. Terry ignored us both.

"Speaking of husbands," he said in a chiding tone and directing the question to me, "where's yours? He didn't want Tar to add another group or Best in Show to his record?"

My scissors were moving fast again, snicking tiny bits of hair off the rounded bracelets on the Standard Poodle's legs. I didn't pause or turn to look at Terry as I replied, but he knew the drill. He hadn't expected me to. "Sam's not here because he didn't think today's judge would be likely to appreciate Tar's better qualities."

"I can't imagine why not. Cruella Melville is a very discerning judge."

"*Drucilla* Melville," Bertie corrected him without missing a beat. "And she is very discerning. She just happens to judge the wrong end of the lead."

Politics. It was a common problem at dog shows, exacerbated by a system that rewarded judges for applying for additional breeds whether they felt qualified to preside over them or not. Judges who had faith in their own abilities rewarded the best dogs. Those who didn't often relied on an exhibitor's reputation to guide them to a correct decision. Professional handlers flocked to judges like that; owner-handlers knew better and stayed home.

"Of course, darling," said Terry. He and Crawford were among Mrs. Melville's favorite exhibitors. "That's why we're here."

"Me, too," Bertie admitted. "I know it's not fair but my dogs will get their share, my owners will be happy, and it pays the bills."

The reality of dog show life.

"Sam and Davey are spending the day building a tree house," I told Terry.

Bertie glanced over. "I thought they were working on that two days ago."

"They were. It's turning out to be a big project. At this rate, I wouldn't be surprised if it keeps them busy all summer."

"Who's busy this summer?" asked Aunt Peg.

I jumped slightly as she came up behind me. Luckily I'd been talking rather than scissoring at the time. You wouldn't think that a woman who was nearly six feet tall would be so light on her feet. Then again, Aunt Peg has plenty of surprising facets. The ability to keep everyone on their toes whenever she was in the vicinity was merely one of them.

"Where did you come from?" I asked.

"Ring six, Tibetan Spaniels. I'm thinking of applying for them next and they had an excellent entry today. It was well worth watching Danny Zimmer sort them out."

After decades of breeding and showing her own Poodles, Aunt Peg had applied for and been granted her judge's license several years ago. Her first breed had been Poodles, of course, then gradually she added other breeds from the Non-Sporting and Toy groups to her roster. Despite her years of experience in the dog show world, she still soaked up knowledge like a sponge. And when Aunt Peg was hired to judge, professional handlers and owner-handlers alike hurried to enter under her.

"Sam and Davey are building a tree house," I said in answer to her first question.

Peg looked at me as though I was daft. "I know that."

"It's why they're not here."

She crossed her arms over her chest and stared. Maybe Terry had been giving her drama lessons. "How about telling me something I don't know?"

"Okay," I said. "According to Terry, half the people who entered that ridiculous dog food contest are here today."

"Really?" Her gaze swung his way, eyes passing over the lavender boa without comment. "How do you know that?"

"I *always* have the latest gossip."

All too true. Terry usually had the best haircut and the smallest waist, too.

"I presume you called and relinquished your spot as one of the five finalists?" Aunt Peg said to me.

"I called and tried."

"You didn't succeed?" The notion was as foreign to Peg as it was repugnant. "How is that possible?"

"Apparently by submitting the entry, I agreed to abide by the contest rules, one of which was that I couldn't back out."

"Except that you didn't submit the entry."

"Semantics," I said. "Under the circumstances."

"Well, then." Aunt Peg rubbed her hands together. She didn't sound entirely displeased. "If that's the way things are going to be, let's have ourselves a look at the competition."

"Terry was telling us about a Brittany named Ginger," said Bertie. "Did she make the finals?"

"So I've heard," Terry replied. "Ad nauseam, if you'd like to know."

"That would be the Reddings," said Aunt Peg. She knows just about everybody. "They'll be hard to beat."

"Not a problem." I'd finished scissoring, now I was spraying up. "I don't want to win, remember?"

"Of course you're going to win, you're the one with the Poodle." Aunt Peg didn't think twice about overriding my objection. She turned back to Terry. "Who else?"

"Lisa and Larry Kim."

Peg looked briefly stumped but Bertie was able to fill us in. "Yorkies," she said. "Nice ones, too. I've shown against them plenty. Larry's tough, I wouldn't want to get in his way."

Aunt Peg nodded her approval. Toughness she understands. I knew she was handicapping the race in her head and I suspected she was finding her relatives wanting. "And?"

"Dorothy Foyle and MacDuff."

"Hey, wait a minute! I love MacDuff," I said, surprised. The Scottish Terrier was a relentless and venerable campaigner, winner of countless Best in

Shows. He'd been retired with great fanfare the previous year. "You'd think he'd have done enough already. I wonder why he was entered in the contest."

"Probably because he's won everything else but," Terry sniped.

"That's four," said Bertie, looking down at her watch. "Hurry up, Terry. We're almost due at the ring."

He stopped brushing the Maltese and counted silently on his fingers. Luckily there were only five finalists. "Who'd I miss?"

"*We* don't know," I said impatiently. Bertie was right, we needed to get the Poodles down off their tables and start heading over to the ring. I saw Crawford threading his way through the other setups, probably coming back to get his own Poodles. "You're the guy with the gossip."

"Shhh, not so loud." Terry dropped his voice. He saw Crawford coming, too. "It's Brando."

Bertie's head whipped around. Aunt Peg's eyes widened. Either response would have gotten my attention. Both, brought me up short.

"Who?" I asked.

"Brando the Boxer."

"Oh dear," said Aunt Peg.

"Ditto," said Bertie.

That didn't sound good, did it?

4

"What are you doing standing around talking?" Crawford asked. "Toy bitches are already in the ring." He leveled a look at Terry. "Were you going to bring me my specials dog or did you expect Drucilla to come over here and judge him at the setup?"

"Oops," Terry muttered. He slid the Maltese into an empty crate and swept Crawford's Toy Poodle up off another grooming table. Fortunately, aside from the bright pink vet wrap holding the little dog's ear hair in place, he was ready to go.

Crawford reached over and plucked the silver Toy out of Terry's arms. "This late, you'd better bring the Minis. You know Drucilla, she doesn't waste any time. Hey Peg, nice to see you."

The handler spun around and was gone again before anyone had a chance to utter a word.

"Who put a bee in his bonnet?" asked Bertie.

"It's nothing," Terry said quickly. "Absolutely nothing. All my fault."

Interesting, I thought. Terry never voluntarily took the blame for anything; indeed he never needed to. The man was made of Teflon. He'd never seen a sticky situation he couldn't wiggle out of with aplomb. Something was definitely up.

I would have asked Aunt Peg what she thought but, ever practical, she was already moving to lend a hand. She slipped between the rows of crates that marked the end of Bertie's setup and the beginning of Crawford's. Terry had three Miniature Poodles—all brushed out, sprayed up, and ready to go to ringside—and two arms.

"I've got one," Peg told him. "Let's go."

That left Bertie and me with her two, the Standard dog I'd been working on, and her Mini entry that was apparently due in the ring shortly. We loaded up gear and Poodles and joined the caravan heading across the grassy expanse between the grooming tent and the rings.

By the time we reached Drucilla Melville's ring, Crawford and his silver special were already inside and being judged. He'd been right, we were running late. Quickly I consulted with the steward and picked up our numbered armbands. I was sliding a rubber band up Bertie's arm to hold the numbers in place when Crawford was awarded Best of Variety.

Mrs. Melville made short work of her Mini dogs, then it was Bertie's turn in the ring with the bitch. She beat Crawford to win the Open class, then picked up two points and the purple Winners ribbon. Minutes later, both handlers lost to another pro in Best of Variety.

Waiting next to the gate, I took Bertie's Mini when she exited the ring and handed over her Standard dog. Since Bertie had already gotten her share of the winnings in Minis, neither one of us was surprised when her Standard Poodle managed to garner only a low ribbon in his class.

"How stupid is that," she said, as we headed back to the setup. "He's a better Poodle than the Mini. And he was better than the competition he was showing against."

"Yes, but Drucilla didn't know that," I pointed out. It was easy for me to be sanguine about the outcome. I wasn't the one who had just lost when I should have won. "All she knows is that if each of the pros who gave her an entry gets *something* to show for his efforts, everyone will go home happy."

Aunt Peg clucked her tongue. Crawford and Terry had gone back to the grooming tent after the Minis had finished, but Peg had stayed behind to watch the Standard judging. "You're beginning to sound like a cynic."

"Make that a realist," I said. "I didn't see you showing under her."

"You're right about that," Aunt Peg admitted. "On the other hand, I hardly show under anyone anymore."

Now that Peg was judging more frequently, she was concerned about the perceived conflict of interest in exhibiting under her peers. Instead, agility had become her new love. She and her Poodles had begun to compete in trials all over New England.

"I shouldn't complain," said Bertie. "Gina got two points. Her owners will be thrilled. I'm just sorry my other dog got robbed."

Back at the setups, Terry was drinking a diet soda. Crawford had disappeared again. I deposited the Mini I was carrying onto a grooming table and said, "*So?*"

Three pairs of eyes turned my way.

"Brando?" I prompted.

Surely I shouldn't have had to remind them. Before Crawford had interrupted us, both Peg and Bertie had looked like impending doom at the mere mention of the Boxer's name. Our half-hour break to show dogs—admittedly the reason we'd come in the first place—hadn't been exciting enough that I would have forgotten *that*.

"Oh right," said Bertie. She was running the end of a comb through the Standard Poodle's topknot, popping out the tiny colored rubber bands that had held the elaborate structure in place. "Bad news there."

"He belongs to Ben O'Donnell," said Aunt Peg. As if that explained everything. Which of course it didn't.

Since my relatives weren't proving to be much help, I turned to Terry. His Minis were back in their crates. The silver Toy was lying daintily on a folded towel, awaiting his turn in the group. And Terry was plucking at the Maltese again.

"Who is Ben O'Donnell?" I asked. "And if you want to throw in a little information on Brando, I wouldn't mind that, either."

"Ben's an actor," said Terry.

"He was an actor," Bertie corrected. "I'm surprised you haven't heard of him. *Moments in the Sun?*"

"The soap opera?" I asked. "Definitely not my thing. I work during the day, remember? What else might I have seen him in?"

"There was a corn chip commercial," said Terry. "And another for a new pickup truck."

"That one was a hoot," Bertie said. "Ben was

dressed up in cowboy boots and a big hat, and cows were milling around everywhere. Bear in mind we're talking about a guy who thinks that suburbs are the wide-open spaces. He looked pretty silly trying to walk bowlegged and pretending he was chewing tobacco."

"I saw that," said Peg. "Ben looked like he was afraid all those cattle might stampede and take him along for the ride. And I don't think he ever managed to drive the truck."

"Okay, so he's an actor," I said. "Perhaps not a very good one. And Brando's a Boxer. There must be more to the story than that. Is Brando a good dog?"

"It doesn't matter," said Bertie. "He doesn't have to be. Ben only shows to women judges."

"He's very hetero." Terry sighed. "More's the pity."

I was beginning to get the picture. "And very good-looking, I assume?"

"Enough to put a championship on a Boxer with a bad bite."

Ouch. "So Ben is handsome. And he apparently doesn't mind manipulating people. Anything else?"

Aunt Peg nodded. "Bertie was probably correct to talk about Ben's career in the past tense. At one point when he was younger and starting out, it seemed as though anything at all might be possible: parts on Broadway, character roles in movies, Shakespeare in the Park. But somehow years went by and none of that ever came to pass."

She paused for breath, and Terry took up the explanation. "After the stint in the soap opera, Ben's career pretty much stagnated. In any other business, he'd be in his prime. And Lord knows, the man looks *good*. But as an actor in his early forties, he's already a has-been."

"Don't let Ben hear you say that," Bertie warned. "He'd probably lop your head off and hand it to you on a plate. Facing reality has never been Ben's strong suit. His career might be fading, but he's not going down without a fight."

"Which brings us back to you," said Peg. "And this contest offering national exposure to the winner. Everybody knows how desperate Ben O'Donnell is to make a comeback. I'm betting he sees this as the way to make it happen."

"I read the contest rules," I said. No point in mentioning that I'd read them after the fact. "Chow Down is offering exposure to the winner's dog, not the owner."

"Don't kid yourself, Ben will find a way to shoehorn himself into the publicity even if he has to handcuff Brando to his wrist." Terry paused reflectively. "Though now that I think about it, the notion of Ben with a pair of handcuffs—"

"Terry." Aunt Peg glared.

"Yes, ma'am." He ducked his head.

"You guys must be exaggerating." I held up my hands as if forming a scale. "Chow Down dog food?" One hand rose. "Shakespeare in the Park?" The other plummeted. "What's wrong with this picture?"

"Plenty," said Bertie. "And the worst part about it is that Ben and Brando are in it at all. But you don't have to take our word for it. You can see for yourself what a sweetheart Ben is because here he comes now."

"Really?" Peg swiveled to look. I did, too. Then

Terry joined in for good measure. Which meant that by the time Ben O'Donnell reached us we were all standing there staring at him like a quartet of idiots with nothing useful on our minds at all.

I supposed he could be forgiven for tipping his head sideways and staring back. We must have looked rather odd. Not to mention the fact that we'd all suddenly fallen silent at his approach.

"Ben!" Aunt Peg said heartily into the awkward silence. "Imagine that. We were just talking about you."

"Really? Saying only good things, I hope."

The actor's smile was smooth and practiced and, all right, pretty darn appealing. He possessed the kind of rugged good looks that, at one time, would have been perfect for cigarette commercials; I could see why he'd been cast as a cowboy. Idly I noted that he was probably the only person on the show ground with better hair than Terry.

Whom, as it happened, he was staring at right now. "Nice feathers," he said.

"Thanks." Terry's grin was cheeky. Like maybe he was hoping the jury was still out on the whole hetero thing.

Ben didn't rise to the bait. Instead he turned and focused his attention on me. Beneath the cool shade of the grooming tent, being the object of his regard was like having a beam of sunlight turned in my direction.

"I know everyone else here," he said. "Which means that you must be Melanie Travis. I've been looking for you."

"You have?"

"Of course. Haven't you been looking for me?"

"Umm . . . No."

"That surprises me." His voice was low and smoky. His words sounded teasingly seductive.

"Why?" So help me, it was an effort to form the thought, much less the word. Behind Ben's back, Bertie was biting her lip. Terry was laughing at me openly.

"Because I understand you and I are going to share an adventure together."

"*We are?*" Belatedly I realized he was talking about the contest. Idiot. "So you're here today checking out the other finalists?"

"Of course. I'm surprised you're not doing the same."

"I guess I've been a little busy since I got to the show," I said vaguely.

"I see. I guess that's where we differ, then. I *make* time for the things that are important to me."

"Maybe the contest is more important to you than it is to me."

"Excellent." Ben smiled again.

This time I could see the tiny lines that creased his cheeks. They didn't diminish his appeal at all.

"It is?"

"Of course. That way you won't be too upset when Brando is chosen to represent Chow Down and Faith isn't. I hate to disappoint a lady."

Suddenly, unexpectedly, I felt my competitive juices rising. "Don't worry. I don't plan on being disappointed."

"That's the spirit!" Aunt Peg clapped a hand between my shoulder blades and almost sent me sprawling.

"I understand Faith is a Standard Poodle," Ben said. "I saw her picture on the contest web site, she's a real beauty."

"Thank you."

"I meant to watch the Poodle judging, but I was occupied with Brando earlier. He won the breed, and we'll be competing in the group later. How did Faith do today?"

If Ben had seen one of the pictures Davey had submitted, he had to have known that Faith was cut down. She hadn't worn the labor-intensive continental trim since she'd retired from the show ring two years earlier. Now Faith wore a sporty-looking kennel trim. Her face, feet, and the base of her tail were clipped close, and a dense blanket of short black curls covered the rest of her body.

Was Ben that ignorant about the mores of showing Poodles or was the question intended to psych me out? I wondered. He'd certainly wasted no time in letting me know that his dog was still showing—and winning.

"Faith is retired," Aunt Peg cut in smoothly. "Rather like one of the other competitors, Mac-Duff."

"I see. She's an older dog, then." His lip curled slightly.

"No," I said, ignoring the implied insult. "Just one that finished very quickly." It was a lie, but what the heck. I figured Aunt Peg would back me up, as well she should. The only reason Faith had taken a while to achieve her championship was because I'd been new and hadn't known what I was doing. "You know how it is. When they're that good, they seem to be in and out of the ring in a flash."

"Well then, I guess I'll just have to meet her Monday morning."

"Monday morning?" I echoed.

"At the reception Champions Dog Food is hosting for the five finalists. Didn't you get the email?"

My bad. "I don't always check my email on weekends," I admitted. "I'll have a look when I get home."

"Do that," Ben advised. "You and Faith wouldn't want to miss that all-important first opportunity to wow the judges." He nodded to the others and left.

I waited until Ben was out of earshot, then said, "That didn't go too badly."

Terry snorted. "The man wiped the floor with you."

"He did not."

"He came close." Bertie was shaking her head. "You're going to have to ramp it up a notch if you want Faith to beat Brando."

"Not to mention MacDuff and Ginger and . . ." Aunt Peg turned to Bertie for guidance. "What's the Yorkie's name?"

"Yoda."

"*Yoda?*"

"Don't yell at me. I didn't name her. I think it's an ear thing. You know."

"No, I don't." Aunt Peg didn't sound like she particularly wanted to, either.

The three of them spent the rest of the afternoon plotting—unsolicited, mind you—my potential plan of attack for the contest. I spent the rest of the afternoon mostly ignoring them. Bertie and Crawford showed their other dogs. Then, for the first time I could ever remember, Crawford and

Terry packed up and headed home before Bertie was done for the day.

"Doesn't that seem odd to you?" I asked Bertie, as the Bedford Kennels van drove slowly away from the grooming tent, bumping from rut to rut as it crossed the grassy field.

"What?" She was busy prepping a Cocker Spaniel to go in the last group of the day.

"That Crawford and Terry have left and you're still here." With Poodles having finished, Aunt Peg had left, too, but that didn't strike me as being nearly as strange as this did.

"Maybe they were showing fewer dogs than they usually do."

"That's my point. That's unusual, too. Crawford didn't have any Standard Poodles entered. Think about it. Crawford's Standard Poodles are his showcase dogs. He loves showing them. When was the last time you saw him at a show and he didn't have *any* entered?"

"I don't know." Bertie shrugged. She was relatively new to Poodles. She probably hadn't noticed.

"Today he only had little dogs. Easy dogs. Not only that, but he was awfully crabby, didn't you think?"

"For Pete's sake, Mel. Crawford's always crabby when Terry doesn't keep his mind on business. Where are you going with this?"

"I don't know," I said. "I guess I'm just thinking out loud."

"Well, for once, try thinking a little less, okay?"

Advice worth living by, if only I could ever manage to do it.

5

It was a good thing it was summer, otherwise it would have been dark by the time I got home. As it was, Sam and Davey were able to show me the progress they were making on the tree house. A foundation of beams had been laid across the span between two sturdy branches, and most of the floor was in place.

For the time being, a ladder was providing access to the project. Sam had left it leaning against the trunk of the tree and while I examined their handiwork from the ground, Davey scrambled up and maneuvered himself out the thick branch and onto the partially completed frame.

My first, automatic response was to call him back down; but then I reconsidered. Years spent as a single mother had honed my protective instincts to a fine point. Maybe too fine, I thought, noting that Sam—busy wresting a tennis ball from Raven's mouth so he could throw it for the canine crew to chase—seemed totally unconcerned by the fact that

Davey was all but dangling in the air. Now that my son finally had a solid, reliable male relationship back in his everyday life, maybe I didn't always have to be the one who decided what was best.

"Don't worry," said Sam under his breath. He tipped back his arm and let fly with the ball. Five big black dogs went sprinting away across the yard. "Davey's been all over that tree for the last week. He climbs like a monkey."

"Am I that easy to read?"

He swallowed a bark of laughter. "Yes."

"Oh." Now I was miffed.

"Come on." Sam looped an arm around my shoulder and pulled me close to his side in the gathering dusk. "I love your transparency."

Like that was a good quality?

His hand began to roam, inching downward. "Almost as much as I love your breasts."

"I appreciate the thought," I said. "But your timing stinks."

His hand was still moving. Now the other one had joined it. One by one, the Poodles came trotting back. This time, Tar had the ball. He dropped it at Sam's feet. Sam kicked it hard and they raced away again.

"Nah, this is just a little warm-up for later."

"Kind of like a pregame show?"

"Careful now," Sam murmured, his lips close to my ear. "Men get turned on by sports metaphors."

I insinuated my hips into his. "I thought you were already—"

"Hey, Sam-Dad, look!"

We jumped apart like a pair of guilty teenagers. Sam's hands fell away. He cleared his throat, yanked on his waistband. We both looked up.

Then abruptly I realized what Davey had said. *"Sam-Dad?"*

"Yeah." Davey grinned. He was lying on the boards, looking down at us over the rim of the tree house floor. "Sam said I could call him that."

"He did, huh?"

I glanced sideways, my eyes suddenly moist. Sam was looking away—perhaps purposely—his eyes following the trajectory of the ball he'd just lobbed again. A minute earlier I'd felt desired, but now my heart swelled with emotion. I couldn't imagine ever loving a man more than I loved Sam right that moment.

When I didn't speak right away, he looked back. "Maybe I should have asked you first . . . That's okay, isn't it?"

"It's better than okay," I said with a sniffle. "It's perfect."

Now he looked embarrassed. "It's no big deal."

"It's a huge deal."

"It's a name," Davey said practically, still watching from above us. "I couldn't call him Dad because . . . you know . . ."

Davey's real father lived only a couple of miles away. After being mostly absent for the first five years of his son's life, Bob was now making a concerted effort to play a role in Davey's upbringing. In fact, the house we were now living in—a spacious colonial on two acres of land—had belonged to my ex-husband before we'd traded homes in the spring.

"So I thought of this instead," Davey said.

"It's a great name," I agreed, trying not to sound too watery.

"So when you guys finally get around to having a baby—"

"Davey!"

"What?" He slid back from the edge of the floor, disappearing briefly before popping, legs first, out onto the branch. He shinnied back to the ladder and was on the ground before I'd even managed to formulate an answer. "Sam said that someday I'm going to have a little brother or sister, but in the meantime I just have to be patient."

"Really?" My conversational skills seemed to be deteriorating rapidly.

"Really," Davey confirmed. "I told Sam-Dad I wanted a brother and he said he was trying as hard as he knew how."

"Good to know," I said.

"So . . ." Davey fixed me with a level stare. "I hope you're trying, too."

"Trust me," I said, "it's a joint effort."

"Well, hurry up."

I'd heard much the same thing from Aunt Peg, Bertie, and just about everyone else I knew. Sam and I had been married only three months, for Pete's sake. On several occasions, I'd been sorely tempted to mention that upping the pressure didn't increase fertility. But not to my eight-year-old son.

Instead I looked at him and smiled. "I'll do my best," I said.

When I finally got around to opening my email I found out that the reception Ben had told me about was scheduled to be held at the Champions Company headquarters in Norwalk on Monday morning. Though the event was billed as a social occasion, a chance for everyone involved to meet one another, it seemed pretty clear that this would be the first step in the judging process.

With that in mind, I spent Sunday evening clipping, bathing, and scissoring Faith, devoting as much time to her coiffure as I would have had we been heading to a show. The effort left me feeling like the poster child for ambivalence. I certainly hadn't intended for Faith to remain a contestant, but now that she had, it had become a matter of pride that she appear at her best before the judges. My Poodle might not win the grand prize, but we weren't about to give the game away, either.

The Champions Dog Food Company was housed in a large, boxy brick building located in an industrial zone down near the water in Norwalk. According to the information I'd gleaned from the web site, both manufacturing plant and offices were contained within, though the building's drab exterior looked more in keeping with a factory than a posh company headquarters. The parking lot out front was surrounded by a chain link fence, its gate manned by a bored attendant who waved me inside without bothering to inquire why I was there.

Faith and I entered the building through a double set of glass doors, and found ourselves in a reception area that was surprisingly light and open. Potted ferns wafted gently in the breeze created by the air-conditioning. One wall held a waterfall where streams of water trickled down a backdrop of unmatched rocks and pooled in a basin below.

A middle-aged woman who looked like she'd never outgrown her preppy upbringing, was seated at the reception desk. Her blond hair was held in place by a headband; a light cotton cardigan was knotted around her shoulders. Small pearl studs dotted her earlobes. She stood as we approached and I saw that a border of puppies and kittens were chasing each other around the hem of her A-line skirt. Only in Fairfield County could an adult get away with wearing an outfit like that.

"You must be Faith and Melanie," she said.

I nodded and Faith wagged her tail.

"We've been expecting you. Would you mind signing in, please?"

"Not at all." I pulled the book toward me.

"Can Faith have a biscuit?"

"Sure, but I'll have to give it to her. She doesn't take food from strangers."

"Oh." The woman's brow furrowed. She lifted a bone-shaped biscuit out of a crystal container on her desk and handed it over. "That might be a problem."

I held out the biscuit and Faith sniffed it politely. She realized immediately that it wasn't one of her favorite peanut-butter snacks.

"Go on," I said. "Take it."

Obligingly, Faith did. Her front teeth closed over the biscuit. She held it carefully in her mouth, but didn't bite down.

"Those are Champions' best licorice biscuits," the receptionist said brightly. "I've never seen a dog that didn't love them."

Obviously she wasn't looking down, I thought. I wondered if the entire episode was being captured on closed-circuit camera to be dissected later by the selection committee. Then I wondered if I was being paranoid.

Probably.

"The gathering is upstairs on the third floor.

Take the elevator and turn right when you get off. You're looking for the Cerberus Room. You can't miss it."

Most dogs heartily dislike elevators and Faith was no exception. She dropped her tail and flattened her ears against her head when the doors slid open and she realized we'd be getting in. "It's only three floors," I told her. "And only because we don't know where we're going. On the way back down, we'll walk."

When the doors had closed, I took the still-unchewed biscuit out of her mouth and slipped it into my pocket. Hopefully there weren't any cameras in the elevator.

As we rose to the third floor, I wondered whether whoever had named the room where we were heading knew that Cerberus—the most famous canine in Greek mythology—was actually a three-headed canine that guarded the gates of hell. Or maybe I was just still being paranoid.

Though we'd come a little early, when Faith and I reached the Cerberus Room I saw that we weren't the first to arrive. It looked as though most of the other finalists were hoping to make a good impression by appearing eager. A quick look around the room revealed that Ben and his Boxer, Brando, were the only ones missing. Having browsed the web site the night before, I was able to recognize the rest of the competitors.

Lisa and Larry Kim were an Asian couple in their thirties, both slender and meticulously groomed. Though the other dogs in the room stood beside their owners on leashes, Larry held Yoda the Yorkie in his arms. The Kims weren't mingling; instead they stood off to one side, reserved and unsmiling.

Lisa looked unsure of herself; Larry merely appeared impatient for the proceedings to begin.

I'd never met Dorothy Foyle, though I'd seen her at plenty of shows with MacDuff. She was every bit as durable a campaigner as the black Scottish Terrier that sat on the floor pressed up against her sensible, low-heeled pumps. In her fifties, Dorothy had been a part of the dog show world nearly as long as Aunt Peg. Her sturdy figure and relentlessly cheery demeanor masked a steely sense of resolve that had served the pair well in the show ring.

Bill and Allison Redding, owners of Ginger the triple-threat Brittany, were another young couple. Bill was formally dressed in a suit and tie, and looked as though he might have dashed over to the meet-and-greet from work. He met my gaze and offered a quick smile in return. Allison, kneeling on the floor beside Ginger, was oblivious to the rest of the room. She spoke to the orange and white Brittany in a low voice, her arm lifting and falling in a nervous rhythm as her hand stroked repeatedly from the dog's head to her short tail.

Faith and I had barely stepped inside the room before a man detached himself from a small group standing beside the door.

"Doug Allen, contest chair," he said. "You must be Melanie and Faith. Welcome! We're so glad you could join us."

Doug took my hand in his and pulled me forward. "Let me introduce you to the rest of our committee. These are the people you have to worry about impressing over the next few weeks. They're the ones whose opinions have the power to make your dog a star or send you packing."

Doug sounded like the host of a TV reality show

and the broad wink he trained in my direction did nothing to diminish the self-importance of his tone. He ushered me to the edge of the group by the door and pointed quickly from one committee member to the next. "Cindy Burrows, Chris Hovick, Simone Dorsey."

I started to say hello but quickly realized that none of the three judges was paying even the slightest attention to me. Instead they were all staring with avid curiosity at Faith. Displaying that her manners were better than theirs, the Poodle ignored their scrutiny and stood quietly by my side.

"Beautiful," Simone Dorsey said. Everything about the woman was polished: from her shoes, to her nails, to her shiny lips. "What a classy-looking dog."

Chris, bespectacled, balding, and as rumpled as Simone was sleek, shook his head. "She's too composed. That won't play well on television."

"Maybe she can animate?" Cindy asked. The youngest of the trio, she was also the first to reach out and give Faith a tentative pat. "You know, like on command?" She lifted her eyes to me. "She does tricks, doesn't she?"

"A few," I said. "I really haven't spent any time on that. But Faith's a fast learner. She's always been able to pick up anything I want her to know without any problem."

"Ginger does tricks," Bill Redding said from across the room. Belatedly I realized that our introduction was being minutely observed by the other finalists. Allison was already rising and tugging the Brittany to her feet. "She can do all sorts of things. What would you like to see?"

As soon as Ginger began to move in our direction, Larry Kim did, too. His little Yorkie appeared to be dancing with eagerness in his arms. Or maybe Larry was shaking her. I was beginning to think I wouldn't put anything past this group.

"We don't need to see anything just yet." Doug held up a hand to stop the sudden flurry of activity. "There will be plenty of time for that later. For now, let's just all relax and get to know one another."

"We're missing a participant," Dorothy pointed out. "I guess Ben doesn't appreciate this opportunity as much as the rest of us do."

"Now Dorothy, don't go putting words in my mouth. You might give our esteemed judges the wrong idea."

Ben and Brando came sweeping through the doorway together and they made a striking pair. Owner and dog were both trim and muscular. Brando's compact body was enhanced by his fawn coloring, set off to perfection by the dark mask that covered his muzzle and eyes. Looking at the duo, I wondered whether Ben had timed his arrival to the minute, choosing to be last and make a dramatic entrance into an already full room.

"Here we are, everybody accounted for," Ben continued cheerfully. "You must be Doug. We spoke on the phone. Brando and I are *thrilled* to be included in your happy group." He managed to subtly shoulder me aside and stuck out his hand. "I know the rest of the participants, but perhaps you might introduce me to your colleagues?"

While Doug took care of that, I walked Faith over to a sideboard where tea and coffee were being served. Next to the drinks were three silver serving trays. One held cookies, the second an assortment of muffins, the third was filled with dog biscuits.

Faith was just below eye level with the offerings on the table. She lifted her nose and sniffed the air, but didn't ask for a biscuit. Clearly the Champions products didn't meet the standards of her finicky palate.

As soon as the introductions were finished, we all found seats around the large conference table. I placed Faith in a down-stay on the floor beside my chair. Allison Redding followed suit with Ginger. Ben unhooked Brando's leash and left the Boxer free to wander the room.

Larry Kim, his hands full with Yoda, hadn't taken a cup of coffee. Now, when he sat at the table, his dog was the only one still readily visible to the committee members. Dorothy caught on to that fact at the same time I did. She deliberately chose a chair that had another empty one beside it.

Like Miniature and Toy Poodles, Scotties are shown on top of grooming tables, so I was quite sure that MacDuff was accustomed to finding himself plopped on top of things and expected to stay. As I watched, Dorothy lifted the small dog and placed him on the padded leather seat. The Scottie balanced himself on his haunches as she pushed the chair in.

When it reached the table, MacDuff lifted both front legs, placed them on the polished wooden edge, and put his wiry black muzzle down between his paws. His dark eyes looked up and around the assembled group, gazing at each of us as if he was simply another participant in the meeting.

Now that was cute.

Simone pulled out a small pad of paper and made an unobtrusive note. Dorothy looked complacently pleased. Ben rolled his eyes. Lisa Kim was smiling. Really, it was hard not to. Then Larry caught his wife's eye and glared. Immediately her eyes dropped to the hands she'd folded in her lap.

"Well, MacDuff," Doug said jovially. "What do you say? Shall we call this meeting to order?"

Let the games begin.

6

"Let's start by introducing ourselves again," Doug said. "Since most of us are meeting for the first time, I think it would be a good idea if we each took a minute to talk about who we are, what we do, and why Champions dog food is important to us."

He paused and looked expectantly around the table. Everyone nodded in agreement except Mac-Duff who seemed to be eyeing a muffin Chris had placed next to his laptop.

"Since I'm the contest chairperson, I'll start. I'm also vice president of marketing for Champions Dog Food, which means that I'm the one in charge of telling the world that we manufacture the best canine nutritional products on earth."

Doug sounded as peppy as a high school cheerleader, and I found myself grinning at his extravagant job description. Nothing like a little hyperbole to get the meeting off to a good start. Then I looked around the table and realized that everyone else was taking his pronouncements seriously. Oops.

He nodded to Simone, who was seated at his right.

"Simone Dorsey," she said. Her tone was flat, modulated. "I'm director of public relations. My job is to keep this company and our products in front of the public eye, so that when the time comes for people to choose a healthy, balanced diet for their dogs, they'll think of us first. This contest was my idea, and I think we've come up with five superb finalists. Any one of your dogs would make a fine representative for Chow Down dog food."

This time everyone smiled when she finished speaking. I was relieved to join in; finally I was beginning to catch on to the important cues.

Chris Hovick went next. "Hey," he said, sketching a small wave in the air. "I'm Chris, more formally known as director of advertising. I'm the one who comes up with the specific campaigns that best illustrate to the public what our products are all about. And Chow Down is going to be big, man. I'm proud to be part of the campaign and I know you will be, too."

More cheerleading. I guessed the intended effect was to get our competitive juices flowing. If so, judging by the intent expressions I saw on the other finalists' faces, it was working.

"Cindy Burrows." The last member of the team flipped her long French braid back over her shoulder and introduced herself. "Product manager for Chow Down and delighted to be here. I hope you all are, too. Champions Dog Food is important to me because I believe in the quality of the products." She stopped and smiled slyly, her gaze sliding around the table. "And because they sign my paycheck."

Finally, I thought, as we all laughed together. Someone who was willing to inject a small dose of reality into the proceedings. Doug and Simone, I noted, both joined in the merriment, but neither looked amused by the comment.

"Now you know who we are," Doug said when the laughter had died down. "It's your turn to tell us something about you."

"What do you want to know?" The rest of us had hesitated; but not Ben, he spoke right up.

"Whatever you feel is important for the selection committee to consider," said Simone.

Chris nodded. "Surprise us."

Nothing like a little pressure.

Ben, however, didn't seem to mind. He was in his element and happy to go first.

"I'm an actor," he said. "You've probably seen my work on television and on the stage. And Brando is an actor's dog. Aside from being a gorgeous Boxer, that's something else we bring to the table that none of the other finalists can. Brando and I are professionals. We won't require a lot of coaching to put in a good performance. We both know how to get the job done and to look good doing it."

"Thank you," Doug said when Ben paused to draw a breath.

The actor looked disgruntled by the interruption. Clearly he hadn't intended to give up the spotlight so quickly. "No, thank *you*. Brando and I would also like you to know that we appreciate this wonderful opportunity and that if we're the ones chosen to represent Chow Down dog food, we will devote the full range of our considerable talents to the project. I promise you we won't let you down."

"Excellent," said Simone. I wondered if she was responding to Ben's words or the fact that he'd been flirting with her shamelessly since the moment he'd first entered the room.

"Moving on . . ." Doug prompted. "Bill and Allison, what would you like to tell us about Ginger?"

"First and foremost, that she's a great dog," Allison said, her voice pumped with enthusiasm. "With a wonderful personality. She's almost been like a child to us . . ." She paused and a blush rose to her cheek. "I mean, not that we think she's human or anything—"

"It's all right, honey, they know what you mean," Bill took over for her. "Allison and I aren't breeders. Ginger is the only dog we own. And look what she's accomplished. She's a conformation champion, she's working on her Utility degree in obedience and she's also qualified for her field championship. Having the opportunity to own a dog of this caliber is kind of like hitting the lottery, they just don't come along every day—"

"What Bill's trying to say is that Ginger can do it all." Allison was speaking again now. I felt like we were being tag-teamed. On the other hand, I could see how the committee might find the couple's energy infectious.

Bill reached down and patted the Brittany's head. "Once you stop and think about it, I know you'll realize that Ginger is exactly the kind of dog you want representing Chow Down dog food."

"You might be right," Doug agreed smoothly. "Dorothy, what would you like to tell us?"

The older woman took a moment to gather her

thoughts. She looked slowly around the table, her gaze pausing on each of the committee members in turn. "After listening to what other people have to say, I'm afraid maybe MacDuff and I are going to look a little shabby by comparison."

"No way!" Chris disagreed.

A small, satisfied smile lifted Dorothy's lips. That was just the response she'd been angling for, I thought.

"Now MacDuff and I, we're not as young and flashy as some of your other contestants. But I guess you'd have to say that we do have experience on our side. Those of you who go to dog shows, I bet most of you know who MacDuff is from his record in the ring."

She stopped and waited for us to nod. Dutifully, most of us did.

"This dog . . ." Her hand reached over to stroke his head fondly. "He pretty much won everything there was and then some. I retired him at Westminster in February. He'd earned his chance to do nothing but sit in the sun and snore.

"But funny thing about that. When it came right down to it, that wasn't what MacDuff wanted. He missed the excitement of being on the road all the time. Retirement just seemed to bore him silly. In a nutshell, that's why we're here. I figure I owe this old dog anything he wants that will make him happy. And if one more chance in the limelight will do it, then I'm just pleased to be along for the ride."

Wow, I thought, she was good. That appeal had to tug at the judges' hearts. In her own quiet, unassuming, way, Dorothy had just moved MacDuff up to the top of the list.

Simone was writing furiously on her notepad. Chris had his laptop open. I couldn't see the screen but I assumed he was doing the same. It occurred to me that I probably didn't have to worry about Faith winning the contest. There was no way I was going to be able to top these performances.

"I'm Larry Kim and this is my wife, Lisa," Larry said from the other end of the table. Lisa inclined her head slightly. "And this lovely Yorkshire Terrier you see in my arms is Yoda. Others have told you about their dogs' lofty accomplishments. Of course I could do the same but instead I would rather get right to the point.

"Yoda loves to eat. Yes, she is a small dog, but don't let her size fool you. This is a dog who always enjoys a good meal. We feed only Champions dog food in our kennel and Yoda was raised on it. She has been eating, and loving, Champions since she was a tiny puppy."

Approval wafted around the table like a smooth wave. The committee was lapping up this pitch.

"Recently we were fortunate to receive some free samples. You should have seen Yoda dive right in. I barely had the bag open before she was begging for a morsel to eat."

Seated beside her husband, Lisa was nodding as he spoke. I wondered why she didn't say anything herself. It occurred to me that she was the only one in the room who had yet to speak. Well, except for me.

"Let's be honest," Larry said. "What you're looking for is an adorable canine representative who loves your product and can sell it to others. Yoda is that dog."

Another top-notch appeal. As I listened to my

fellow contestants speak, they had me half convinced to vote for them myself.

"Melanie?" Doug turned to me. "What would you like us to know about Faith?"

Oh right. My turn. Unfortunately I hadn't prepared something to say like the rest of the participants clearly had. Now I needed something fast. Something fresh and catchy. A slogan. A soundbite. An irresistible anecdote . . .

And my mind was a total blank. I hate it when that happens.

"Umm . . ." I said, "she's a Standard Poodle."

Doug smiled encouragingly. Cindy nodded. Chris, waiting with fingers poised above his keyboard, was reserving judgment. As for Simone, she already looked bored.

"The thing about Poodles is . . . that they're a terrific breed of dog. It's true of Faith, but I can't take too much credit because, really, it's true of all of them. Poodles are just wonderful members of the family. They're intelligent, they have a sense of humor, they're empathetic. They're the perfect pet.

"Whatever their owner's lifestyle, they adapt and fit right in. That's why so many people have owned Poodles over the years. And why others have fond memories of the Poodles they knew when they were children. Poodles make people happy. They're evocative of everything that's good about owning a dog."

"I see," said Cindy.

I don't think she really saw anything. I think she just wanted to stop my disjointed rambling. And it was probably just as well that she had.

"You know," Chris said, "now that you mention

it, our neighbors had a Poodle when I was little. Smaller than yours. A Mini, I think. His name was Chester and, man, that was some great dog. I bet plenty of people would see a Poodle in an ad and be drawn to it for just that reason. They might not even know why, but seeing a Poodle would make them feel good."

"Subliminal," Simone said thoughtfully. "I like it."

"Definitely something to consider," Doug agreed.

The other contestants shifted in their seats and regarded me with wary respect. Desperate for something to say, all I'd done was describe how great Poodles were to be around. It was the committee members who had taken my idea—or lack thereof—and run with it. Unexpectedly, it looked as though I'd pulled a rabbit out of a hat.

Doug leaned forward and braced both his hands on the table. "Okay, now we know who we are and why we're all here. Cindy and Chris, why don't you tell everyone what's up next."

"As you know," the young woman began, "Chow Down is a new product for us. One we're going to be introducing to the marketplace shortly. To be perfectly honest, it's not like there's a shortage of good kibbles already available. So it's vital that we do something to set our dog food apart in the minds of the consumers.

"That's where the role of spokesdog comes in. We're looking for a dog that's every bit as much of a standout as we feel our product to be. A dog that's not only beautiful to look at, but that has personality and charisma, too. A dog that's one in a million."

"Obviously all your dogs are beautiful specimens of their respective breeds," Chris told us. "Otherwise you wouldn't be here. But now they need to show us something more. What we thought we'd do next is have you take them off their leashes and let them interact with one another. Kind of a "free play" situation where we could observe what they're like when they're just being themselves."

Five strange dogs, all turned loose simultaneously in a small room and encouraged to be entertaining? It certainly wasn't the best idea I'd ever heard. Years earlier, I had taken Davey to an interview for a preschool where they used a similar evaluation technique. That meeting had turned into a train wreck. This one, I thought, had similar potential.

"Fine by me," Doug said happily. Brando was already loose. The Boxer had been roaming freely around the room for the last ten minutes.

Allison shrugged, reached down, and unsnapped Ginger's leash. The Brittany was beautifully trained. She knew she'd been released, but even so she maintained her down-stay position.

"I'm not sure this is a good idea," said Dorothy. "Terriers can be territorial. Nothing wrong with that, it's their nature." It was also the reason why terriers were sometimes asked to spar in the show ring. MacDuff was one of the smallest dogs in the room. If he decided to pick a fight, he would be at a real disadvantage in the fray that followed.

Chris looked as though he was about to argue, but Larry Kim's voice, speaking calmly and deliberately, brought the room to a standstill. "This will not be happening," he said.

"Pardon me?" Simone sounded shocked. I was willing to bet she wasn't accustomed to having people deny her what she wanted.

All eyes at the table turned Larry's way.

"Your idea is not a good one. In such a circumstance, the smaller dogs' safety cannot be ensured, and in fact if something should go wrong, any one of the five might be at risk. I suggest that we find a different way for you to observe the dogs' personalities. Either that, or we take the time to carefully introduce them to each other before turning them loose."

"That won't be the same." Chris was already shaking his head. "What we're looking for is excitement, spontaneity. Something fresh and fun, and entirely out of the ordinary."

Larry's nod was curt. Yorkie still cradled in his arms, he rose to his feet. "Then what you are looking for is not Yoda."

For a moment, Lisa merely stared at him, wide-eyed. Then she scrambled to her feet as well. "It was a pleasure to have met you," she said softly, addressing the group. "But our coming here was obviously a mistake. Now we must go."

"Wait!" Doug jumped up.

The sudden movement startled Brando. The Boxer had been standing with his back to the table, sniffing the trash can next to the sideboard. Now his body stiffened as he spun around to face us. He landed with his feet braced in a pugnacious stance and jutted his jaw forward as he weighed the situation.

Instantly Ben was on his feet as well. He crossed the room quickly to stand beside his dog. "Easy boy," he said, his hand reaching down to cup Brando's muzzle.

At first glance the gesture looked like a caress. But watching a moment longer I realized he was holding the Boxer's mouth shut. And maybe muffling a low growl.

Interesting. It looked like there might be aggression issues there that Ben was trying to downplay.

Bill must have seen the same thing I did. Out of the corner of my eye, I watched as he unobtrusively slipped a hand down and refastened Ginger's leash.

"Maybe you're right," Doug said to Larry. "We certainly wouldn't want to force any of you to place your dogs in a situation that makes you uncomfortable. This is only our first get-together, after all. We're still feeling our way here, finding out what works and what doesn't."

Larry slowly sat back down. Lisa followed suit.

"Fine," said Cindy. "Then let's try this a different way. Everybody up and out into the middle of the room. Dogs on leashes." She glanced at Ben, who quickly complied. "Now that everyone's under control, just let your dogs be dogs. Let them do what they want to do. And we'll just observe and see what happens."

All of us liked that idea much better. Each of the five contestants was well socialized, each had been to dog shows. They all knew how to behave in polite company.

Faith and Ginger had touched noses and wagged their tails. MacDuff ignored the others and sniffed around for crumbs under the table. Yoda circled the room looking elegant and composed, her blue-grey coat rippling as she moved. Brando sidled over and discreetly stole a biscuit off the sideboard, which he swallowed in one quick gulp.

Meanwhile, the committee stood together off to

one side, watching the various antics and taking notes. Twenty minutes later, they decided they had what they'd wanted. Good thing because the dogs were beginning to tire. I wished I'd thought to bring a thermos of water for Faith.

"That's a wrap," Doug announced. "Thank you all for coming. Everyone was great. Chris, Cindy, Simone, and I will get together this afternoon and compare first impressions. Sometime in the next couple days, you'll receive an email letting you know what the next test is going to be. Please feel free to stop at the reception desk on the way out and pick up a gift basket of Champions products."

I heaved a sigh of relief and headed straight for the door. Some of the other contestants hung back—probably wanting to curry more favor with the judges—but Faith and I had had enough. We were more than ready to go home.

I'd promised the Poodle we'd take the stairs on the way out. Exiting the conference room, I saw that a red-lettered EXIT sign marked their location at the end of the hallway. But it was hot outside, our car would be stifling from sitting in the sun, and we were twenty minutes from home. Before heading down, I detoured into the ladies' room to get Faith something to drink.

Lacking a bowl or a cup, I filled the nearest sink with cold water. Then I hopped the Poodle's front feet up onto the porcelain rim and let her lap. I was glad I'd taken the time to stop; Faith drank thirstily.

When we emerged from the ladies' room, the hallway was empty. I pushed open the heavy fire door that led to the stairwell and Faith ran on ahead. Quickly she trotted down two flights of stairs with me hurrying to keep up. We had only one flight to go when I heard a door open above us.

The sound of hushed voices echoed through the vertical chamber. More of my fellow contestants, I guessed. I probably wasn't the only one whose dog didn't like elevators.

Quick footsteps tapped a staccato beat on the metal steps above us. Then I heard a sudden scream. It was followed quickly by a series of thumps. Faith and I both froze where we stood.

"Hello?" I called out. No one answered. Only my own word echoed back.

A door slammed. I thought I heard someone moan.

Then I heard the patter of little feet and Yoda came flying down the steps, trailing her gossamer ribbon leash. Without even stopping to think, I leaned down and opened my arms. The little Yorkie flew right into them.

"It's all right," I said, as she pushed her tiny body into me and burrowed close to my chest. "You're going to be all right."

Damn, I thought. I really hated lying to a dog.

7

It was lucky I'd stopped to get Faith that drink of water. As things turned out, she and I didn't get back home to Stamford until midafternoon.

On the other hand, if we hadn't paused for those few minutes on the third floor of the Champions building, we wouldn't have been in the stairwell when Larry Kim went tumbling down the flight of steps and broke his neck on the landing. Timing is everything, or so they say.

In my case, I think it might be more like bad luck just tends to follow me around.

Aunt Peg would probably be the first to agree with that assessment. She was the one I'd ended up pouring out the whole story to, when Faith and I finally got home. Davey had had a play date scheduled that afternoon with his best friend, Joey Brickman. Sam had gone to drop him off and then run some errands.

We'd settled all that by cell phone. What Sam hadn't mentioned was that I would find Aunt Peg waiting for me when I got home. She was sitting on the deck, sipping a tall glass of ice tea, and reading through a book of breed standards. Not surprisingly, she was surrounded by my bevy of besotted Poodles.

"What are you doing here?" I asked.

Aunt Peg loves to drop in without warning but usually she manages to make her visits coincide with times when someone's home.

"Holding down the fort, apparently." Peg slapped her book shut and set it aside.

Imagine that. I hadn't even been aware that we'd needed holding down. Just in case I was missing something, I ran quickly through a mental checklist. The house was standing, the Poodles looked healthy, no Indians were attacking . . .

Nope, we were good.

"You're white as a sheet," said Aunt Peg. "Let me pour you a glass of tea. Maybe you're pregnant."

She threw in that last bit like it was a casual afterthought. Nobody in the vicinity was fooled.

"I don't think so." I poured my own glass of tea and added a mint leaf to it. "If I look pale, it's probably because we just got back from the opening reception at the Champions Dog Food—"

"I thought you were due back several hours ago."

"We were. The reception ended before noon. But unfortunately, as we were leaving the building one of the other contestants fell down the fire stairs and broke his neck. He was dead before the ambulance got there."

"Oh, dear." Aunt Peg didn't sound nearly as upset as most people would have under the circumstances. There's nothing she likes more than a good set of complications. "Accident?"

"I don't think so."

"Let's go back outside and sit down. You'd better tell me *all* about it."

As if from the moment that I'd first seen her minivan parked in the driveway, there'd ever been any doubt of that.

Davey's and my previous house had been a small Cape Cod in a tightly packed family neighborhood. Lots were cramped; privacy almost nonexistent. Sitting outside in our other yard, with houses so close on either side that we could almost reach out and touch them, Davey and I never knew whether we might be subjected to the blare of a nearby radio, the aroma of dinner cooking on someone's barbecue, or uninvited visits from the neighbor's cats.

Things were very different at the new house. Our deck was beautiful, and the backyard was spacious and tranquil. If the residents of this neighborhood made any noise, they did so within the privacy of their own homes. Occasionally there were moments when I missed the constant bustle of our old block, but this wasn't one of them.

Now I wanted to sit down and have a serious discussion about murder, and having serenity for a backdrop suited me just fine.

"First things first," Aunt Peg said when we'd gotten settled. "Who died?"

"Larry Kim. He and his wife, Lisa, are the owners of Yoda the Yorkie."

"Aside from that, what do we know about them?"

I remembered our conversation about the other finalists at the dog show. Bertie had been the one who knew the Kims, not Aunt Peg.

"Not much, I'm afraid. I'd only met them both an hour earlier. We were together in a conference room with our dogs for a group interview with the contest committee. Larry seemed like a nice enough man, I guess. Very protective of his dog."

"Nice enough people don't usually get murdered," Aunt Peg commented acerbically.

"Well . . ." I admitted, "the police aren't exactly calling it a murder."

"What are they calling it?"

"They're not sure. It was obvious that Larry died as a result of his fall. But they don't know why he fell."

"You mean maybe he just tripped?"

I nodded slowly. "That seemed to be what they were thinking before I told the officer that I'd heard someone in the stairwell with him shortly before he died."

"Well then," Aunt Peg said happily, "the plot thickens."

"Oh please." I'd injected enough exasperation into the comment to wilt a lesser woman. Peg wasn't even daunted. "The only thing my information got me was the opportunity to hang around Norwalk a couple of extra hours and be interviewed two more times by the police."

"So you've done your civic duty, now do the same by your family. I want you to tell me everything. But before we get started, did you miss lunch? Are you hungry? Shall I make you a sandwich while you talk?"

Only Aunt Peg could skip back and forth between murder and food without missing a beat, and make the juxtaposition sound perfectly natural.

"Yes, I missed lunch, and no, I'm not hungry."

"Maybe that's good news! Maybe you're—"

"Don't say it."

"All right, I won't." Peg frowned. "But that doesn't stop me from thinking it. Now, back to a topic you *will* discuss without getting cranky for no good reason, which, by the way, is another possible sign . . ."

Not trusting myself to speak, I simply leveled a glare.

Aunt Peg shrugged. She recognizes outrage only when it suits her. When I'm the outraged party it usually doesn't.

"So we're back to Mr. Perfectly Nice Yorkie Owner and his presumably perfectly nice wife," she said. "Tell me more about them."

"My first impression was that they were both rather quiet. The entire time we were there, Lisa let Larry do almost all the talking. But halfway through the interview, the two of them stood up and threatened to walk out."

"It's always the quiet ones that surprise you."

"This surprised everyone. But they were right. Chris—he's director of advertising for the company and one of the judges—wanted us all to let our dogs loose in the room so they could run around and jump on one another."

"No wonder the man with the Yorkie balked at that. It sounds like good common sense to me."

"It sounded like common sense to all of us. Well, except Ben O'Donnell. He'd already turned Brando loose."

"He would have. Anything to draw attention to himself."

"By the way, does that Boxer bite?"

"How would I know?" Aunt Peg snorted. "Despite appearances to the contrary, I am not privy to every single little thing that goes on in the dog show world."

"Oh."

That was a shame. My life had been easier when I'd thought Aunt Peg was omniscient.

"Does it matter?"

"Probably not, but I just saw something that made me wonder. Anyway, Chris and the committee backed down. The meeting concluded amicably and we were told we'd all be contacted about our next assignment."

"This is beginning to be a very long story," Aunt Peg said. "The stairway will be making an appearance soon, won't it?"

"Very soon. The meeting took place on the third floor of the building. And when it was over, we all had to go back down to the lobby."

"Elevator?"

"Faith hates them."

"Not surprising, lots of dogs do. So you looked for steps."

"First we stopped in the ladies' room for a drink of water."

"I assume we're talking about Faith?"

I nodded.

"A long group interview on a hot summer day and nobody thought to supply water for the dogs?"

"They supplied biscuits instead."

"Not those horrid licorice ones?"

"The very same."

Aunt Peg shuddered slightly. She reached down and patted Faith, who was lying between us, her fingers combing lightly through the dense, dark hair. "Poor girl. The things your mother puts you through."

I considered mentioning that it was Davey who'd signed Faith up for this particular ordeal, then thought better of it. Peg wasn't the only one to whom this recounting of events was beginning to seem long.

"Anyway, because we were in the ladies' room, I didn't see how people split up or which way they went. All I know is that when I pushed open the fire door, the stairwell appeared to be empty. I figured everyone else was either ahead of us or behind us, or else they'd taken the elevator."

"A logical assumption. Then what happened?"

"We'd gone partway down when I heard a door open above us. I heard voices, too."

Aunt Peg sat up in her chair. "Saying what?"

"That's the problem, I don't have any idea. It sounded like there were two people. They must have been pretty far above me in the stairwell and I wasn't really paying attention. I mean, why would I?"

"Why, indeed?" Aunt Peg said tartly. Like Terry, she tends to eavesdrop as a matter of course.

"Next thing I knew, somebody screamed, and then Larry Kim came tumbling down the steps."

"Did you see him fall?"

"No. I heard him, though. He ended up on the landing above us. And then Yoda came flying down to where we were, trailing her leash along behind her. Larry must have been holding her in his arms when he fell."

"Lucky she wasn't injured," Aunt Peg mused. Trust her to gloss over the fact that a man had died and worry about the dog's welfare. "And where was Mrs. Kim when all this was happening?"

"Lisa told the police that Larry had hung around

after the meeting was over because he wanted to have a word with the judges. He'd sent her ahead to the parking lot to open up the car and get the air conditioner started."

Aunt Peg didn't comment but I knew what she was thinking, because the same thought had crossed my mind. Lisa Kim must have been more biddable than we were. Neither one of us was particularly good at taking orders.

"So she was outside when her husband fell to his death," Peg said. "Or at least she claims she was. Did anyone see her out in the parking lot?"

"You'd have to ask the police about that. Though I didn't see them asking very many questions. They seemed more concerned with consoling the grieving widow."

Aunt Peg nodded. "Because they assumed the fall was an accident."

"I told them about what I'd heard—"

"Which was woefully vague, if you ask me. How do you know Mr. Kim wasn't speaking to Yoda? Lots of people hold conversations with their dogs."

Including the two of us, I thought.

"Yes, but what about the scream?"

"Good point. Unusual for a man to scream, don't you think? Are you sure it was Mr. Kim that you heard?"

"No, but since he was the one who fell, I think it's a pretty logical assumption."

"So you and Mr. Kim were in the stairwell, possibly along with at least one other unspecified person. And Lisa Kim was outside. Where were the other contestants while all this excitement was taking place?"

"I believe the Reddings had already left. By the time the police got around to talking to us, they were long gone. Dorothy and Ben were still somewhere in the building, though both claimed not to have heard or seen anything."

"So you were the only witness, so to speak."

"Yes."

"And a reasonably poor one, too."

No way to refute that.

Aunt Peg patted her knee and Eve stood up. Peg hauled the Poodle up into her lap, ran her fingers through the dog's coat absently, and thought for a minute. She always concentrates better when she has her hands on a dog.

I sipped my tea and said nothing. I'm good at that.

"Who called the police?" she asked after a bit.

"That was Doug Allen. He's the VP of marketing and also the contest chair. I heard Larry fall, but I was a flight down and busy grabbing Yoda. Before I could get back up the stairs, Doug opened the fire door on the third floor and saw the body on the landing below."

"Interesting timing," Peg commented. "Did he say why he happened to open the door at that particular moment?"

"He told the police that he was on his way outside to sneak a smoke. He said he had no idea anything was wrong until he saw Larry lying there."

"Surely he must have seen *something*. Or more importantly, someone. If he was in the third-floor hallway, he should have seen someone exit the stairwell in a big hurry, don't you think?"

"The same thought occurred to me. I asked

Doug about it, but he said that he'd been in his office grabbing his cigarettes and when he stepped out into the hallway it was empty."

"Pity," Aunt Peg muttered. She hates it when potential witnesses refuse to cooperate.

"Indeed."

Neither one of us was entirely convinced by Doug's version of events. We both filed the information away for further consideration.

"What about security cameras?" Aunt Peg asked. "Lots of companies have them in the fire stairs."

"Lots do. This one doesn't. The police asked."

"I wonder who knew that."

"Probably anyone who'd bothered to look into it. Possibly anyone who worked for the company. Why?"

"Because most murderers would like to be reasonably assured that they're not being observed in the act. At first I was thinking that the killing must have been a spontaneous deed—a crime of passion, if you will. But now I'm wondering about that. Perhaps the killer chose to murder the unfortunate Mr. Kim in the stairwell precisely because he knew there weren't any cameras there."

As she so often did, Aunt Peg had clarified the situation; taking what I'd told her and ferreting out interesting nuggets of information that I hadn't managed to come up with on my own.

"You should mention that to the police," I said.

"Or you should." Aunt Peg gently eased Eve from her lap and stood. "They know you."

"I wouldn't go that far."

"They have your name in the report. Same thing, more or less."

We stashed our glasses in the kitchen sink and I followed Aunt Peg out the front of the house to her minivan.

"You never did tell me why you'd come," I said.

Door open, foot on the running board, Aunt Peg paused. "Considering everything else that's happened to you today, it hardly seems important now."

"But?"

"I was going to bug you about Eve. She's a beautiful bitch and nearly two years old. It's high time you got her back in the show ring and finished her championship. Of course, that was before I knew that you already had a task for the summer."

"Winning the contest?"

"Oh pish," said Peg. "Nobody cares a fig about who wins that silly contest except perhaps for Davey. But the morning's events have put a whole new spin on things. You've got your work cut out for you now. I imagine you're going to have to go and figure out what happened to Larry Kim, aren't you?"

8

I supposed I would. At least that was how things always seemed to work out. So rather than fighting the inevitable, I got up the next morning and thought about who might be able to answer some questions for me. My sister-in-law, Bertie, was right at the top of the list.

Growing up, I had always wanted a sister. Instead I'd had a younger brother, whose chief goal in life seemed to be to discover exactly how much mayhem he could get away with causing. It had taken us years to work out our differences, and the prickly relationship we'd forged as children had lasted well into our adulthood.

Then Frank had met Bertie and fallen head over heels in love. For him, it was an event of life-altering proportions. The relationship had not only changed my brother into a new and better man, it had also resulted in the birth of my wonderful niece, Maggie. And as an added bonus, Frank had provided me with the sister I'd always coveted. It was a win-win situation all the way around.

Bertie and Frank lived in the northern edge of Wilton, just below the Ridgefield border. The house had been Bertie's before their marriage, bought with the proceeds from her handling business. She'd built a kennel in the basement and added a dozen outside dog runs to accommodate boarders. Fortunately, with land that nestled up against a nature preserve, she didn't have to worry about noise restrictions.

When I mentioned over breakfast that I was going to be visiting Davey's aunt and new baby cousin, he had opted to come along. Sam stayed home to work on a new software idea that had piqued his interest. Frank was down in Stamford at his coffeehouse, The Bean Counter, preparing for the midday rush. Bertie and Maggie were waiting for us on the porch when we arrived.

My niece, who'd seemed so tiny when she was born, was now growing rapidly into her own little person. At six months of age, Maggie wasn't quite walking yet but she could crawl almost anywhere. I'd advised Bertie to hang a bell around her daughter's neck to match the one worn by her cat, Beagle, but so far Bertie had declined.

"Ga!" Maggie said, lifting a hand in greeting as Davey and I came up the steps. Or maybe she was just trying to throw Cheerios at us. The latter seemed likely when a spray of cereal landed at our feet.

"Ga back at you," said Davey. He was really getting into the whole baby thing. "When is she going to start talking?" he asked Bertie.

"She's talking." Bertie laughed. "You heard her."

"I mean words I can understand."

"Me, me, me, me, me . . ." Maggie sang out.

"She's her mother's daughter, all right," I teased.

"Bite your tongue. I'll have you know that child has just about turned me into a selfless paragon of virtue. I'm damn near unrecognizable. Some days even I wonder what's come over me. Has anyone else noticed that it's friggin' hot out here? Who besides me wants some lemonade? Davey?"

"Yes, please." He'd immediately sunk to the floor of the porch to sit beside Maggie. Now he was rolling a rubber ball back and forth to entertain her. Knowing Bertie, the toy probably belonged to Beagle.

"I'll help," I said, stopping to latch a baby gate across the top of the steps as Bertie headed inside.

She paused and looked back at Davey. "I'll leave the door open and we'll only be two rooms away. If you need us for any reason, just yell, okay?"

"We can be back out here in five seconds if we need to," I added.

"Don't worry," said Davey, sounding very grown-up. "We'll be fine."

"He's great with her," Bertie said as we walked through the house.

"I know." I heaved a windy sigh. "And we're *trying*."

"I'm just mentioning . . ."

"So is everybody else. It's gotten to the point where I feel as though I ought to be sending out daily email updates to any and all interested parties."

"Great, can I get on that list?"

"I'm kidding, Bertie!"

"So was I." She turned and peered at me. "Getting a little touchy, aren't you?"

"Maybe just a bit," I admitted. "Let's talk about something else."

"Name it."

"Lisa and Larry Kim."

"Can't say that I didn't expect that." Bertie opened the refrigerator and pulled out a pitcher of lemonade. I got three glasses out of the cabinet and lined them up on the counter. "I read about what happened in this morning's paper. The article made reference to the contest. I wondered if you were there."

"Not only there, but in the stairwell when he fell."

"You certainly know how to attract trouble." Bertie held her hand over the spout and gave the pitcher a good shake. "Maybe you're the one who ought to have a warning bell hung around your neck."

I'd always thought I was just unlucky. It had never occurred to me that I might be a jinx. Quickly I shook off the thought.

"The article was a little vague on the specifics," Bertie said. "It implied that the incident was a tragic accident. But since you're asking questions, I'm guessing that you don't agree?"

"There was someone up on the landing with Larry right before he fell. Someone who ran away afterward, rather than staying and trying to help."

"I can see why you're feeling suspicious, then. Where was Lisa while all this was happening?"

"Larry had sent her outside. At least that's what she told the police."

Bertie had filled the three glasses. I picked one up and lifted it to my lips. The lemonade was strong and tart. It tasted great.

"I'll run one of these out to Davey," Bertie said. "If everything's copacetic out there, we can let the kids entertain each other for a few minutes and talk in here."

Neither one of us had to mention that since the topic under discussion was murder, we would both rather that our children didn't overhear.

Three minutes later, Bertie was back. In the meantime I'd taken a seat at the kitchen table. "Everything okay?" I asked.

"Perfect. Davey's got Maggie in his lap and he's reading her a book. The two of them looked so cute together that I grabbed the camera and sneaked a picture or two."

"I'll want copies."

"I'm holding them hostage. Maybe I'll bring one to your baby shower."

"I used to think you were a good influence on my brother," I said. "Now I'm beginning to see it's worked the other way around. He's turned you into a fiend."

"That wasn't Frank, that was motherhood. I just want everyone to experience the same maternal joys that I have."

"Stretch marks, sleepless nights, varicose veins . . . It's no wonder I can't wait." I stopped abruptly. "I can't believe you managed to get me back to *that* subject again."

Bertie laughed. "You're the one who keeps digressing."

Maybe I was, I realized. These days it seemed like I had babies on the brain.

"Back to the Kims," I said firmly. "At the show last weekend, you said you knew them."

"It was more like I knew *of* them," Bertie corrected. "I wouldn't say we're friends or anything, I know them as fellow competitors. They're big into Yorkies and I've shown against them lots of times over the years. Actually I guess I should say that I've shown against Larry. Lisa doesn't go in the ring, or at least I've never seen her there."

"She was pretty quiet at the meeting, too. Larry was the one that was holding Yoda and he did all the talking for both of them."

Bertie nodded. "Larry's the one that runs that show. It always looked like Lisa preferred to stay in the background. Almost blending in, if you know what I mean. She grooms the dogs back at their setup but Larry's the one who shows them to the judge."

"Kind of like you and me," I said.

Bertie snorted. "You? Blend into the background? Not on this planet."

"Hey, I think I make a pretty good support staff."

"Nobody's disputing that. It's the other part that would have anyone who knows you in hysterics. And speaking of people we know, here's something you might be interested in."

"What?"

"Yesterday I got a call from a potential client. A man in Massachusetts with a Standard Poodle puppy he needed a handler for. Of course the guy knew who Crawford was, so he'd called him first. Terry told him they were totally booked and referred him over to me."

"Is that so unusual?"

Bertie looked at me as though I was daft. "*Yes.* It's hard to make a living as a professional handler. I don't know anyone in the business who turns clients away."

"Crawford's a little different though. He's at the top of the game. Maybe he gets offered more dogs than he has time to compete."

"How do you think Crawford got to the top?" Bertie asked. "He never says no to anyone. His kennel is huge. You know that, you've seen it. Crawford isn't only a gifted handler, he's also a savvy businessman. At some shows, he has half the Poodle entry. Owner can't find a major for his less-than-deserving Mini? No problem, Crawford can bring along a couple extra dogs and build one for you."

Majors were the necessary evil of the dog show world. To complete a championship, a dog needed to amass a total of fifteen points. The point scale ran from one to five; and the number of points awarded was based on the number of same-sex competitors that a dog beat. Included in those fifteen points had to be at least two majors: outings where a dog defeated enough competition to be awarded three or more points.

The idea was a good one, in theory. It prevented mediocre dogs from gaining a championship by piling up single point wins in undistinguished competition. But it also made life difficult when, for a variety of reasons—winter, bad judges, scarcity of puppies—major entries were sparse, and good dogs either had to wait for months or travel long distances to find them.

Building a major might be frowned upon but it was not unheard of. Usually the competitor in need would call around to get friends to supply entrants. It was a rare exhibitor who could, like Crawford, simply engineer the task on his own.

"True," I said. "Crawford's never been known to

be overly discriminating in the dogs he accepts to show. The fact of the matter is, he doesn't have to be. He and Terry are such masters that by the time they get done preparing their Poodles to go in the ring, they all look good enough to win."

"Precisely. And this is the second client he's referred to me recently. The first time I thought he was just being nice. You know how Crawford is . . . He wants people to think he's such a gruff, hardened professional, but inside he's really just a big marshmallow."

The assessment was accurate, if a bit exaggerated. Close enough to make me laugh, though.

"Better not let him hear you say that," I warned.

"I wouldn't dare. But Crawford knows that I recently added Poodles to my string. I thought at first that maybe he was just trying to help me get started."

"And now you've changed your mind?"

"I don't know. Maybe."

As we were speaking, Bertie's cat, Beagle, stood up on top of one of the high cabinets and made her presence known. Lying down, she'd been invisible. Now the tiger-striped cat wanted our attention. She stretched sinuously, extending each white tipped forefoot slowly, then followed the procedure with her hind feet.

When she was satisfied we were watching, Beagle hopped down onto the top of the refrigerator, from there to the countertop, and then down onto the floor. Gracefully she sauntered over and deigned to honor us with her presence. Beagle wrapped her body around my legs, her tail curling upward over my knees.

"It took her long enough," I said. "Beagle usually shows up the minute we arrive."

"New routine," Bertie informed me. "Now that Maggie's crawling everywhere, that poor cat has learned she either has to stay somewhere that Maggie can't reach or else run the risk of being mauled. Beagle is *not* amused. Mags means well but she thinks Beagle is the most fascinating creature on earth. And Maggie's too young to know how to treat her respectfully."

Pets and new babies were always an uneasy mix. I could sympathize with what Bertie was going through. "It'll get better as Maggie gets older."

"*I* know that. It's Beagle who needs to be convinced. She came to me as a stray, you know. Some days I'm half-afraid she'll simply get fed up and take off again."

"Beagle? No way. She's your cat now. She loves it here." I reached down to give the tiger cat's back a long scratch.

"I hope so. And I hope everything's okay with Crawford, too. It hadn't even crossed my mind that it might not be, until you brought it up the other day at the show. Now you've got me wondering, too."

Bad sign, I thought. I'd been hoping that my concern was merely the product of an overactive imagination. But Bertie was much more level-headed than I was. If she was worried, too, maybe there really was something to worry about.

I got up, walked through the dining room, and looked out the front door. Davey and Maggie were just where we'd left them, sitting in the sun on the porch. Now they were building a pyramid out of blocks. Actually Davey was doing most of the building. Maggie was playing the part of a baby wrecking ball.

Davey glanced up, winked at me over Maggie's head, and went back to describing the tree house that he and Sam were building. Maggie made an appreciative audience. Heart warmed, I went back to the kitchen with a few final questions.

"Tell me how people felt about the Kims," I said to Bertie. In my absence, she'd pulled Beagle into her lap and was stroking the cat's long, taut body. "Did they like them?"

"I guess. The two of them tended to keep pretty much to themselves. You know how crowded things can get underneath a grooming tent . . ."

I nodded.

"Sometimes it feels like we're all working right on top of one another. It's hard to stay out of people's way in a situation like that. But Larry and Lisa always seemed to hold themselves somewhat apart. I don't know that people liked them or disliked them so much as they didn't really know them."

"What about Larry? You said he was a tough competitor. Did he have any enemies?"

"He must have," said Bertie. "Think about it, Mel. He's dead, isn't he?"

9

There was an email waiting for me when we got home. Faith and I had been issued an invitation to the next phase of the contest competition. Individual interviews were to be held Thursday morning at the company headquarters.

I sat and stared at the email for a minute before shooting back a reply. Obviously the fact that one of the finalists had died after the previous meeting wasn't going to be allowed to slow down the process at all.

Under the circumstances, I assumed that Lisa and Yoda would drop out of the competition. Doug might have held me to my commitment, but surely he would have to accept the Yorkie's withdrawal. In any event, I didn't expect the pair to take part in the interviews on Thursday. Which was why I was so surprised to run into Lisa when Faith and I arrived a few minutes ahead of our scheduled appointment at eleven.

Exiting the building, Lisa saw us coming across the parking lot and paused to hold the door. She was dressed in a simple black linen sheath that fell to just above her knees. Her arms and legs were bare, and a pair of black strappy sandals set off her dainty feet.

I wondered whether she'd chosen the outfit as a foil for her creamy skin and shiny black hair or whether the dark color was meant to show that she was in mourning. Either way, the clothing complimented her slender figure.

Looking at her, I had the nagging impression that something was missing. After a moment I realized what it was: the little Yorkie, Yoda, was nowhere in sight. Maybe Lisa had come to the dog food company alone to tender her resignation.

"I'm so sorry for your loss," I said, when Faith and I reached the door.

"Thank you." Lisa's eyes lifted briefly. They met mine, then skittered away. Her expression was somber. "I appreciate your concern."

"If there's anything I can do . . ."

"No, there's nothing." Her voice was soft and melodious, the kind of voice that dogs would respond to instinctively. Indeed, Faith had lifted her head and was watching Lisa intently.

"I'd only just met Larry, but he seemed like a very fine man."

"My husband was a man of many admirable traits. He knew what he wanted in life and he went after it. He worked hard and he accomplished many things."

There was something almost routine about her response. The words sounded as though they'd been rehearsed. Then again, I thought, everyone dealt with grief differently. At our previous meeting, Lisa had struck me as an intensely private person. It shouldn't have come as a surprise that she wouldn't want to display her emotions in front of a virtual stranger.

"Yoda is all right?" I asked, venturing to a safer topic.

"Yes, physically she's fine. You were the one who came to her rescue on the steps, correct? I'm sorry I didn't get a chance to thank you the other day."

"You're welcome. It was nothing. I knew you wouldn't want her to be running loose. I merely picked her up and held her until help arrived."

"So then . . . you were there? You saw my husband fall?"

"No. I was in the stairwell when it happened, but I was two flights lower down. I didn't see anything until after I heard the crash—" Abruptly I stopped speaking. I was sure Lisa wouldn't want to hear the gory details.

"Doug Allen called 9-1-1," I finished lamely. "And Chris Hovick came running to see what was wrong. He took Yoda from me. I assume he gave her back to you?"

Lisa nodded. "He came outside and told me what had happened. At first I didn't believe him, I was sure he must have been mistaken. I had just been with Larry five minutes earlier. I couldn't imagine that he could be gone. Especially in the manner in which I was told it happened."

Faith and I had an appointment inside. If we were to be on time, we needed to get moving. But now what Lisa had said brought me up short. I dropped my hand and gave Faith a silent signal to sit.

"Why do you say that?" I asked.

"Larry would not have liked me to talk about this before. But now that he's gone, I suppose it doesn't matter. My husband suffered from vertigo. Heights made him very uncomfortable. Usually he avoided places like that stairwell. It came as a great surprise to me that he would have chosen to go there."

And yet he had. That was clear to both of us.

"Perhaps he didn't want to take Yoda on the elevator?" I suggested.

"We had come up on the elevator. Yoda doesn't mind. She's traveled all over the country with us. She goes wherever we do and it's never been a problem."

So much for that theory. In that case, what *had* Larry been doing in the stairwell? Could he have ducked in there for the purpose of holding a private conversation with the person I'd heard him speaking to?

"It's not surprising to me that Larry lost his balance and fell," Lisa said. "Just being in that stairwell would have made him dizzy. And with Yoda in his arms, he wouldn't have been holding on to the banister. I can't imagine what he was thinking."

"Are you sure your husband's death was an accident?" I asked gently.

"Of course." Lisa didn't seem offended by the question, but she didn't give it much credence, either. "How could it have been anything else?"

"I was just wondering because I thought I heard voices right before Larry fell." And a scream, I thought, but I didn't add that. "I thought maybe he was talking to someone . . ."

"Who?"

"I don't know. They were pretty high above me. I couldn't hear what was being said."

Lisa was shaking her head, as if trying to make sense of this new information. "And this person Larry was supposedly with . . . He wouldn't have tried to help him? To prevent him from falling?"

Actually I'd been thinking just the opposite. But right that moment, looking at Lisa's pale face and dark, red-rimmed eyes, I would no sooner have brought up that possibility than I would have kicked a defenseless puppy.

Besides, I thought, Lisa's revelation about her husband's vertigo had cast the incident in a whole new light. Maybe I was the one who was wrong. Perhaps I'd been entangled in so many mysteries, that I'd begun to see evidence of wrongdoing where it didn't even exist.

Belatedly I realized that Lisa was still holding the glass door. I reached out and took it from her.

"You and Faith are having your private interview this morning?" she asked.

"Right." I glanced at my watch. "We're running a little late."

"Don't worry, I was just up there. The Reddings had the appointment ahead of yours and they seemed to have a lot to say. I'm sure nobody's noticed that you haven't arrived yet."

"So you came to speak to the contest committee. Does that mean you'll be withdrawing Yoda from the competition?"

Nothing I'd said earlier—offering my condolences, describing what I knew of her husband's fall, implying it might not have been an accident—had thrown Lisa. This did.

"Pardon me?" she said.

"I just thought that since—"

"You thought wrong." Lisa didn't wait for me to finish. "Yoda is a strong competitor and so am I. She is still very much a finalist in the contest." Her eyes dropped to Faith, waiting patiently by my side. "Your Poodle may yet be the winner, but we won't be conceding the victory. She will have to beat us to get the prize."

Rather than jamming my foot any farther into my mouth, I simply said, "Good luck to you."

"And to you," Lisa replied. "May the best dog win."

Upstairs I found that the committee was indeed waiting for us. And they had noticed we were late—at least Doug Allen had.

Not wanting to revisit the stairwell, Faith and I ended up taking the elevator again. The Poodle looked at me reproachfully as I steered her in that direction. As soon as the doors opened on the third floor, she went bounding out into the hallway. And straight into Doug, who was walking by.

"Well hello!" he said, nimbly sidestepping a canine charge that might have felled a slower man. "I'd been wondering where you two were. It's nice to see one of our finalists arrive with such enthusiasm."

I didn't feel the need to mention that Faith's eagerness had less to do with the contest or Champions dog food than it did with exiting the dreaded elevator.

"Sorry we're late. I ran into Lisa downstairs and I wanted to offer my condolences."

"Lisa Kim?" Doug looked surprised. "I didn't realize she was here."

"She said she'd been up here . . . She mentioned seeing the Reddings . . . ?" My voice trailed away. This all looked like news to Doug.

He quickly rallied, however. "I'm sorry I missed her. This has to be very difficult for her. I would have wanted to offer my support as well. We at Champions are ready to do anything we can to ease her way through this terrible time."

Spoken like a true marketing man. Or maybe like a vice president who was concerned that his company might find itself with some liability in Larry's death. I wondered whether Doug's offer of support would be intended to mitigate the possibility that Lisa might decide to seek financial compensation.

Then I had another thought. Doug was the one who'd steered me to the fine print when I had tried to drop out of the contest. No doubt Yoda's withdrawal under these circumstances would generate even more adverse publicity.

Doug had never been shy about voicing his determination to do what was best for his company. He said he hadn't seen Lisa that morning, but that didn't mean he hadn't spoken to her previously. I wondered if he'd offered her some sort of incentive to keep the little Yorkie as a participant in the contest. And whether perhaps the rest of us were now competing for second place.

"Faith and I had better be going," I said. "I believe we're supposed to see Simone Dorsey first?"

"Down the hall and to the left. Last office on the right. I'm sure she's waiting for you."

Since I'd known we'd be meeting with Simone that morning, I'd taken extra care with my appearance. Rather than my usual summer outfit of shorts and a T-shirt, I'd actually donned a skirt and put on a little makeup. My efforts didn't help. Rising from behind her desk to greet us as we entered her office, the PR director still made me feel like I hadn't tried hard enough.

As before, Simone appeared cool and poised. The designer dress she was wearing probably cost more than I'd spent on clothes in a year. A scarf was tied jauntily around her shoulders. It didn't come unknotted or slip to one side when she reached out a hand to shake mine, as it would have done if I'd been wearing it.

Taking a seat in a chair opposite her desk, I took small consolation from the fact that her stiletto, pointy-toed pumps probably pinched her feet.

"Thank you so much for coming," Simone said gracefully. "I want you to know that I found Faith to be absolutely delightful the other day. I probably shouldn't admit this, I'm supposed to be impartial after all, but I absolutely adore Poodles."

Wasn't it amazing, I thought, how quickly a few well-chosen words could totally change your opinion of someone?

Simone beamed down at Faith, who'd taken a seat at my side. "They're the glamour girls of the dog world, aren't they?"

"Well . . . yes." The ability to dress up a Poodle's hair in all manner of intricate designs had never been the breed's appeal to me. "But they're also much, much more than that."

"Of course they are! And I want you to tell me all about Faith. How old she is, how long you've had her, how you came to get her in the first place. I want to hear everything."

Most of that information had been covered on the entry blank. But since I hadn't filled out the form, I didn't mind repeating the story if Simone wanted to hear it again. I sat back in my seat and told her about Aunt Peg, doyen of the dog show world, Faith's breeder, and the woman who had initiated and orchestrated my involvement in dogs.

"She sounds like a remarkable woman," Simone said when I'd stopped speaking. "Does she feed our products to her dogs?"

Expediency warred with honesty. After a brief internal struggle, honesty won.

"I'm afraid not," I admitted. "Aunt Peg cooks for her dogs, mostly stews with chicken and vegetables and broth that she pours over kibble."

Champions made kibble. In fact as far as I could tell, the signature product of the new Chow Down line was its kibble. Tactfully neither one of us remarked on that point.

"It's a point in Faith's favor that she comes from such a distinguished line of Poodles," said Simone. "It's very important to us that the dog we select to promote Chow Down has a background that's above reproach. As I'm sure you can understand, we're looking to avoid any sort of negative behavior on the part of our spokesdog that might reflect badly on our company."

Well . . . No, I thought, I didn't understand. When it came to dogs, what precisely might constitute negative behavior? Did she think that Faith went out barhopping at night after I was in bed? Or that the Poodle'd had a DUI conviction, or maybe had once checked herself in at Betty Ford? Sitting there thinking about it, I was hard-pressed to come up with any activity that Faith—or any other dog, for that matter—might have indulged in that would shed an unflattering light on the Champions Dog Food Company.

Simone, however, was still regarding me eagerly across the desk. As if it was my turn to speak. As if now was my chance to confess any past transgressions Faith might be guilty of committing.

Off the top of my head, I could think of only one thing to say. It would have come out sounding like, *Are you crazy?*

Fortunately for both of us, I didn't say a thing.

"Well then." Simone braced her hands on her desk and stood. "I guess we're good. There's only one more thing . . ."

I'd risen when she did, thinking the interview was over. Apparently I'd been wrong.

Simone turned and opened a cabinet behind her desk. She withdrew a small, unmarked sack. A clean stainless steel bowl came out with it.

"Chow Down," Simone said in a low, confidential tone. "Aside from the dogs in our testing labs and focus groups, you five contest finalists are going to be among the first to sample it."

I truly hoped she was speaking to Faith and not to me.

"Isn't that exciting?"

Faith didn't seem to think so. She was looking distinctly indifferent to the opportunity about to be accorded her. Knowing how finicky my Poodle could be, I could only hope that this wouldn't get too ugly.

Simone didn't wait for us to answer. She poured a generous amount of kibble into the bowl and set it down on the floor.

Faith sniffed the air delicately, but didn't move toward the food. Her nose was stronger than mine. I sincerely hoped she wasn't smelling licorice.

"Go ahead, girl!" Simone urged. "That's for you. Go get it!"

I supposed she hoped Faith would leap forward eagerly. It didn't happen. Indeed, I had to nudge Faith with my knee to even get her moving in the right direction.

The Poodle hesitated and looked up at me for permission. "It's okay," I said. "Go take a bite."

What she took was a sniff. And then a tentative nibble. Faith picked up one small nugget of kibble and rolled it around in her mouth.

I held my breath, praying that she wouldn't spit it back out. Finally, Faith swallowed.

"There," I said, trying not to sound too relieved. "She likes it."

Simone looked disgruntled. She reached down and snatched the bowl away. Faith watched it leave without apparent regret.

"Well, that was underwhelming."

"Faith had a big breakfast." I was lying but what the heck. The contest seemed to have that effect on me.

"Most dogs *love* Chow Down." Simone's tone was

so insistent that I found myself wondering if she was lying, too. "They can't get enough of it."

Fortunately for me, Faith wasn't anything like *most* dogs. And if that cost her the contest, so be it. That thought brightened my day enormously.

10

Faith and I were sent back around the corner to Cindy Burrows's office next. Simone's work space had been elegantly spare. By contrast, the product manager's office was small and cluttered.

File folders and piles of papers were stacked everywhere. Any surface that wasn't littered with papers held framed photographs. I saw at least half a dozen pictures of a flashy black-and-white Border Collie. Cindy was with the dog in some of the photos. In others he seemed to be performing, making impossible twisting leaps to snatch a Frisbee out of the air.

"Great dog," I said by way of a greeting.

Cindy immediately grinned. "Thanks. That's Gus. And he *is* a great dog. He was tristate disc dog champ last year."

"He looks like he'd be a natural for the Chow Down contest. Did you think about entering him?"

"I wish I could have. He'd be a great spokesdog for the product. But it wouldn't have been fair."

She waved me toward a chair and leaned back to perch on the edge of her desk. "You know, nepotism rearing its ugly head and all. Besides, I adore Gus. He's my best friend. I wasn't sure how I'd feel, sitting in the committee meetings and listening to the other judges rip him apart."

"So that's what you've been doing to us? Ripping our dogs apart?"

"Not usually, no." Cindy looked like she wished she'd kept her mouth shut. "Well, sometimes. But only because it's necessary."

I sat down and patted my knees. Faith hopped her front legs up into my lap. I pulled her toward me protectively.

"We have five excellent finalists. And there's only going to be one winner. Under the circumstances, we don't have any choice but to be critical of every little aspect. It's a big responsibility, being in charge of a major product launch like this. None of us wants to screw up."

I read between the lines and decided Cindy was the one who was worried about making a mistake. Doug, Simone, and Chris were all older than she was. Their positions within the company were probably more secure. Certainly their jobs were at a higher level; each had probably handled pressure like this before.

Judging by their titles, the other three committee members all had wide-ranging responsibilities within the company. Cindy was a product manager. Chow Down was her product. This launch was a make-or-break proposition for her.

"I can see your point about favoritism," I said. "Especially if the other committee members have dogs themselves . . ."

I let the thought dangle, hoping that Cindy would feel obliged to fill in the blanks. Getting to know the judges a little better could only be a good thing. Besides, it didn't seem fair that the contestants were the only ones giving up personal information.

"Doug's got a Lab," she said with a nod. "Chocolate. His name's Hershey, Doug's kids named him. Then his wife divorced him and took the kids. Doug ended up with the dog."

I wasn't about to comment on the contest chairman's marital difficulties. Instead I went for an observation that seemed safe enough. "Doug looks like he'd be a Lab kind of guy."

The two of us smiled. Spend enough time around dogs and their owners and you realize it isn't a myth that people tend to look like their pets.

"What about Simone?" Cindy asked. "What kind of dog do you see her with?"

I thought for a moment. "A Saluki."

"Good guess, but no."

"Chinese Crested?"

Cindy giggled at that. "No way. You'd never catch Simone with a dog that was nearly hairless. Not enough to primp. No, she's got a Pomeranian named Chloe. Sometimes Simone sticks Chloe inside her purse and brings her to work." She glanced down at Faith. "Not on the days when we're going to have other dogs visiting, though."

"What about Chris?" I asked.

"He has a Scottie."

"Like MacDuff."

"That's right."

She looked over her shoulder and pushed some papers around her desk, as if she'd suddenly remembered a task that needed attending to. I wasn't fooled. Cindy didn't want to talk about Chris's pet. Which made me want to discuss him all the more.

"So I guess he was pretty happy to see MacDuff chosen as a finalist," I said.

"I guess so."

Her tone was carefully neutral. I guessed there might be some resentment there that she was holding tightly in check. Worried about appearances, Cindy had tried hard not to practice favoritism. It must have rankled to see Chris do the opposite in making his selections.

"How were the five finalists chosen?" I asked.

"You know that. The procedure was outlined in the contest rules. You must have read them before you entered."

"Sure, but I was wondering how things worked within the committee itself. Did each of the judges look at every single entry? Did you vote on which ones you liked the best? Did all your votes count equally?"

Queried about an easier topic, Cindy relaxed a bit. "Doug and Simone were much too busy to be involved at the beginning of the selection process. The contest was incredibly popular, there were several thousand individual entries that needed to be sorted through. That was Chris's and my job. Between the two of us, we looked at and evaluated every one."

"That must have been a huge undertaking."

"Believe me, it was. Although some of the entries were obviously more serious than others. You wouldn't believe how many submissions we got from little kids who thought that their pet Fluffy or Fido was the best dog in the world."

Little did she know, I thought.

"Of course we had to put those aside. But even so, there was still a huge number to consider. Finally Chris and I had to split them up. Each of us did half and came up with our ten favorites. That left us with twenty semifinalists for the whole committee to consider."

"How many of your choices ended up as finalists?" I asked curiously.

"Three," she said with satisfaction. "And before you ask, yes, Faith was one of them. As soon as I saw your entry, I knew that she would be a perfect candidate."

"Who else did you pick?"

I wasn't sure Cindy would answer, but she did.

"Ginger and Brando were mine, too. All three of my choices were dogs with great charisma. Actually I was quite certain that at least seven or eight out of the ten I presented could have won the whole thing. But when we got the entire committee together to choose the finalists, I think Doug and Simone felt kind of bad when the first three we selected came from my pile. After that they made a conscious effort to take the last two from Chris."

"Not an entirely fair way to do things. Maybe your semifinalists were a better group."

Cindy only shrugged. If she'd had a problem with the outcome, she wasn't about to discuss it with me.

"So your selections were all big dogs."

"Not intentionally, that's just the way it worked out. I was looking for a dog that I thought would have a certain kind of presence in the print ads and on TV. In my mind, I guess that translated into using one of the bigger breeds."

"Clearly your director of advertising didn't feel the same way."

"Not necessarily. I saw Chris's whole group, and he had several large dogs among his final ten. A Weimeraner, I think, and maybe a Scottish Deerhound. But the two he was really pulling for were Yoda and MacDuff."

"And Doug and Simone agreed with him."

"Eventually, yes. In the beginning our choices were all over the place. And it didn't help that there were four of us on the committee, which naturally led to some tie votes."

"What did you do about those?"

"Doug dealt with them," Cindy said with a small, humorless laugh. "Or rather, he announced that in the case of a tie, his vote carried more weight than the rest of ours did."

There we were, right back to that favoritism thing again.

"Doug and Simone weren't sold on MacDuff at first because of his age. He turned six a few months ago. It won't be long before he starts getting gray around the whiskers. We're looking for someone who's willing to make a long-term commitment to the product. There's no way we're going to go through this procedure again any time soon."

"I take it Chris managed to convince them that MacDuff would be a good choice?"

"Did he ever. Chris really went to the mat for that dog. And Yoda too, I guess. Anyway, they both ended up in the final five. Which is okay. Over all, I think it turned out to be a pretty good group."

Cindy glanced down at Faith who was still half-sprawled across my lap. While we'd been speaking, the Poodle had laid her long muzzle down between her front paws and fallen asleep. Now she was snoring softly, her body rising and falling gently with each deep breath.

"Geez, I can't believe you let me go on like that," she said, pushing herself up off the desk. "My mother always told me that I talked too much. It looks like our time's just about up. You and Faith are seeing Chris next, right?"

"If you say so."

I'd seen a story on TV once about something called speed dating. These quick, back-to-back interviews, where Faith and I had only a very limited amount of time to make a good impression, were beginning to feel pretty similar. Except for the lack of alcohol and the fact that we'd be leaving by ourselves at the end.

"Don't worry about Chris," Cindy said, misreading my silence. "He's really a big teddy bear."

"One who likes smaller dogs, apparently."

"I don't think he has anything against big breeds necessarily. It's just the way things shook out."

Like the other judges we'd already seen, Chris Hovick was waiting for us. He welcomed us into an office that looked rumpled and well-used. Kind of like Chris himself.

Faith, refreshed from the catnap she'd taken while I was talking to Cindy, danced happily through the doorway. I followed more slowly behind. The pressure of having to be eager and enthusiastic all over again each time we changed judges was beginning to wear me out. Maybe it was time to let the Poodle speak for herself.

"Greetings," Chris said. When he stooped down to Faith's eye level, she sat down and offered him a paw, a trick I'd taught her several months earlier when we'd been making nursing home visits.

"Cute." He accepted the paw, shook it gently, then returned it to the floor. "Did you give her a cue to make her do that, or did she come up with it all on her own?"

"That was Faith's idea. Poodles are thinking dogs."

"So I've heard. Have a seat on the couch over there, and we'll talk about what else she knows."

I sat down and Faith hopped up next to me. She turned a tight half-circle on the cushion, then sat down beside me, also facing outward. Chris, busy pulling up a chair for himself, watched curiously.

"You're still not telling her what to do?" he asked.

"No, would you like me to?"

"Hell no. This is fascinating to watch. She behaves just like a person."

"Poodles do that. Most are convinced that they *are* people."

"Fast learners?"

I grinned. "What do you think?"

"Yeah. I guess I could have figured that out for myself. I was just talking to the Reddings. Their dog, Ginger, has all sorts of titles and degrees. How does Faith measure up in that department?"

"She's a champion, for one thing."

"That's for conformation, right? That means she's a good-looking Standard Poodle?"

"Yes."

"She ever win that—what's it called?—Best in Show?"

"No."

Chris leaned back in his seat. He rested his elbows on the chair's arms and steepled his fingers in front of his face. "How come?"

"I showed Faith to her championship myself. And the two of us together weren't good enough to compete at the Best in Show level. Besides I really didn't want her to be a specials dog. Do you know what that means?"

"More or less. Like MacDuff."

"Exactly."

"He won Bests in Show."

"Lots of them," I agreed mildly.

I wasn't about to dispute that. If the point of the contest was to find the dog with the best show record, MacDuff was the winner hands down. The rest of us might as well go home.

"What about obedience? Does she have any titles there?"

"Just one. Faith has her CD."

CD stood for Companion Dog and was the most basic of the obedience degrees. Even so, it was an achievement. A dog had to be pretty well-trained to make it that far.

"It's a start," said Chris. He didn't sound impressed. Since he'd recently met with the Reddings and their triple-threat Brittany, I could understand why he might not be.

"You saw Simone earlier, right?"

I nodded.

"She gave Faith some Chow Down to taste?"

"Yes." Deliberately, I didn't elaborate.

"How'd that go?"

So much for the not elaborating thing. "Okay."

"Just okay?"

There was no point in beating around the bush. I was certain the committee members would be comparing notes later.

"Faith didn't fall in love with the product right away. But that's pretty normal for her. It usually takes her some time to decide whether she likes a new food or not."

"Finicky, huh?"

"She can be."

"I know what you're thinking," said Chris. "That a little thing like that is no big deal. But at this level, everything counts. It has to. This contest is important to me. It was my concept and it's been my baby since the beginning. I really care about the end result. And it wouldn't say much for the dog food, would it, if the company's own spokes-dog didn't love it?"

I sat quietly through Chris's lecture. But that, coming on top of what I'd learned from Cindy— that Faith hadn't been one of the finalists Chris had backed—put me on the defensive. All at once I found myself wondering if Faith wasn't the only one who'd had a problem with her initial sample of Chow Down.

"How'd the others do?" I asked.

"Pardon me?"

He'd heard me. I knew it and he knew it.

"I'm just curious," I said casually. "Brando, Yoda, MacDuff, Ginger—how did they do with their first taste of Chow Down?"

Chris hesitated, as if trying to decide how much to reveal. Then abruptly he seemed to realize that his silence itself was telling enough.

"Some handled it better than others."

I waited in silence. After another minute, Chris continued.

"Brittanys aren't big eaters, at least that's what the Reddings told me. And Brando, well . . . one look at Ben and you can pretty much see that that dog's been spoiled beyond redemption. But they'll come around in time. They'll have to, otherwise what would be the point?"

I wondered if it was just coincidence that the contestants Chris outlined as having problems were the ones he hadn't chosen in the first place.

"What about MacDuff and Yoda?"

Chris smiled happily. "MacDuff was fine. He's always fine. Pretty much no matter what you ask him to do, that guy's a pro."

"And Yoda?"

"She did great. For such a small dog, she really packed it in. Then she danced around on her hind legs and asked for more."

"I'm happy for Lisa's sake," I said. "Actually I was surprised to see her today. You know, so soon after what happened."

"Me, too. None of us expected her to show up. And of course we'd have understood entirely if she hadn't. But Lisa was very determined to go on. That's what she told us. She was sure it was what Larry would have wanted her to do."

I've always done my best thinking when I'm driving in the car. Maybe that's why it wasn't until twenty minutes later, when Faith and I were on our way home, that something occurred to me. When I'd seen Lisa earlier outside the dog food company, she hadn't had Yoda with her. So the Yorkie couldn't have sampled Chow Down that morning like the other finalists had.

Yet Chris was certain that Yoda had tried the product and liked it. I wondered when that had happened.

11

After Faith and I got home, I realized something else. Despite the numerous topics I'd talked about at various meetings that morning, the one thing that hadn't come up in our conversations was any speculation about Larry Kim's death. Oh, we'd danced around the subject a bit, spoken about how bad we felt for Lisa, and discussed the fact that she'd elected to remain in the contest.

But like the proverbial elephant in the corner, everyone had avoided mentioning the obvious questions that still remained. What had Larry been doing in the stairwell? Had another person been there with him? And why might someone have wanted to push him down a flight of steps?

I wondered whether the police had been searching for answers, or if they agreed with Lisa's version of events: that her husband, suffering from vertigo, had lost his balance and fallen. It was interesting that she'd been so quick to assume that Larry's death was an accident, especially in light of the fact that she couldn't imagine why he would have entered the stairwell in the first place. That alone should have raised some red flags.

Why was I the only one who seemed to be seeing them?

I'd missed my chance earlier, I realized. While I might not have wanted to pump the grieving widow for information, I'd had interviews with several other people who'd been in the vicinity at the time of Larry's death. And yet I'd neglected to pose a single question.

What had I been thinking?

The answer to that was immediately apparent. I hadn't been thinking, I'd been competing. I'd been polite and acquiescent. I'd answered questions instead of asking them. I'd showcased Faith's good points to the best of my ability, just like a good contestant was supposed to do. And all I'd gained from that was the knowledge that despite the fact that the details as we knew them didn't add up, everyone else involved in the contest preferred to sweep the episode under the rug and forget about it.

I wished I could dismiss my own curiosity so easily.

That night, I began the arduous task of getting Eve ready to compete in a dog show. Spectators who see the dogs only as they appear in the ring have no idea of the amount of time and effort it takes to get a Poodle ready to compete. In actuality, the preparations begin when a puppy is only a few months old.

The long mane coat that comprises the major element of a Standard Poodle in continental trim takes nearly two years to perfect. The precious hair on the ears, the top of the head, and the back of the neck is allowed to grow nearly undisturbed from birth. Frequently bathed and blown dry, it's brushed often enough to keep it from matting and usually protected by banding and wrapping.

At the age of almost twenty-four months, Eve's coat was in its prime. I'd devoted countless hours over the previous two years to its care and upkeep. Now, with an additional five or six hours of work on my part, Eve would be ready to enter the show ring over the weekend.

I'd been spending so much extra time with Faith recently that I should have realized Eve might be feeling a little neglected. Now when I went to set out the grooming supplies, the younger Poodle followed me eagerly into the grooming room. Some dogs hate to be groomed but Eve, like her dam, was a natural show-off. She loved to look her best.

The Poodle watched as I plugged in the clippers and oiled the blades. *It's about time,* she seemed to be saying.

In our old house, I'd had to do my grooming in the basement. In our new home, there was room for everything. Having been accustomed to a concrete floor, dim lighting, and heat that didn't always kick in, I now felt like I was working in deluxe accommodations.

The room Eve and I were standing in was an area

off the kitchen, intended by the builders to be a laundry room. Sam had taken one look at that arrangement and exchanged it for one he liked better. Some tinkering with the plumbing had allowed him to move the washer and dryer to a walk-in closet upstairs. The empty space that remained had quickly been converted to a state-of-the-art dog grooming room.

Thursday night was dedicated to the task of clipping. Eve's face, feet, and hindquarter all needed to be shaved down to the skin, a deed performed several days in advance, giving the black hair time to grow a short, smooth cover over the silvery skin before the Poodle went in the ring that weekend.

Sam came in, pulled up a stool, and sat down to keep me company while I worked. He and Davey had been occupied with the tree house all afternoon, and the topics over dinner had ranged from Davey's upcoming session of soccer camp to why the tomatoes in our salad were classified as vegetables instead of fruit. This was our first chance to do more than gloss over the highlights of my visit to Norwalk that morning.

"Things must have gone well," he said. "Faith was looking very pleased with herself when she got home."

"Faith always looks pleased with herself. In case you haven't noticed, she's a smug dog." I turned Eve's paw in my hand, clipping carefully between each of her toes. "Faith was a hit this morning. The only way she could have done any better would have been if she'd deigned to eat the Chow Down dog food they offered her."

"She didn't?" Sam laughed. I knew he was picturing the scene in his mind. And enjoying every minute of it, the fiend.

"Thankfully she wasn't the only finalist who found it less than palatable. MacDuff was good, but I gather Yoda was the only one who actually dove right in."

"Odd for a Yorkie."

"You'd think. But this one apparently loves to eat. Also, I suspect she'd been slipped a sample ahead of time to practice with."

"Yoda's the dog who belonged to the man who died?"

I nodded. "Larry Kim. His wife, Lisa, plans to continue with the competition. She says it's what Larry would have wanted her to do."

Sam sat in silence and thought about that. I kept working. Finishing with Eve's second paw, I cooled my blades with a blast of spray, then reached around and picked up the third.

"Okay, here's the thing," he said after a minute's consideration. "If I fall down and break my neck at a dog show, I don't want you to simply continue on as if nothing has happened. Don't keep a stiff upper lip. Don't go marching into the ring anyway. And for God's sake, don't go all out for the win."

"No?" I was amused by his train of thought.

"No way. I want you to dissolve in tears on the spot, maybe scream and rant a little, and tear your hair—"

"My hair, not Eve's?"

"Hell no, don't touch the Poodle's hair."

"Just checking." Nice to know that even in times of crisis, Sam had his priorities straight. "This dissolving thing . . . Would that be like the bad witch in *The Wizard of Oz*?"

"If you can manage it." Sam considered the options. "It would certainly be a nice touch under the circumstances."

"Okay, I'll try."

I finished clipping Eve's feet and turned her around on the tabletop so that her hindquarter faced the best light. Carefully, I began to work the clipper blade up her back legs against the growth of the hair. Meanwhile, my husband was apparently contemplating his own demise.

"Is there anything about this conversation that strikes you as just the tiniest bit strange?" I asked. You know, just to make sure we were on the same page with this life-and-death thing.

"What seems strange to me is that three days after Lisa Kim's husband plunges to his death—accidentally or not, apparently still to be determined—his loving wife seems to care so much about the outcome of a dog food contest."

"I was wondering about that, too."

"Maybe they weren't such a loving couple."

"Hard to say. I hadn't seen enough of them to have an opinion. Could be though, that her behavior has nothing to do with how she feels. Maybe now, especially with Larry gone, Lisa needs the money."

Sam looked up. "How much money?"

"The winner of the contest is guaranteed a hundred-thousand-dollar modeling contract as the spokesdog for Chow Down dog food."

"You never mentioned there was a payoff like that involved."

"I didn't?"

"Nope."

I nudged Eve's tail to one side, concentrating on perfecting the circular line around her hip rosette. "The information is on the web site. I guess I just assumed maybe you'd seen it, or that Davey had mentioned it to you."

"Davey's a little hazy on the details when it comes to high finance," Sam said. "As far as I could tell his major motivation for entering Faith in the contest was getting the chance to see her on TV."

"The thing about that contract is that it's enough of an incentive to give everyone a decent motive. Even without the added bonus of having your dog appear in magazines and on TV."

"I wonder what the police are doing," said Sam. "Coverage in the paper has been pretty sketchy. The first article simply said that they were looking into a suspicious death at Champions's headquarters. I haven't seen anything since that labeled it a homicide."

"Lisa told me this morning that Larry suffered from vertigo. She thinks he must have tripped and fallen. It sounds as though the police might be buying her version of the events." I turned off the clipper and stopped and thought. "Suppose Lisa's right and Larry did fall. Why didn't the other person who was there with him do something? Or say something? Why didn't they raise the alarm?"

"Good questions."

"Instead, I heard a door slam shut. Like maybe someone was running away."

Eve, standing between us on the table, was

watching the conversation like a third participant. Now she turned and looked at Sam as if waiting for him to reply.

"Then Doug Allen showed up," he said, replaying the events as I'd related them to him several days earlier. "He opened the fire door two floors up."

"Right."

"How soon after Larry fell did Doug appear?"

I thought back, remembering standing there frozen, then stooping down to catch Yoda as she came flying down the stairs. "Right away. It couldn't have been more than thirty seconds."

"Or maybe it was no time at all," said Sam.

I set the clipper down. "What do you mean?"

"How sure are you that someone actually left and came back through the fire doors? You couldn't see them from where you were, right? You just heard the doors opening and closing?"

"Damn," I said softly.

Sam was looking very pleased with himself. "I guess that's why you finally married me," he said. "So I'd be handy for pointing out things that you miss."

"Get real, Driver. I married you for your body."

"Oh." He colored slightly.

"Besides, you'd recently inherited a small fortune. Maybe I married you for your money."

"You didn't."

I grinned wickedly. "Want to bet?"

"Sure." Sam reached over and yanked me into his lap. "It seems to me that you started wearing my ring when I was just a poor, struggling software designer."

Good point.

"People will do all sorts of things for money." I was still thinking about Lisa and the rest of the contestants.

"Like bump off the competition?" Sam asked, following my train of thought.

"Maybe."

"Why Larry?"

"Convenience? Opportunity? Or possibly because Yoda was the only one of the finalists that actually liked the dog food? That had to give her a leg up on the rest of us. Maybe whoever pushed Larry down the stairs thought that would eliminate the Yorkie . . ."

I stopped as something else occurred to me. "Chances are, Larry was holding Yoda in his arms when he fell."

"Lucky she didn't get hurt."

"Precisely. What if the killer wasn't after Larry? What if he was trying to hurt Yoda?"

"You think maybe Larry died trying to shield his dog from harm?"

To some people that might have sounded farfetched. Not to me and Sam. Our Poodles were like members of the family. Each of us would have done anything to keep someone from injuring them.

"Maybe Lisa was right," I said. "Larry's death was an accident and Yoda was the target all along."

"If that's the case, you'd better keep an eye on Faith."

As one, our gazes went to the other Poodles, three of whom were lying on the floor near the doorway. A quick glance told me that Sam's Poodles were all accounted for. Davey was in the living room, playing a video game; I could hear the sound effects from where we were. Faith, no doubt, was in her usual position, lying on the couch next to him.

"Greed is one of the oldest motives in the world," said Sam. "And don't forget something else. If and when the police go looking for possible killers, every single one of the contestants will be a suspect. That includes you, babe."

12

Saturday came and I took Eve to a dog show. Exactly as I'd done dozens of times before. This time felt different, however. Most show days, I'm feeling hopeful about our chances. On rare occasions, I'm already resigned that things aren't likely to go my way. But that morning, there was a feeling of expectation in the air.

I had begun showing Eve when she was a young, rambunctious puppy. Dogs are allowed to be entered in A.K.C. shows once they've reached six months of age and I had started taking Eve to shows shortly thereafter. In the beginning, we were going mostly for the experience. But even with my inexpert handling, Eve had begun to pile up points pretty quickly.

By the time she turned a year old, the Poodle had already amassed seven of the fifteen points needed to complete her championship. After that, things had slowed down. For one thing, Eve had

had to take some time off to grow into her new adult trim. For another, there'd been a number of changes in my life in the past year, and I'd been too busy to devote as much time as I previously had to showing dogs.

Another factor was that Aunt Peg had cut back on her own show schedule. At one point, we'd gone to nearly every show together. Now Peg was more involved in agility trials and in handling her own judging assignments. Sam had been specialing Tar, but he'd been picking his group and Best in Show judges carefully. Considering how many less-than-stellar panels kennel clubs managed to put together, that inevitably meant that there were many weeks when the duo opted to remain home.

One thing I've learned over the years about going to dog shows: they're not nearly as much fun when your friends aren't there to share them with.

Showing sporadically, Eve had picked up five more points, including her first, all-important, major. Now, one more major win would make her a champion.

Davey was spending the weekend with his father, but I'd been surprised to discover Friday evening that both Sam and Aunt Peg had put their other plans on hold to accompany me to the show. I was hoping that that didn't mean the two of them were assuming I would get the job done. It was one thing to compete in a major entry, and quite another to actually bring home the points.

Sam and I arrived at the indoor facility in Springfield, Massachusetts, where the show was to be held, in midmorning. Aunt Peg had driven up on her own and beaten us there. Once again, Crawford and Bertie had managed to situate their setups in adjacent rows. Thankfully they'd also saved a little bit of space for me.

Sam backed his SUV up to the nearest door and we spent ten minutes unloading. Crawford and Bertie were busy over at the rings. Terry was grooming a Bichon Frise. Aunt Peg was hovering in the background. Hovering and looking like she was itching to get to work on something.

I'd no sooner set my grooming box down than she had it open and was pawing through it, pulling out combs and brushes and lining them up on top of Eve's crate. Meanwhile, Sam deftly maneuvered me aside and hopped Eve up onto the grooming table.

All at once, I felt distinctly superfluous. The two of them were setting up shop faster than a grifter at a flea market.

"Stop," I said.

Sam paused fractionally. Aunt Peg pretended she didn't hear me.

"What's going on?" I asked. My eyes narrowed suspiciously. "What are you two even *doing* here?"

Sam glanced my way. "Do I need a reason? Last time I checked, I was a newlywed. Of course I would want to accompany my lovely wife wherever her endeavors take her."

"That's so romantic," Terry said. He thinks every conversation within earshot should involve him. And he has very big ears. His idea of earshot covers a pretty wide range.

"It's not romantic," I said. "It's a crock."

"Melanie! Such language." Aunt Peg had found all the tools she needed. She laid Eve down on her left side and began to brush through the Poodle's mane coat in long, even rows.

"How come neither one of you is showing today?" I asked.

"Nothing in hair," Peg replied crisply. Her nimble fingers never even slowed.

"Too lazy," Sam said with a shrug.

"And yet you came all this way just to watch."

"And help out."

"Help me, you mean."

Terry sidled over. "From here, it looks as though it's Eve they're helping."

His voice carried, as I was sure he'd meant it to. I put a hand to his shoulder and pushed him away. Grinning broadly, the troublemaker retreated back to his own setup.

"We wanted Eve to look nice," Aunt Peg said. "You know, in case she needed to have her picture taken."

Only winners had their pictures taken. We all knew that perfectly well.

I gazed at the pair of them in exasperation. "Are you that confident about our chances?"

"If they were *that* confident," said Terry, "would they both be here?"

"What do you mean?"

"It looks to me like they came to do up your dog for you," said Terry. "Best of both worlds, if you ask me. You're here, but you're getting a day off. If I were you, I'd sit back and enjoy it."

"I don't need a day off," I said mildly. "And I'm perfectly capable of preparing my own Poodle to go in the ring."

"Of course you are, dear." Aunt Peg kept right on brushing.

Sam, caught in the act of sliding a comb through the rubber band holding the colored wrap on Eve's ear and snapping it loose, looked only briefly guilty. Then he resumed working, too.

The two of them didn't trust me to do a good enough job, I realized. Sam and Peg hadn't come all the way to Massachusetts to share my potential moment of triumph. They'd come to make sure that I didn't blow it.

Well, that was depressing.

"Oh honey," said Terry. "Don't go getting all crestfallen on us. You *so* do not want to take this personally." He patted an empty grooming table next to the one he was working on. "Let those two work their magic. You come sit by me and we'll dish about everybody at the show."

I had to admit, the idea had a certain appeal. As did the notion that Eve would look perfect when Sam and Aunt Peg were finished working on her. I wouldn't have to lift a finger to achieve that effect; all I'd have to do was accept the end of the leash when they handed it to me and walk into the ring.

Giving Eve's nose a good-bye pat, I turned sideways, slid through the bank of stacked crates that separated our setup from his and went to join Terry. "Okay, I said. "Do your worst. Who do you want to talk about first?"

"You must be joking."

I hiked myself up on the empty table. "Why?"

"Because the answer should be obvious. Rumor has it that you got caught, once again, hanging around at the scene of a murder."

"When you put it like that, I sound like some sort of serial killer." I considered pouting, but decided it wasn't a good look for me. "Two things. Number one, the police haven't decided yet how Larry died. They're calling it a suspicious death—"

"Murder would make me suspicious too, hon."

"And two," I continued as if he hadn't interrupted. "I came to the show to get my mind off of all that. To think about something different."

Aunt Peg snorted indelicately.

I looked across the crates at her. "*Now* what?"

"You came to the show to finish Eve, and it's about time, too. So try to stay focused."

"I don't have to stay focused. You two are doing that for me. I'm not grooming, I'm gossiping."

"Some days it's hard to tell the difference," Terry said. "The mouth has to do something while the fingers are working."

"Words to live by," Sam commented. He was spritzing down and brushing out Eve's ears. "Didn't some great philosopher say that?"

Terry didn't miss a beat. "I'm pretty sure it was Nietzsche."

I looked at him skeptically. "What do you know about Nietzsche?"

"More than most people. I was a philosophy major in college."

I was momentarily shocked into silence. Terry worked so hard at being shallow, I'd had no idea he had hidden depths.

He cocked his head to one side and smiled. "Don't hate me because I'm intellectual."

"All right, Mr. Intellectual. Since you want to talk about murder, here's a philosophical query for you. Would you kill someone for one hundred thousand dollars?"

He didn't even have to stop and think. "Honey, I'd be tempted to kill some of these dog handlers just so I wouldn't have to look at their ugly-ass fashion choices week after week."

And he wondered why people were surprised when he said he read Nietzsche.

Then his fingers stilled. Terry looked up, expression brightening. "Is someone offering to pay me? You know, to perform this service for the greater good of society?"

"Right," Sam muttered. "You'll be issued an uzi and sole discretionary power over its use. Fire at will."

Geez but it was hard to get a word in edgewise.

"Nobody's offering to pay anybody anything. Or arm them, for that matter." I poked Terry. He went back to grooming. "I'm asking a question. A simple question."

"She's fishing for motives," said Aunt Peg.

"What's to fish?" asked Terry. "A hundred grand is a perfectly good motive. I take it we're talking about the Chow Down contest?"

"Right."

"You're thinking that one of the other finalists decided to eliminate Larry Kim from contention?"

"I'm trying the theory on for size."

"Makes sense to me," said Terry. "Especially if it isn't just the money that's at stake. There's the fifteen minutes of fame that goes along with it."

"Fame is highly overrated," Aunt Peg contributed. She stood Eve up and began to scissor her bracelets.

"You can't tell me you wouldn't want to see one of your Poodles on television."

"Of course I can. I don't even watch television." She paused, then added, "Well, except for *Law & Order*."

Like we couldn't have seen that coming.

"Well, as far as some people are concerned,"

Terry said, "I'd imagine that was the primary reason they entered the contest."

"You're talking about Ben?" I guessed.

"Among others."

"Like who?"

The handler glanced over his shoulder in both directions before speaking. He wasn't the only one who had big ears. "I'm talking about Dorothy and MacDuff."

I thought about that. Over in the next setup, Eve was looking better and better by the minute. Sam had her topknot in and Aunt Peg was almost finished scissoring. Now all that remained for them to do was spray her up.

Not only were they doing a better job than I could have done, but they were faster, too. I should have thought to enlist their services a long time ago. Not having to prep my own Poodle for the ring definitely made the whole dog show experience much more relaxing.

"Dorothy did say something at the first meeting about MacDuff missing the limelight. That once she retired him from showing, he got bored."

"*He* got bored?" Terry said with a sniff. "I don't think so. How old is that Scottie anyway? Five? Six? *Seven?* She's been running his little feet off for years. There probably isn't a show on the entire East Coast he hasn't been to."

"And won at."

Terry nodded. "I never said he wasn't a good Scottie. Just that Dorothy kept specialing him long after most owners would have been happy to let that poor old thing enjoy a well deserved retirement."

"It seems to me she did give him some time off

on a couple of different occasions over the years," Aunt Peg said.

"Usually when she was bringing out a puppy of his—one she thought might be good enough to take his place. But none of them panned out the way she hoped. They were good enough to finish and maybe put a couple of groups on. But none were as good as their sire. Dorothy wanted a dog that could win week after week at the highest level. And that had to be MacDuff."

"But she finally did retire him," I pointed out.

"She pretty much had to," said Sam. "I showed Tar against him a couple of times last fall. Mac-Duff had definitely lost a step or two. It was clear even then that he was pretty much just coasting along on his reputation. If she wanted him to go out a winner, it was time to stop."

"But then the contest came along," said Terry. "And next thing you know, they were up and running again. If you think Dorothy was a fierce competitor in the dog show ring, honey, watch out now. Looks to me like Chow Down is offering her and MacDuff wider recognition than anything they could ever have achieved in the dog show world. Dorothy's not about to let an opportunity like that slip through her fingers."

I filed that away for further consideration later, as the other three went back to work. A few minutes later, Bertie and Crawford appeared. Having finished in their respective rings, both were leading winners.

"Eve looks great," said Bertie admiringly. She stowed her Clumber Spaniel in a crate and tucked his purple and gold Best of Breed ribbon in her tack box.

"Thank my capable assistants," I said.

"I'm glad I'm only showing a couple of puppies for experience. She'll be hard to—"

"Don't say it!" Peg snapped. Where dog shows are concerned, she's very superstitious.

Bertie grinned and whispered, "Beat."

Aunt Peg glared.

Bertie ignored her. She'd picked up the Poodle armbands on her way back from the rings. She handed me mine and I slipped it up my arm.

Her two Standard puppies were on their table-tops, waiting patiently. She stood them up and both shook out their coats. The hair lifted, then fell right back into place, the sign of a scissoring job well done.

"Time to head over," she said. "Let's go get 'em."

13

Just like at the previous show, Crawford and Terry didn't have any Standard Poodles entered. The two of them remained behind when our small procession made its way to the ring. Bertie's puppies led the way, hopping and scampering through the crowds.

The two were littermates, and both were bitches. Since Bertie would be handling both of them, one had been entered in the Puppy Class, the other in American-Bred. At their young age, their owner wasn't expecting them to win. But even puppies that were showing to socialize and get experience added to the numbers that produced the solid major.

Eve was eligible for the Bred by Exhibitor class, but I'd put her in Open. That was where the toughest competition would be entered; and showing her there sent a signal to the judge that Eve was ready to be a contender. Open Bitch was also the last of the regular classes to be judged within each breed, which meant that by the time our turn came, I would probably be a nervous wreck.

Sam, who knew me better than anyone, took Eve's leash out of my hands as soon as we reached the ring. Winners Dog was being judged; the competition in bitches would begin shortly.

"Go away for a few minutes," he said.

"Pardon me?"

"Shoo. Get lost." His hand flipped up and down in the air, motioning me away. "If you stand here, you'll begin to fidget. And if you fidget, you'll make Eve nervous. Then both of you will begin to fall apart."

"You don't even trust me to *hold* my own dog?"

"It's not a matter of trust, it's a matter of expediency," said Aunt Peg. "If you start fussing and knock all her hair down, Sam and I will be the ones who have to put it back up."

Well, there was that.

"Here," said Bertie, materializing beside me. "If you want to make yourself useful, you can hold one of these wild things while I go in the ring with the other."

She reached over and shoved a balled-up show leash into my hand. The big brown puppy that was attached to it immediately spun around, leapt up, and planted her front feet on my chest.

"Hello!" I said, grunting slightly with the impact.

"Her name's Snickers," said Bertie. "And trust me, you don't want to encourage her."

I wasn't encouraging her, I was merely trying to remain upright. That in itself was a job since the big puppy probably weighed half as much as I did.

Prudently, I moved Snickers away from Eve so that
her antics wouldn't cause any damage. We walked
around the side of the ring and watched Bertie
show her sister.

The best that could be said for the performance
was that the puppy had a lot of fun, most of it at
Bertie's expense. Even the judge was smiling by the
time she pinned the class. Bertie merely looked resigned to being run ragged by her exuberant charge.
In a class of six, the two of them left without a ribbon.

We switched puppies at the gate and Bertie went
right back into the ring with Snickers. The American-Bred class had two entries. Snickers was only
marginally better behaved than her littermate,
and she and Bertie earned second place by default.

I'd been concentrating so hard on watching one
puppy while keeping the other out of trouble that
I'd completely forgotten about the fact that Eve
and I were due in the ring momentarily. Which
had probably been everyone's plan all along.

Clutching her red ribbon, Bertie came flying
out the gate and grabbed the leash I was holding.
As she pulled the puppies away, Sam led Eve into
place by my left side. Aunt Peg stooped down in
front of my Poodle, making one last check of ears
and topknot. Sam took out his comb, ran it quickly
through my hair, then patted everything down into
place.

"Perfect," he said softly.

"You're sure?" Butterflies, late to arrive, were
now coming on full force.

"Positive."

Sam was looking at me, not Eve; and I saw everything I needed to know in his eyes. God, I loved that man.

"Go have fun," he said.

Nine Standard Poodle bitches were entered in the Open class. As usual, almost all of them were being handled by professionals. The majority of the entry had already filed around us and into the ring. Eve and I took our place at the end of the long line.

Most handlers jockey for position in the front of the line. They like the psychological impact of leading right from the start. But since we'd already missed that opportunity, I decided that Eve and I would make the most of our place in the rear. We were going to make a spectacular last impression.

Sam and Aunt Peg had done me a huge favor by coming to the show to prepare Eve for the ring, I realized. Earlier I'd been feeling a little demoralized, wounded by the fact that they hadn't thought I was capable of doing a good enough job of grooming my own dog. But now I saw that their help had freed me to concentrate on the one important thing I had to do that day: showing off my Poodle to the judge to the best of my ability.

Maybe I'd never have the handling skill that Aunt Peg possessed. Certainly I'd never have Sam's flair. But what I was taking into the ring with me that day was an all-encompassing knowledge of the Poodle at the end of my leash.

The other handlers in the ring were professionals. They hadn't been there when the Poodles they were exhibiting were born. They hadn't watched them grow up; they didn't live with them twenty-four hours a day. In some cases, they might have met the dog they were handling only minutes earlier.

Eve and I had a bond that none of the other exhibitors in the ring could hope to emulate. We were accustomed to working together as a team. Each of us knew what the other was thinking.

I reached down and chucked Eve under the chin. She tipped her head back and caught my eye. We shared a look and the same thought passed between us. We'd been showing together for eighteen months. It was time to get the job done.

The judge was a woman named Charlotte Raines. I'd shown to her before and knew what she liked. When she made her first pass down the long line, I didn't stack Eve as the other handlers were doing. Instead, making use of the extra room I'd gained by being at the end, I stepped back and let Eve choose her own balanced stance, then baited her naturally.

Mrs. Raines's gaze slid quickly down the line, examining dogs and handlers alike and making mental notes of the faces she had to deal with. She wasn't a Poodle specialist but she judged the breed often and knew a good one when she got her hands on it. She appreciated the skill that went into a professional handling job, but she wasn't likely to let the pros con her into thinking that their Poodles were better specimens than they actually were.

In other words, she would reward an owner-handler for bringing her a good dog, but she'd make you work every single minute for the win.

Fine, I thought. Eve and I were up to the task.

The first go-around passed without incident. Mrs. Raines took note of Eve, which was good; but she also gazed favorably upon three or four other bitches. Even that early in the class, the contenders had begun to sort themselves out.

As the judge began her individual examinations, most of the other handlers pulled back out of line and let their Poodles relax while they waited their turns. Another time I might have done the same; but not that day. There was too much at stake.

Instead I left Eve standing on the rubber mat. The Poodle responded as I'd known she would. Her dark eyes fastened on the judge, watching her intently for several minutes. It was long enough to draw Mrs. Raines's attention her way twice.

I looked away, smiled to myself, and let Eve continue to work her magic.

Here's the thing. Eve was an excellent Standard Poodle, but with a four point major on the line, she wasn't the only good one in the class. Gazing up the line, I could see several other bitches that were probably her equal. On a given day, any one of us might deserve to win the class. But I refused to let that knowledge intimidate me. Today was going to be *our* day.

I believed it. Eve believed it. And that was half the battle right there.

Slowly the line moved forward. When Eve's attention began to flag, I pulled a little furry mouse out of my pocket and waved it enticingly under her nose. Immediately the Poodle's head snapped up, and her neck arched. Her tail, already high over her back, waved stiffly to and fro.

I gave the toy a small toss and Eve caught it on the fly. Before she could shake her head to "kill" the mouse, I snatched it back and held it up in the air. Eve stood at attention and woofed softly under her breath. Mrs. Raines glanced our way again.

The best judges, those who really understand the breed standard, know that Poodles have to do more than just look good to win. They also have to display the intelligent and playful temperament that is such an integral part of the breed. Mrs. Raines had entered the ring expecting the Poodles to entertain her, and Eve was doing her part to comply.

When our turn came to be individually examined, I walked Eve into a free stack and left her standing there on her own. *Look Ma, no hands!* I was telling the judge that I didn't have to prop Eve up to make her appear correct. That this Poodle bitch was pretty special all on her own.

Eve stood like she'd been cast in stone while Mrs. Raines conducted her examination. The judge ran her hands over the Poodle's body, checking her bite, examining her bone structure, feeling for muscle tone. When she had finished, Mrs. Raines stepped back and asked us to gait a triangle pattern.

Eve and I were at the top of our game. Not only did the judge watch us move, but I saw that the other handlers were taking note, too. They'd sized up the competition and decided who they had to beat, and Eve was at the head of the list.

Mrs. Raines sent us all the way around the ring to the end of the line, but we didn't remain there for long. Almost immediately she beckoned us forward, waving us to the opposite mat to start a new line. As she made the rest of her selections and Poodles filled in the spots behind us, I took a moment to glance outside the ring.

Aunt Peg was frowning, but that wasn't unusual when I was handling. I'd learned not to take it personally. Bertie was trying to watch, but she was also busy wrangling the two puppies who were trying to play with a nearby Briard. Only Sam, standing with his arms crossed over his chest and gazing in our direction, looked supremely confident.

He caught my eye and dropped one lid in a broad wink. *Having fun yet?* he mouthed.

I grinned in reply, just as the judge stepped back to the head of the line.

"I'd smile, too, if she was my Poodle," she said. Then she lifted her hand and pointed to each of us in turn, awarding the class placements. "I'll take them just as they are. One, two, three, four!"

Quickly I hustled Eve over to the first-place marker. That she'd won the Open class was great. It meant that we'd already defeated a significant portion of the competition. But now Eve needed to defeat the winners of each of the earlier bitch classes to secure the points.

The puppy winner and the American-Bred bitch that had defeated Bertie filed back into the ring. The judge marked her book, then handed me a blue ribbon, which I stashed in my pocket. Then I swung Eve back into the lineup. As winner of the Open class, the place of honor in the front was hers by right.

At this point in the competition, the judge has already seen each of the entrants before. Usually they have a pretty good idea of who they're planning to put up for the points. But occasionally they're still debating the outcome; either that or else they want to ratchet up the suspense. In that case, they'll judge the Winners class almost from scratch. Despite the fact that Mrs. Raines obviously liked Eve, this was not the time to take anything for granted.

Since the routine had worked for us earlier, I didn't stack my Poodle this time, either. Instead I stood back and let her free bait. I stepped out of line and angled my body slightly in the judge's direction so that Eve, while looking at me, could also focus on Mrs. Raines.

Of course the problem with that was that now I had my back to the judge. Good handlers pick up a lot of information by watching the judge. Approval or disapproval can often be read in expressions or body language. And some judges use hand signals rather than their voices to advise the exhibitors what they want them to do next. So I was placing myself in a somewhat vulnerable position.

On the other hand Eve was baiting like the champion I hoped she soon would be. Standing square and tall, she cocked her head and watched my hands with an expression of rapt attention. Hopefully Mrs. Raines, whom I couldn't see, was noticing my Poodle's performance.

"Take them around, please."

I flipped Eve the piece of dried liver I was holding in my hand and turned to face front. Pausing only long enough to make sure that the two handlers behind me were ready to go, I shot the Poodle out to the end of the leash and took off at a brisk trot. This was the part Eve liked best, flying around the ring in a spectacular, showy fashion, and daring anyone to believe that she wasn't the best.

As for me, I just tried not to lose my footing in the tight corners of the ring and to stay out of the way. This was Eve's moment to shine; my job was merely to remain inconspicuous.

Mrs. Raines gazed quickly up and down the line. Then her focus returned to Eve and stayed there for the remainder of the circuit. Her hand raised and my heart leapt.

"Winners Bitch," she said. Her finger pointed in our direction.

Someone screamed a little. I'm afraid it might have been me.

Eve bounded into the air, landed on the mat, and then bounced up again. The second time I caught her in my arms and hugged her tight. I was crushing her carefully coifed hair but for the first time in nearly two years, I didn't care.

I had a brand new champion.

14

Eve and I exited the ring just long enough for the judge to award Reserve Winners to the next most deserving bitch. Actually we kind of danced out.

You'd think Sam might have given me a hug. Or maybe a high five. But he and Aunt Peg barely glanced at me. Instead the two of them pulled out scissors, comb, and hair spray, and went right back to work on Eve.

Remember that crushed hair? They had only a minute or two to put it back where it belonged. Even though the part I really cared about was over, Eve was now eligible to compete for Best of Variety.

Only moments later, we were called back into the ring. In that short amount of time Sam and Peg had worked a remarkable transformation. Eve once again looked like a contender.

"Keep up the good work," Sam said cheerfully.

"There's not much here to speak of in specials," Aunt Peg whispered in my ear. "Eve's got a real shot at taking the whole thing. So *please* try not to blow it."

My aunt considered that to be encouragement. It never occurred to her that her pep talks often came out sounding more like threats.

Eve and I strode back through the gate. In the Best of Variety competition, the finished champions were at the head of the line, followed by the Winners Dog. Once again, our place was at the rear.

As we moved into position, I stole a quick glance up the length of the mat, evaluating our competition. Two champions had been entered, a silver and a cream. Neither was a seasoned campaigner; most weeks Tar beat them both handily. Maybe Aunt Peg was right and we did have a chance.

Mrs. Raines judged the class like a woman who'd already seen what she wanted and was only going through the motions until it reappeared. She examined the two specials and had another cursory look at the Winners Dog. Then she quickly pulled Eve out and placed her at the front of the line.

This time she didn't even bother to send us around again. "I'll take the Winners Bitch for Best of Variety," she announced in a loud voice. "Winners Dog is Best of Opposite Sex."

Some days, it's just that easy. Now not only did I have a new champion, but we'd also qualified to compete in the Non-Sporting group. As we waited for the photographer to set up for our picture, I handed the ribbons back to the judge, thanked her for the points, and told her that she'd just created a new champion.

"She's a lovely Poodle," Mrs. Raines said graciously. "I'm delighted to have finished her. I hope she does something for you in the group."

I started to pose Eve next to the plaque, then stopped. "Come on," I said, waving Sam and Aunt Peg into the ring to join us. "I want you both to be in the picture with us."

"No way," Sam replied quickly. "This is your day. Yours and Eve's."

Aunt Peg hung back beside him.

"I couldn't have done it without your help."

"She does have a point," Aunt Peg mentioned.

"Come along," Mrs. Raines said. "The more the merrier."

Invited by the judge herself, Sam and Peg lined up beside us in a row behind Eve. This was, after all, all about the Poodle. The photographer waited until we were ready, then tossed a squeaky toy across the mat.

Eve's ears pricked. The camera flashed. I was grinning like a veritable idiot. Sam had his hand on my ass. Perfect.

The Poodle judging over, we now had time to kill before the groups took place later that afternoon. Aunt Peg and Sam went off in search of edible food, not always an easy thing to find at a dog show. I was on a different mission. According to the catalogue, Bill and Allison Redding had Ginger entered in obedience. Their class was currently being held on the other side of the facility.

Though they both take place at dog shows, conformation and obedience are two entirely different kinds of competitions. It takes a rare dog to excel at both; and it also demands a versatile dog owner. The fact that Ginger had achieved her championship in both events was a testament to the Reddings' skill and their determination.

Three large, fully matted obedience rings filled the area at the far end of the building. Three classes of varying difficulty were being judged. In the Novice ring, a jaunty Norwich Terrier was heeling on leash. In the Open ring, a sleek Rhodesian Ridgeback was skimming over a broad jump. And in the Utility ring, a Bulldog was shuffling across the mat in search of a glove he'd been directed to retrieve.

A Bulldog, I thought. Imagine that. I had to stop and watch. The brindle dog went straight to the glove in the corner, pushed it briefly along the floor with his nose as he attempted to get his teeth around it, then lifted his head in success and carried the glove directly back to his delighted owner. Well done.

I was smiling when I turned away from the ring and spotted Bill and Allison standing together behind the row of seated spectators. Beside them was a wire crate. Inside the crate, Ginger was curled up, asleep, on a thick sheepskin pad.

Bill saw me coming as I approached. He lifted a hand in greeting. "Melanie, right?"

"That's right. It's nice to see you both again. How's Ginger doing today?"

The Brittany opened one eye briefly at the sound of her name. She looked up, saw nothing that required her attention, then tuned us back out. Clearly accustomed to the rigors of competition, Ginger knew enough to grab some rest when she could get it.

"She's great," Allison replied eagerly. Everything the Reddings said and did seemed to be delivered with enthusiasm. "She aced the Open B class this morning. Now we're just waiting for our turn in Utility."

"Which one of you shows her?" I asked curiously.

"That would be me," Bill replied. "At least in obedience. We use a professional handler for breed."

"I get too nervous," said Allison. The two of them spoke so quickly that they seemed to be finishing each other's sentences. "Obedience is tough, every little move you make matters."

"I've tried to tell her it's no big deal," Bill said. "What's the worst that could happen? Ginger already has her OTCH, and besides there's always another day and another dog show—"

"But I want her to be the best every single time," Allison said with a small laugh. "And that means everything has to go just right. I'm always afraid I'll give the wrong signal, or start with the wrong foot, or trip over a mat."

Bill smiled and shook his head. Clearly, he didn't take his wife's fears too seriously. "The truth of the matter is, Ginger's such an old hand that she could probably show herself."

"That's just Bill talking. He doesn't like to take too much credit for himself. The real truth is, Ginger never would have gotten as far as she has without him."

"I'm with you," I said to Allison. "I found showing in obedience to be much harder than competing in the breed ring. There were so many little things I had to keep track of that I found the whole experience pretty nerve wracking."

"Were you showing Faith?" asked Bill.

I nodded and the two of them exchanged a look.

"I didn't realize your Poodle had competed in obedience, too," Allison said. "We thought Faith was just a breed champion."

Just a breed champion. Well, that got my hackles up. Even if Faith wasn't as well-rounded as Ginger, having a breed championship was still a pretty big accomplishment.

"Sometimes Allison speaks before she thinks," Bill said quickly. "She didn't mean that the way it sounded. We were just surprised, that's all."

"Faith's full of surprises," I said cryptically. Let them worry about that for a while. We stood and watched the action in the ring for a few minutes. When there was a brief break between competitors, I said, "Do you mind if I ask you two a couple of questions?"

Bill checked on Ginger. Now the Brittany had her nose tucked beneath one of her paws and was snoring softly.

"Nah," he said. "It looks like we're going to be here a while. Shoot."

"Last Monday, when we were all at Champions, did you leave as soon as the meeting was over, or did you hang around afterward to talk to the judges?"

Bill slid a quick glance over at Allison. For once, neither one of them was in a hurry to speak first. Or maybe they were checking with each other to see what their story was going to be.

And wasn't it interesting that they would feel the need to concoct a story at all?

"I guess you're talking about when Larry died," said Allison. "What a shock that was. We'd just been sitting in a room talking to him only moments earlier . . . and bang, just like that, he was gone. Something like that makes you really stop and appreciate every single day, doesn't it?"

I nodded but didn't speak. Just because Allison was busy trying to change the subject didn't mean that I was going to help her do so.

"Let me see . . ." Bill stroked his chin thoughtfully. He looked less like a man who was trying to remember than like a play actor who was trying to convey that idea.

Come on folks, I thought. The question wasn't that hard. I knew exactly where I'd been when Larry Kim died. If the man's death had come as such a surprise to the Reddings, you'd think they would have had that information at their fingertips, too.

"Honey?" Bill looked at his wife. "Did we leave before or after Larry and Lisa?"

"I don't know," she said vaguely. "I guess I wasn't paying any attention to them at that point."

"The Kims split up when they left the meeting," I said to help things along. "Lisa took the elevator down and Larry went by the stairs."

If someone had said that to me, I'd have asked why. But either the Reddings lacked my curiosity, or else they already knew the answer. Neither one commented.

"So when you left the conference room to go home, you weren't with either one of them?"

"No," Bill said slowly, "not that I recall."

"What about Dorothy and Ben?"

"What about them?" asked Allison.

"Were they on the elevator with you?"

"Oh, we didn't take the elevator." Bill seemed happy to finally be able to supply an answer. "Ginger hates them. We took the steps."

I tried to work that information into my timeline. "So if you didn't see Larry in the stairwell—or Faith and me, for that matter—you must have gone down ahead of us."

"Maybe," Allison said with a shrug. "The police asked us about that and it turned out that we hadn't taken the same set of stairs that you and Larry did. There was another stairwell at the other end of the hallway. That's how we got down."

Damn, I thought. I hadn't realized that. Having another potential exit was going to make it that much harder to pin down where everyone had been when Larry died.

"One more thing," I said. "Where were the two of you when you heard about what had happened to Larry?"

"Outside in the parking lot. We were just about to leave when Chris Hovick came outside and said there'd been an accident. We didn't realize he was talking about something serious. We had no idea that Larry had died until later that afternoon."

"How did you find out?"

"The Norwalk police called us. A Detective Sheridan," Bill said. "He said he just had a couple of routine questions, but when he found out that we left before anything happened, he didn't even ask those."

But they hadn't left, I thought. Hadn't they just told me that? They'd still been outside the building.

"Lisa was outside then, too," I said. "Maybe you saw her?"

Allison shook her head. "Not me."

"Me either," said Bill. "I guess the Kims must have been parked on the other side of the lot."

I stifled a sigh. Under the guise of trying to be helpful, the Reddings had managed to tell me exactly nothing of any value. I wondered if it was by accident or design that their collective recollection of the previous Monday was so vague.

"Now I have a question for you," said Bill.

"Go ahead," I said.

"Are you asking everyone what they were up to when Larry Kim died, or just us?"

"Sooner or later I guess I'll talk to everyone."

"Why?" asked Allison.

"Because I want to know what happened."

The two of them stared at me blankly.

"Aren't you curious?" I asked.

"Not really," said Bill. "It's none of our business."

"One less contestant to beat," said Allison. "His loss. Our gain."

15

That was just cold.

And though the Reddings apparently didn't know it yet, Yoda and Lisa weren't dropping out of the contest. So if either one of them had had anything to do with Larry Kim's demise, they hadn't gained much.

When I got back to the setup, Aunt Peg and Sam were leaning against either side of a bank of stacked crates and sharing a funnel cake. Judging by the evidence, they'd also eaten burgers and fries. Bertie, whose crates they were draped over, was brushing out an Otterhound, munching on a power bar, and looking as though she'd rather be eating a funnel cake.

"There you are," said Peg. "You missed lunch. We picked up a hamburger for you at the food stand but Bertie ate it."

I glanced at my sister-in-law and lifted a brow.

"It was getting cold," she said without remorse. Bertie was still breast feeding Maggie. Always slen-

der, she now ate like a stevedore just to keep her
weight up. "Trust me, it was bad enough already.
You really wouldn't have wanted it once the grease
had congealed."

"Don't worry about it. I'm not hungry anyway."

"There might be another power bar in my bag,"
Bertie said. Then she stopped eating and held out
the snack in her hand. "Or you could finish this
one."

The small rectangular bar looked like something
you might consider feeding to a horse. Actually,
upon closer inspection, it looked like something a
horse might reject.

"No thanks. I'm fine, really."

"You're not fine," said Aunt Peg. "You're missing a meal."

Having gotten up early to get to the show, I'd
missed breakfast too, but who was counting?

"I miss lots of meals," I said. "It's never bothered
you before."

"That was then. Now—" Abruptly my aunt stopped
speaking.

As well she might. I'd just figured out where this
conversation was heading. And it wasn't in a direction I had any intention of discussing. Again.

"*Now* what?" I demanded.

"Now you should be taking better care of yourself."

"Good save," Sam said, laughing.

He could read Aunt Peg just as easily as I could,
and knew exactly which topic we were dancing
around. But while I thought that my pregnancy—
or lack thereof—was my own business, Sam didn't
seem to mind our relatives' interfering ways. Then
again, he wasn't the one who felt deficient every

time another month passed without good news to share.

"New subject," said Bertie. "Where'd you go anyway?"

"Over to the obedience rings. I wanted to talk to Bill and Allison Redding."

"Wait, wait, wait!" cried Terry. He was striding toward the setup from the direction of the rings. A Chihuahua was tucked securely beneath each of his arms. "Don't start talking yet. I don't want to miss anything."

"I've been talking all day," I pointed out as he stashed the Toy dogs in their little crates. "You've missed most of it."

"You missed seeing Eve finish her championship, too," Aunt Peg said.

"Gawd!" Terry swore. "Don't you just hate it when work gets in the way of your good time?" He scooted between the grooming tables and wrapped his arms around me. "Congratulations! It's about time. You kept us waiting for*ever*."

"I was enjoying the journey."

"Pish," Aunt Peg muttered. "You just kept allowing yourself to get side-tracked—"

"By real life," I said. "Imagine that."

Where dog show people are concerned, there often is no such thing. And most think that's a perfectly normal state of affairs. Ask any exhibitor who won Best in Show last March in Louisville and they can probably tell you. Ask that same person who the current secretary of state is and you might well get a blank stare.

"But Eve's done now," Sam said. "And she and Melanie are going in the group this afternoon."

"You won the variety, too?" Terry leaned in and

hugged me again. It was a little depressing to realize that he smelled better than I did. "Good job!"

"Mrs. Raines liked her," I said modestly.

"As well she should have." Peg was brisk. "Did anyone check and see who's doing the Non-Sporting group?"

"Harry Bumgartner," Terry said.

"Oh my."

"Bad news?" I asked.

"Harry's a Whippet specialist," said Bertie. "He likes his dogs skinny and fast. And he has no idea what to do with hair. The Non-Sporting group just confuses him. He usually goes with the Dalmatian."

I knew there had to be a reason why Sam hadn't entered Tar in the show. But when I'd entered Eve under Charlotte Raines it hadn't occurred to me that I'd need to worry about the group judge.

"Never mind," said Aunt Peg. "Eve has finished her championship in grand style and that's what really matters."

Terry flapped his hand in the air. "Enough about Harry Bumgartner, who has to be one of the least interesting people one would ever meet at a dog show. Back to the Reddings, whom you were about to spill the beans about. Presumably they're your second set of suspects?"

I looked at him with interest. "Who were the first?"

"Dorothy Foyle and MacDuff, of course. You *do* remember talking about them earlier, don't you?"

"MacDuff is a suspect?" Bertie said with a laugh. "That must be one very talented Scottie. Do you suppose Dorothy sent him into the stairwell to trip Larry?"

"Do shut up," Terry said pleasantly. "We're trying to do some serious detecting over here. Melanie has the floor."

"Melanie doesn't need the floor," I said. "Unfortunately Melanie doesn't have anything terribly useful to say."

"You went and talked to Bill and Allison . . ." He refused to be deterred.

"And they didn't have anything useful to say, either. That's what I'm trying to tell you."

"Then make something up. Tell us a good story."

Aunt Peg glared in Terry's direction. "Don't listen to him. And don't make up a thing. We're supposed to be looking for clues here, not spinning fairy tales. The Reddings must have seen something. They were there."

Murder solving by committee. It was enough to make my head spin. Is it any wonder that Kinsey Millhone works alone?

"*I* was there," I pointed out. "And I didn't see anything."

"You heard Larry fall down the steps. That's something. Where were the Reddings while that was happening?"

"They were out in the parking lot. They said they left as soon as the meeting ended. Lisa Kim said she did the same thing. She told the police she was outside when Larry fell, but neither Bill nor Allison saw her there."

"Maybe Lisa was lying," said Terry. I think he watches *Law & Order,* too. "Maybe she was actually in the stairwell with Larry. I'll bet she's the one who screamed."

"What makes you think that?" asked Sam. He doesn't really approve of my mystery solving predilection, but sometimes he gets interested in spite of himself.

"Because women always lie. It's the nature of the beast."

Wrong answer. All four of us glared at him.

Terry wasn't even slightly fazed. "Oh, like you think that isn't true. Try asking any woman her weight. What about dress size? Age? Do you color your hair? Did you buy that on sale? Who ate the half pound box of chocolate I left sitting on the counter?"

"Women lie *sometimes*," Bertie said. Pointedly she ignored Sam who'd begun to snicker. "And what makes you think men are any better? Just try asking a man what sports he played in college. Or when he's going to mow the lawn. Or whose idea it was to meet the guys for lunch at Hooters."

"Hooters?" asked Aunt Peg.

"Use your imagination," I told her.

"I am," she muttered unhappily.

"Maybe Lisa was in the parking lot," Bertie mused, "and the Reddings are the ones who weren't where they said they were."

"Or maybe they'd split up," Sam offered. "Bill could have been outside with Ginger while Allison was screaming in the stairwell with Larry."

"Now there's a visual to make your hair curl," said Terry.

"Not mine," said Peg. "I'm still stuck on the Hooters thing."

I lifted my hands and cradled the sides of my face. "You people are giving me a headache!"

Aunt Peg leaned over and peered at me closely. "That's not our fault, you're just hungry. Eat something, dear, you'll feel better."

The Non-Sporting group was scheduled second to last, which meant that we had to hang around the show nearly all afternoon. Bertie continued to show her clients' dogs, Aunt Peg wandered off to talk to various other people she knew, and Sam and I gave Eve a breather in her crate and went to watch the judging in other breeds.

Even though I've reached the point where I know quite a bit about Poodles, I'm still a novice when it comes to dogs like German Shorthaired Pointers or Great Pyrenees or Rhodesian Ridgebacks. I could usually pick out the soundest entries but the intricacies of breed type eluded me. It seemed nothing short of astounding that there were judges who were licensed to judge every single one of the A.K.C.'s more than one hundred and fifty breeds. No matter how long I was involved in dogs, I was certain that I'd never succeed in compiling that comprehensive a body of knowledge.

An hour before our group was due to start, we headed back to the setup. The handlers' section of the large hall had emptied out considerably. Space had been tight earlier, but now, as exhibitors finished for the day and went home, areas had begun to open.

My single crate and grooming table had been tucked in beside Crawford and Terry's much larger setup, with Bertie's equipment and supplies on the other side. But as Sam and I approached we saw only empty space where the Bedford Kennels setup had been earlier. Even Bertie was packing up for the day.

"Good, you're back," she said. "I was about to start loading up and I didn't want to leave Eve sitting here all by herself."

"I hope we didn't hold you up," I said. "I just assumed Crawford and Terry would still be here. I can't believe they've left already."

Normally it wasn't unusual for Crawford to have an entry in at least two or three of the seven groups. On many occasions, he needed to stay through Best in Show. Aside from the event the previous week, I couldn't remember a time when the professional handler hadn't remained at a show ground until the bitter end.

"He and Terry finished with their class dogs an hour ago," Bertie said. "Crawford took a Maltese in the Toy group, and then they packed up and left."

I leaned against the edge of the grooming table and frowned. "Something's wrong. This is *so* unlike Crawford. He lives for dog shows. He and Terry are always the first to arrive and the last to leave at night."

"Not only that," Bertie added for Sam's benefit, "but he's been sending me clients."

Sam looked back and forth between us. "That doesn't necessarily mean that anything's wrong. Maybe Crawford's just overbooked. I'd imagine plenty of people would love to have a handler with his reputation showing their dogs. It wouldn't surprise me to know that he has to turn people away."

"But that's just it," I said. "He's bringing fewer dogs than ever to the shows. And what happened to all his specials? When was the last time you went to a show where Crawford only went into one group and didn't even pick up a ribbon?"

"How old do you suppose Crawford is?" Bertie mused.

Sam and I both thought about that.

"Maybe Aunt Peg's age?" I guessed. "Early sixties?"

"No," said Sam. "Crawford looks great for his age but he's older than that. I think he might be approaching seventy."

"Wow," I exhaled slowly. "I wouldn't have guessed that."

"Funny thing is," said Bertie, "a couple of years ago it looked like Crawford's career was beginning to wind down. He just didn't have the same oomph he'd had earlier. But then Terry came along and it was as though he'd gotten a second wind. Maybe this time he really is getting ready to retire."

"Don't you think he'd have said something?" I asked.

"Crawford?" Sam shook his head. "He's about as private as they come. The last thing he would want would be for people to make any sort of fuss over him."

"Precisely," I said, "and that's what worries me. Look at what's been going on recently. Crawford's been working half days and showing only little dogs. He doesn't spend any time socializing with us and when he is around he acts like a real bear."

"Who's a real bear?" Aunt Peg asked. Heading

our way across the grooming area, she was eating a powdered doughnut, carrying two shopping bags, and frowning at Eve, who was still lying in her crate. "And why isn't that Poodle out on a table getting ready for the group?"

"We were getting to that," said Sam. He leaned down to remedy the situation, flipping the latch on Eve's metal door, then catching her deftly as she leapt out into the aisle.

"No you weren't," Peg replied. "You were talking again. Who's the unlucky subject this time?"

"Crawford," I told her. "We're hoping he's all right."

"Of course he's all right," Peg said briskly. She polished off the last of the doughnut and dusted off her hands. "Why wouldn't he be?"

I gestured toward the empty space that earlier had been filled by the Bedford Kennels setup. "Because all of a sudden, he seems to be taking things pretty easy."

"So? He's entitled."

"Of course he's entitled," said Bertie. "He can do whatever he wants—"

"I'm sure he'll be delighted to know that you think so." Aunt Peg watched as Sam hoisted Eve onto the grooming table. Her practiced eye skimmed over the Poodle's topknot, deciding what needed to be repaired.

"That's not the point," I said. My aunt was being deliberately obtuse. "I'm worried about Crawford. He loves being a handler. Dog shows are his whole life. I just wouldn't want to think that anything is wrong—"

"Then don't think it." Peg's tone was short. She

picked up a comb and a can of hair spray and
began the delicate task of smoothing Eve's topknot back into place. "Nobody asked you to. Crawford doesn't want anyone worrying about him,
and why should he? There's nothing the matter.
Nothing in the slightest."

Case closed. Or at least that was what the others
seemed to think.

Sam retrieved some tools from the tack box; he
began to fluff Eve's tail with a comb. Bertie went
back to packing up her things. They all had jobs to
do and I just stood there worrying.

I should have found Aunt Peg's words reassuring but instead they had the opposite effect. My
aunt loves to solve problems. She's a master at digging around for clues and ferreting out hidden
motivations. She's endlessly curious about what
other people are up to and she tends to think that
their secrets are fair game.

So the fact that she didn't want to discuss my
concerns about Crawford was worrisome. It made
me think that maybe she knew a whole lot more
about the subject than I did. And that maybe what
she knew wasn't good.

Thanks to Sam and Peg's dedication to the
cause of Poodle pulchritude, Eve looked like a star
in the group. Unfortunately, the judge, Harry
Bumgartner, didn't notice. Rather quickly he put
up the Shiba Inu, followed by the Dalmatian, the
Schipperke, and the Boston Terrier. The rest of us
were thanked for our participation and politely
sent on our way.

That small disappointment, however, did nothing to detract from the triumph I'd felt earlier. At

long last, Eve was a champion. She was the second I had finished all by myself, and the second produced by her dam, Faith. Those accomplishments were more than enough to keep me smiling for the long drive home to Connecticut.

16

That evening, there was another email from the contest committee waiting for me when I turned on my computer. Once again, Faith and I were being summoned to a test of the Poodle's suitability to represent Chow Down. This one would take place on Tuesday in Manhattan.

The five finalists and their owners were going to be transported to Central Park where the judges planned to observe how members of the dog food–buying public responded to each of the different contestants. The judges also wanted to see how the dogs comported themselves in a new and unfamiliar environment, as that was something they'd be subjected to regularly if chosen to fill the role of spokesdog.

I read the email through twice, then sat back in my chair and sighed. It was beginning to look as though my entire summer vacation was going to be taken over by this silly contest.

"Something the matter?" asked Sam. He walked into the bedroom and sat down on the bed.

Davey was still with Bob, he wouldn't be returning until the next afternoon; but Sam wasn't alone. As usual, he was trailed by a procession of Poodles. One thing about owning a dog: you never lacked for company.

"Not really. It's just annoying. Though perfectly predictable, I suppose."

"Chow Down?"

I nodded. "Faith and I have been summoned again. We're going into the city on Tuesday."

Sam leaned forward and read over my shoulder. "It's an interesting idea, I suppose. But what if you guys don't draw any response at all? This is New York we're talking about. Everyone from rock stars to Donald Trump wanders around there on a daily basis. A group of people with five nice looking dogs? Nothing unusual about that. You might not even get noticed."

I clicked the email closed and signed off. "I hope we're not meant to do stupid things to draw attention to ourselves."

"And, by association, the product?"

"Right. That's what this whole thing is about, after all, publicity. The more buzz the company creates around the product, the bigger the Chow Down launch is going to be."

"All those MBAs sitting over at Champions Dog Food are no dummies," said Sam.

"And this is only the beginning. Doug Allen mentioned something about a press conference and maybe an appearance on a morning show."

Sam reached over, laid both hands on my shoulders, and began to knead the knotted muscles gently. "I'd imagine the contest committee must be thrilled at the extra press they're getting from the coverage of Larry Kim's death. Now that the police have finally decided to open an investigation, the papers have been all over the story. And every time some reporter writes a piece about it, they mention Champions Dog Food and the Chow Down contest."

"Somehow I don't think that's the kind of attention they were hoping for."

"I disagree," said Sam. "What those marketing types really want is brand recognition. And that involves getting their name in front of the public as often as possible. The context isn't nearly as important as the fact that it's there. People tend to skip over ads and commercials but they read news stories. They want to feel like they're staying informed.

"This kind of press is like gold for the Champions Company. Larry Kim died at their headquarters, but not through any negligence or wrongdoing on their part. Chow Down wasn't to blame, it just happened to be in the vicinity. That puts them in the enviable position of receiving lots of free publicity with virtually no downside."

Sam was probably right, I realized. And now that the press had begun to pay attention to the story they probably wouldn't let go of it any time soon. Reporters from more than one paper had already noticed that the tale had several great hooks: a grieving widow, a cute little dog, and the fact that Larry had been on the premises to compete in a contest for Chow Down dog food.

"It's a win-win situation for Champions," said

Sam. "Of course they'd deny in public that they're capitalizing on Larry's death. But in private, I bet they're reading the papers every day and congratulating each other on how lucky they got."

"Sad to think that somebody's death could be considered a stroke of luck." I leaned back and let my husband's hands work their magic. The kinks in my neck and shoulders were melting away. My bones were turning to liquid.

I closed my eyes and sighed again. This time there was bliss in the sound.

"You don't really want to keep talking about dog food, do you?" I asked.

"Not if you have a better idea."

Oh yeah, I thought. I was pretty sure I did.

Tuesday midmorning found Faith and me standing in the parking lot of the Champions Dog Food Company, preparing to board a large bus. The vehicle had been procured and customized for the express purpose of conveying the finalists, their owners, and the contest committee into the city. A colorful banner wrapped around three sides of the bus. It featured the Chow Down logo, along with larger-than-life-size pictures of Brando, Ginger, Yoda, MacDuff, and Faith.

"Pretty exciting stuff," said Ben. He sidled over to stand beside me.

"Something like that," I said.

Ben didn't seem to notice my lack of enthusiasm. He chattered on about how much he and Brando were enjoying the competition and how he was looking forward to the day when his Boxer would be chosen as the Chow Down spokesdog.

One thing I had to say for the actor, he wasn't short on confidence.

Unfortunately Ben was so busy listening to himself talk that he was paying only minimal attention to Brando. The dog's leash was looped around his fingers, but its six-foot expanse still gave the Boxer plenty of leeway to explore. When Brando looked at Faith, measured the space between them and curled his upper lip, I quickly took several judicious steps back.

And walked right into Lisa who'd been coming up behind me.

"Sorry," she said quickly, even though I was the one who had landed squarely on her foot. "I thought we were ready to start boarding."

As usual, Lisa was holding Yoda in her arms. The Yorkie leaned over and gazed down at Brando. You didn't have to be a psychic to read the disdain in her gaze.

"I don't know what's holding us up," said Ben. He looked around at the assembled group. Everyone seemed to be accounted for, but no one had yet climbed up into the bus.

He'd barely finished speaking before a late-model sedan came flying into the parking lot and slipped into an empty spot.

"Finally," Doug muttered.

A middle-aged man in battered khakis and a faded baseball cap opened the car door and slid out from behind the steering wheel, dragging a leather camera bag along behind him.

"People!" Doug clapped loudly to get everyone's attention. "This is Charlie Dunbar. Charlie's a photographer and he'll be traveling into New York with us to record the day's outing."

"Hey," Charlie mumbled. He didn't look very impressed either by us or the assignment. "How about we start with a group shot in front of the bus?"

"Good idea!" Doug was in cheerleader mode now. As if maybe he was hoping that some of his excess energy would transfer itself to the photographer. "Let's line up, everyone. Little dogs in front, bigger dogs in the back."

We probably could have figured that out for ourselves, I thought, then realized I was wrong. Because evidently Ben was under the impression that Brando was a small dog. When Dorothy and Lisa stepped to the front of the group, he went with them.

"We'll crouch," he said, placing himself and the Boxer front and center.

"Whatever." Charlie pulled out a camera that looked to be loaded with bells and whistles. He didn't touch any of them before desultorily snapping off a few shots. "Got it," he said before half the group had even had time to pose and smile.

"Great!" said Doug. "Let's load up, then."

By the time Faith's and my turn came to climb up onto the bus, all the seats near the front were already taken. Chris, Simone, and Cindy were sitting in a tight little group just behind the driver.

Lisa came next. She and Yoda had a seat to themselves. Though the benches were wide enough to accommodate two people comfortably, no one had joined her. I glanced her way briefly but when she didn't return my look, I kept walking too.

Doug had seated himself with Charlie. Perhaps they had work to do. At any rate, I had no desire to join them.

The Reddings and Ginger were in the next row and Ben had slipped in across from them with Brando. That left Dorothy and me to share the long bench that ran along the back of the bus. We settled down next to each other, both of us directing our dogs to our outer sides. Faith and MacDuff were both experienced travelers. As soon as the bus began to move, they laid down next to our feet and closed their eyes.

Dorothy and I had met the previous week at the initial meeting, but we hadn't had occasion to speak to one another. Now, even though we were seated side by side, it didn't look as though that was going to change. Dorothy turned her head away and stared out a side window. As the bus lumbered through Norwalk's industrial zone on its way to I-95, all that could be seen was a dreary visage of worn brick buildings and hulking factories. I doubted that Dorothy was enjoying the view.

Maybe a little judicious name-dropping would break the ice, I decided. It wouldn't be the first time I'd invoked Aunt Peg's name to shore up my own credibility. The two women were of similar age and status within their respective breeds, and the dog show world was, at its core, a very small community. Just as Peg had known immediately who Dorothy and MacDuff were, I was quite certain the reverse would also be true.

"I'm wondering if you know my aunt," I said. "Margaret Turnbull?"

As I had hoped, the question got Dorothy's attention. She swiveled her head my way. "Of course I know Peg. She's your aunt?"

"Yes. She's the one who got me started showing dogs. In fact, she's Faith's breeder."

Dorothy's gaze drifted downward to the Poodle reclining on the floor of the bus. "No wonder she's such a good one. Your aunt has produced a wonderful family of dogs. These days, she doesn't seem to be showing as much as she used to. At one point I was accustomed to seeing her in the group ring nearly every weekend."

"She cut back a lot after my Uncle Max died. Now you're much more likely to find her judging than competing."

Dorothy nodded. "So many exhibitors make that leap eventually. After you've devoted your life to learning everything there is to know about your breed, it seems like the natural progression."

"Does that mean you're thinking about applying for a judge's license, too?"

"I'm always thinking about it." Dorothy laughed. "I just never seem to get around to doing the paperwork. And competing with MacDuff kept me so busy for so long . . ."

"I always enjoyed watching the two of you in the ring," I said, and my enthusiasm was genuine. "MacDuff seemed to love what he was doing and you made a great team."

"He adored it," Dorothy said fondly. "He absolutely reveled in the applause and the attention. As soon as I walked him into the ring, MacDuff just turned on. He enjoyed every single minute. So much so that it seemed almost unfair to make him stop. Now I'm really hoping that we can find something for the second phase of his life that he'll love just as much."

A moment of awkward silence followed. As if we'd both briefly forgotten why we were there, until Dorothy's comment reminded us. For Dorothy and

MacDuff to get their wish, Faith and I would have
to lose. It wasn't the worst thing that could happen
by my estimation; but Dorothy didn't know I felt
that way.

"Is your aunt still breeding?" she asked after a
minute.

The bus had found the entrance ramp to the
turnpike. It pulled on and merged into traffic. We
were moving faster now but Central Park was still
at least an hour away. Now that we'd established
our credentials, Dorothy had evidently decided
that she might as well while away the time in conversation.

"Occasionally. No more than a litter a year.
Sometimes not even that."

"I know how that goes. Puppies are more fun
than anything. But if you're determined to do
everything right, having a litter can be a very time-
consuming project."

I suddenly thought back to the conversation I'd
had with Cindy during our individual interview.
We'd spoken about how determined Chris Hovick
had been in his support of Yoda and MacDuff.
He'd fought hard for their inclusion in the final
five.

And, as it happened, his own dog was a Scottie,
just like the one lying near my feet.

Coincidences happen more often than you
might think; but I tend to be a naturally suspicious
person. What were the chances, I wondered, that
Chris had just happened to pull MacDuff's entry
out of his pile of submissions? I was willing to bet
that it wasn't very likely.

"Not to mention," I said, "how hard it can be

sometimes to find enough really great homes for all of them."

"Fortunately I've never had to worry about that," the older woman said. "As you might expect, MacDuff's reputation enhanced the desirability of everything I produced. I usually have a waiting list for my puppies."

Aunt Peg did too, but I feigned surprised anyway. As if Dorothy had attained a level of achievement with her breeding program that most mere mortals could only dream about.

"Really?" I said casually. "Is that how you first met Chris?"

Dorothy shook her head slightly. As if maybe she was trying to place the name. Her confusion didn't appear any more real than my surprise had. Regardless of how she answered the question, I knew that my suspicions had already been confirmed.

"Chris?"

"You know"—I nodded toward the front of the bus—"Chris Hovick?"

For a moment, Dorothy looked as though she might deny the connection. But since she wasn't sure how much or how little I knew, I guess she quickly realized that doing so might lead to complications later.

"Did Chris tell you that?" she asked instead.

"No, but Cindy told me he had a Scottie." I pasted a goofy smile on my face and tried to look as though I'd ventured a lucky guess. "I suppose I just put two and two together . . ."

"Sometimes when people do that, they come up with five," Dorothy said tartly. "But in this instance, as it happens, you're correct. Chris acquired a puppy from me last year. A very nice male. I believe he calls him Duffy."

"A nod to his illustrious sire."

"Quite so."

Dorothy didn't look at all pleased by the turn the conversation had taken. I wondered if the fact that she and Chris had had a prior connection was against the rules. Of course to know that, I would have had to have actually read the rules. Usually contests barred family members from entering. In this case it seemed as though the same ought to apply to canine families.

In any event, I was willing to bet that neither Chris nor Dorothy had advertised their previous acquaintance. Probably the other committee members had no idea. Which meant that Dorothy was right to be concerned.

As far as conversation was concerned, most people wouldn't have considered a question about murder to be an improvement. But right about then, Dorothy was looking like she'd be very receptive to a change of topic.

"That was too bad about what happened to Larry Kim, wasn't it?" I said.

"Indeed." Dorothy had gone back to staring out the window. She didn't choose to elaborate.

"Had you known him and Lisa from the shows?"

"I'd certainly seen them around. You know what the dog show world is like. The two of them had been breeding Yorkies for quite a while. Occasionally they've even had a good one."

She didn't even bother to veil the insult. I gathered she hadn't thought very highly of the Kims.

"You don't seem surprised that someone might have wanted to hurt Larry."

Dorothy swiveled in the seat to face me. "Should I be?"

"I don't know. I never met either of the Kims until last week at the meet-and-greet. Why don't you tell me about them?"

"If you're waiting for me to say that it was a huge loss to the dog show community, don't bother."

I didn't respond, just waited in silence until she continued.

"Larry wasn't a particularly nice person," she said after a minute. "He wasn't a good winner and he wasn't a good loser. Frankly I don't know how Lisa ever managed to live with him. He was always bossing her around, telling her what to do and where to go, as if she didn't have a single original thought in her head."

"So . . ." I said slowly, "you think maybe Lisa just got fed up?" Certainly Dorothy seemed to be leading me that way.

"All I know is that I wouldn't blame her if she had. If I'd been married to Larry Kim, I would have pushed him down a flight of stairs a long time ago."

17

Come on, I thought, tell me how you really feel. There was no need to encourage Dorothy to continue, however. She was warming to her subject now.

"There's nothing more annoying than a young woman who looks to a man to make her decisions for her. Good Lord, what do they think women's liberation was all about? My generation burned their bras and marched on Washington. We had to. Nobody would have listened to us otherwise. Now the girls that are coming up behind us take our accomplishments for granted, and that's a huge mistake."

"So you think Lisa was too subservient? A moment ago, I thought you were implying that she might be the one who had pushed him down the stairs."

"Perhaps she simply snapped," said Dorothy. "And bravo to her if she finally gave Larry some of his own medicine back. It was probably no more than he deserved. I'd like to think that times have changed, but they haven't, not really. This is a man's world and sometimes a woman has got to look out for her own."

"You really disliked him," I said.

"On the contrary, I didn't know Larry Kim well enough to like or dislike him. What I abhorred was the way he treated his wife in public. One could only imagine what their private life must have been like."

Pretty strong words and a surprising amount of emotion coming from someone who claimed not to have known the murder victim very well.

I'd always enjoyed watching Dorothy and MacDuff in the show ring. She'd looked like such a sweet and unassuming little old lady. But she definitely had a core of steel. And perhaps—considering the way she and the Scottie had made their way into the contest—a duplicitous side as well.

Faith shifted at my feet, snoring softly in her sleep and turning from one side onto the other as the bus rolled beneath us. I reached down and flicked several long, silky strands of ear hair out of her mouth. We were crossing the Triboro Bridge and entering Manhattan. It wouldn't be long now until we arrived at our destination.

"I think it's rather odd, don't you?" Dorothy asked abruptly.

I turned and looked at her. "What is?"

"The way nobody talks about the fact that one of our contestants died right in our midst. Everybody, including the dearly departed's wife, just soldiers on as if nothing even happened."

"It seems very odd," I agreed. "I can only think that the judges are afraid that talking about it will cast a pall over the proceedings."

"Maybe the company is worried about liability," said Dorothy. "That's what everyone does these days, isn't it? They go off and sue someone?" She paused, gazing up one side of the bus and then back down the other. "Frankly if I were them I'd be more concerned about the fact that this tight little group they've put together is, in all likelihood, harboring a murderer. It makes you stop and think, doesn't it? Maybe Larry was only the first target."

Dorothy didn't look like the sort of woman who would be afraid of much. I wondered if she actually felt threatened; or whether, considering that we'd started the conversation by talking about her own impropriety, she was simply trying to deflect attention in another direction.

"Would you kill someone for a hundred-thousand–dollar modeling contract?" I queried. It was a question I seemed to be asking a lot.

"My ethical code isn't what's under discussion here. But since you've asked, I will point out that wars have been fought for less. And with luck, the initial contract is only the beginning. Assuming that Chow Down is successful, there will be further commercials and public appearances. The promotion could go on for years, and the value to the winner could increase substantially."

I decided to take that as a yes. Which led to my next question.

"What did you do at the end of that first meeting?"

Dorothy's eyes narrowed. "I assume you're asking where I was when Larry took his unfortunate fall?"

I nodded.

"To tell you the truth, I don't have any idea. I stayed behind for a few minutes to chat with Simone. I used to work in public relations myself back in the day. I thought perhaps we might find a common chord."

Or more likely, she'd thought to increase MacDuff's chances of winning by ingratiating herself with yet another of the judges.

"Then I made a pit stop at the loo. After that, MacDuff and I took the elevator down to the lobby. I'll tell you exactly the same thing I told those two officers. Since I don't have any idea exactly when Larry met his demise, I could have been doing any number of things at the time."

That didn't help much, did it? I sat back in my seat. My toe nudged Faith, who lifted her head. "Good girl," I murmured. "We're almost there."

"And?" Dorothy said sharply. I realized she was still staring in my direction.

"And what?"

"I certainly don't see why I should be the only one to furnish a description of my whereabouts. Where were you when the dire deed occurred?"

"On the stairwell," I mumbled. As if there was any hope she would find that answer satisfactory. When Dorothy continued to stare, I offered up a more detailed explanation.

"Too bad you weren't paying more attention," she said at the end. Her tone was more than a little accusatory. "The police could have this whole thing wrapped up by now, and we wouldn't have to go around wondering which one of us was busy hatching plots against the others. As if we didn't have enough to worry about already."

"You mean the contest."

"Of course I mean the contest. What else would I be talking about? MacDuff and I have made it this far, and we intend to go all the way. All I can say is, nobody had better try and stop us or they'll be sorry they ever got in our way."

"You realize," I said mildly, "that now it sounds as though you're the one making threats."

"Don't be silly. How could anyone possibly find MacDuff and me threatening? We're the senior citizens of the group. You know what that means, don't you?"

The first answer that came to mind was that it didn't require either youth or strength to push someone down a flight of steps if you caught them off guard. Since I doubted that that was where Dorothy was headed, however, I kept that thought to myself and shook my head.

"It means that we've been around the block a few times. We've got the experience and the know-how to be winners. Maybe we don't look as formidable as some of the other finalists, but nobody should make the mistake of underestimating us. We've got a few tricks left up our sleeves yet."

Perfect, I thought. That was just what this contest needed. More tricks.

The bus double parked on a busy cross street just around the corner from the south end of Central Park. Horns blared, streams of pedestrians filled the sidewalks, traffic eddied around us in fits and starts. Welcome to the big city.

Faith had her ears flattened against her head. I wished I could do the same.

Instead I reached down and checked the clasp on her leash and collar, making sure that everything was hooked up tight. My Poodle was dependable off leash, but in the midst of this much noise and confusion I wasn't about to take any chances.

As soon as the bus stopped moving, Doug stepped up to the front to make a brief announcement. "In just a minute, we'll be heading across Fifth Avenue and into the park. Once we're there, I want each of you to do whatever makes you feel comfortable with regard to your own dog. My only request is that you try to stay at least somewhat loosely grouped. We, the judges, will be observing your interaction with the public and Charlie will be capturing much of what happens on film. So we don't want to have to be looking all over trying to figure out where everyone went. Okay?"

Dutifully we all nodded.

"Field trips," Ben muttered under his breath. "You gotta love them. It's just like being back in elementary school."

"At least we don't have to wear name tags and hold hands," Allison Redding replied. Ginger had ridden into the city on the seat beside Allison and her husband. Now she hopped the Brittany down to the floor and prepared to disembark.

One by one, we made our way down the narrow aisle. The judges, sitting in the front, had followed Doug and gotten off first. Dorothy and I, seated in the back, were bringing up the rear.

By the time Faith and I reached the door, I could see that Sam had been wrong. Despite New Yorkers' reputation for being blasé, a small crowd had gathered on the sidewalk to watch us unload. Kind of like watching clowns emerge from a Volkswagen at the circus, I imagined.

Though the human contestants were largely ignored, murmurs of approval greeted each newly revealed canine. I had to give credit to Simone and Chris. With our dogs' pictures plastered all over the sides of the bus, the Champions PR team had created the impression that the five finalists were celebrities, even though they had yet to do anything to justify their fame.

Faith and I hopped down the two steps onto the street. The judges had moved to one side to give us room. Faith and I joined Dorothy, the Reddings, and Lisa, who'd pressed together in a tight little group between the bus and the sidewalk. We all awaited further instruction.

Ben, however, had ideas of his own. Dragging Brando behind him, he slithered between two parked cars and went to greet the assembled crowd.

"Wow," I heard a teenage girl say. "Are these movie dogs?"

"No, stupid," her friend replied. "They're on TV. Read the sign."

"The sign says they eat dog food," someone called out. "Hey, my dog eats dog food. Can he be famous, too?"

Standing on the street with the bus and bumper-to-bumper traffic behind me, and parked cars and a crowd of spectators in front, I slid a hand down and pressed Faith closer to my thigh. She didn't seem perturbed but I knew that was because she trusted me not to put her in harm's way. Breathing in exhaust fumes, and waiting impatiently, I hoped I was going to be able to keep my word.

I glanced over at Doug and the other judges. They were engrossed in watching Ben and Brando work the crowd and seemed to have forgotten all about the rest of us. The actor was busy explaining to the teenage girls that he had been a soap opera star. One of them was fishing around in her purse for a piece of paper for him to sign. How that was supposed to help Brando's cause I had no idea.

Charlie walked around onto the sidewalk and began to take pictures. Predictably that made even more people stop to see what was happening.

I waited a minute, then stepped forward and caught Doug's eye. "Maybe we should get moving into the park? You probably don't want us to do this here in the street, do you?"

Doug didn't respond right away, but Simone did. "You're absolutely right," she said. "Ben? Brando? Wrap it up here, we're moving over to the park."

The command she barked out was enough to finally galvanize Doug into action. He hopped up onto the sidewalk and addressed the crowd.

"On behalf of Champions' new dog food, Chow Down, welcome! The dogs you see here are five finalists, one of whom will become our new spokesdog and be featured on television and in print advertising. We'll be heading over to Central Park now, where we'll be handing out free samples of the product. Of course you're welcome to come and join us. You'll be able to meet all the dogs, then later you can go to our web site and vote for your favorite. Thank you all for your support!"

Doug's rousing speech didn't have the effect he

seemed to be hoping for. Nobody applauded. In fact nobody even looked terribly interested. As celebrities, our dogs had had potential. As advertising for a dog food company, they were boring.

"Yeah, whatever," said a young man with multiple piercings.

He turned and walked away. Others followed. In less than a minute, we were all by ourselves again. Looking disgruntled, Ben rejoined the fold.

"Way to shut down a party, man," Chris said with a grin.

Simone quickly turned away; I suspected she might have been hiding a smile. Cindy, standing beside Chris, looked worried; obviously she was new to insurrection in the ranks. Doug ignored all of them and rounded us up.

Bunched together like a Brownie troop on a mission, we crossed Fifth Avenue and took the path that led into the park. Now that we weren't hemmed in by traffic and pedestrians, everyone relaxed and let out their leashes.

The dogs, confined during the long bus ride, began to hop and play. Several lowered their noses to the ground to sniff out likely spots. I hoped everyone had remembered to bring baggies for cleanup.

Faith and Ginger were eager to stretch their legs. When we came to a small meadow, dotted here and there by picnickers and mothers with small children, Allison reached down and unfastened Ginger's lead. Bill pulled out a tennis ball and gave it a toss. The Brittany went flying across the grass after it.

Faith watched the action and whined softly under her breath. I could understand her desire to run, but

I wasn't at all sure I liked the idea of turning her loose. A glance at the others seemed to confirm my feelings of trepidation.

Yoda was on the ground for once, but Lisa had a tight hold on her slender leash. Ditto Dorothy and MacDuff. Ben, so eager to set Brando free in an enclosed room, seemed to have no intention of doing so here.

"Can I touch?" asked a small voice.

I turned back and saw a girl of perhaps three, her chubby hand extended toward Faith's nose. The Poodle was bigger than she was, but the child showed no fear. Her mother grasped the little girl's other hand firmly.

"That's a Poodle, right?" she said. "Taylor *loves* Poodles, but we've never seen one that big before. Is she like a super-size, or what?"

And so the fun began.

18

After that initial, tentative approach, Faith and I were seldom alone for more than a few minutes at a time. I'd bathed the Poodle and blown her dry the previous evening and even though her trim was nothing fancy by dog show standards, its precise lines and plush look drew a lot of favorable attention. After the fifth person in a row asked me how I got the pom pon on Faith's tail so perfectly round, I began to think that I should have printed up answer cards to hand out.

"Having fun?" asked Doug, coming over to see how we were doing.

Several hours had already passed. During that time, I'd been acutely aware of Doug and the other judges, wandering among the members of our group, observing the interactions, and surreptitiously taking notes. Meanwhile Charlie was busy snapping pictures, recording the day's events for what, no doubt, would be further discussion and dissection by the committee.

I'm normally not a self-conscious person but being the object of that kind of intense scrutiny had quickly led to paranoia. Though I'd devoted a decent amount of energy to promoting Faith, it was clear that I was neither as outgoing nor as motivated as some of the other contestants. Nor was I about to change my ways in an effort to keep up.

Ben continued to work the area effortlessly; drawing attention to himself seemed to come naturally. Dorothy, meanwhile, had mastered the consummate handler's trick of fading into the background and letting her dog shine. The Reddings played in the meadow with Ginger, the three of them gamboling in the grass like there was nothing else in the world that they'd rather be doing. Only Lisa looked strained and wary when people loomed above her little Yorkie and gushed about how cute she was. She seemed to dislike all the fuss and public adulation just as much as I did.

When Doug approached me, I was more than ready to take a break. Being center stage was a wearying experience. Even at dog shows, we'd never had to be "on" for hours at a time. Now both of us were beginning to feel the strain.

"Some of it's fun," I replied honestly in answer to Doug's question. "But it's hard work, too."

"I'm sorry if you expected differently." He motioned toward a bench in the shade beneath a large elm tree and Faith and I followed him there. As the three of us got settled, Doug continued to talk.

"We on the committee spent quite a lot of time considering just that very issue before we initiated the contest. It's one thing to hire a 'professional' dog to represent a product. Those dogs and their handlers know exactly what to expect from a job like this. They've seen the hard work that goes on behind the surface glamour, and that makes them easier to work with. But it also means that you lose the personal connection that comes with dealing with somebody's real pet."

"You also forfeit the free publicity that a contest like this is able to generate in the media."

"There's that, too," Doug agreed. "At any rate, Faith seems to be handling things well. Better, I'd venture to say, than some of the others. She really is a people dog, isn't she?"

That went a long way toward softening some of the prickliness I'd been feeling. What can I say? Praise my dog and I'll love you forever.

"I wish I could take special credit, but honestly that's just the way Poodles are. It's highly unusual to find one that doesn't love people. Poodles would much rather spend time with their owners than with other dogs."

As if on cue, Faith sat down, nestled herself next to my legs and rested her head on my thigh. Her dark eyes lifted to link with mine and she blew out a happy sigh.

The effect wasn't lost on Doug. Actually it was my impression that the contest chairman didn't miss much of anything. I was also cynical enough to believe that even this seemingly spontaneous break we were sharing had probably been scripted ahead of time.

"We tried to take breed characteristics into account when we were choosing our finalists," Doug said. "Not that every breed doesn't have some great qualities, but I think most people would agree that not every breed is equally suited for the unique function we have in mind."

He leaned back, rested his arm across the top of the bench, and gazed out across the meadow. Even while sitting with Faith and me, he was still evaluating the other finalists' performances.

I wondered whether he'd been picking up on the same things I had: That Brando didn't always respond favorably to unwanted attention from strangers. That MacDuff could be aloof, showing more interest in the chipmunks and squirrels that crossed his path than in the people. That Yoda was sometimes overwhelmed by all the fuss; small children poking their fingers in her direction intimidated the Yorkie enough to make her hide behind Lisa's legs.

Not that I was trying to be overly critical of my fellow contestants. What the committee was asking us to do was a difficult task. But if the spokesdog for Chow Down was going to be required to make numerous personal appearances on behalf of the product, I supposed we'd all just better buckle down and get used to it.

"Picked a favorite yet?" I asked idly.

I didn't really expect an answer, so I was surprised when Doug said, "We all have our favorites. I suppose that's human nature. Right or wrong, it's been that way from the very beginning."

As he spoke, he was watching Yoda. Lisa had gathered the Yorkie up in her arms and was standing off to one side. Body hunched protectively around the small dog as if shielding her from potential harm, Lisa's demeanor clearly proclaimed that the two of them wished to be left alone.

It wasn't to be. Simone strode purposefully toward the pair. She reached out and draped a comforting arm around Lisa's shoulders. I half-expected the dog owner to shrug her off, but she didn't. Instead, heads tipped toward each other, the two women quickly became engrossed in conversation.

"We're trying to cut her some slack," Doug said when he realized I was watching, just as he was. "I'm sure none of this is easy for Lisa."

"And yet it was her choice to stay in the contest," I pointed out. "Some people would find that an odd decision under the circumstances."

Doug only shrugged. "Who knows how other people's minds work? Especially women. Certainly not me."

Charlie had been tracking Ginger, who'd been romping with some teenagers, but now he zeroed in on Lisa and Simone. The photographer started to head in their direction, but Doug caught his eye and waved him off. Then Dorothy plucked at the photographer's sleeve. Charlie turned and focused his lens on MacDuff. Doug relaxed and went back to speaking.

"We all noticed right away that Lisa and Yoda were uncomfortable out here. Then Simone pointed out that according to the information we'd received, Larry was the one who always took the dog in the show ring. Lisa was accustomed to remaining in the background."

I hadn't thought about that either. I supposed it put a new spin on Lisa's somewhat defensive behavior.

"So maybe it was unfair of us to spring a test like this on her."

"You sprang it on all of us. If Lisa and Yoda can't cope now, what's going to happen if they win?"

"Good question. And something we'll have to take into consideration when we make our decision."

Doug's eyes were still following the two women. With all the activity going on around us, something about the pair continued to draw his interest.

I thought about Dorothy and Chris, who'd met the previous year over a Scottie puppy. I considered the fact that Doug had shown up within seconds of Larry's fall and yet somehow managed not to see anything. And I decided to ask another question.

"How long have you known the Kims?"

He looked around quickly. "What do you mean?"

It seemed like a relatively simple question to me. It was interesting that he didn't have a similarly simple answer.

"When did you first meet?"

"Last week. Monday morning it must have been. You know, at the opening reception."

In the space of mere seconds he'd gone from being confused by the question to being so sure of his answer that he'd felt compelled to give it three times.

"The day that Larry Kim died."

"Right."

"So you hadn't had any prior contact with them?"

Doug paused to ponder his reply. "I imagine I might have spoken with them after Yoda was named as one of our finalists," he said after a minute. "Just like I spoke with you."

The difference wasn't lost on me. Doug remembered speaking with me. He merely imagined he might have spoken with the Kims. My ego is pretty healthy but even I know I'm not necessarily that memorable.

"So then—"

"Sorry," said Doug. He quickly rose. "I've got to go see what Cindy wants."

The product manager was standing on the dirt path with Ben and Brando. Though she was gazing in our direction, I wouldn't have guessed from that fact that she wanted anything.

It didn't matter. Doug was already gone, striding away across the field.

And I was left to wonder why my questions had made him so uncomfortable.

After that, things wrapped up pretty quickly. The contest committee decided that they'd seen enough. Unfortunately, if the judges had formed any opinions about which of the finalists might be best suited to fill the position, they weren't sharing the news with us.

Our group had been giddy with enthusiasm and anticipation on our way into the park. Exiting, we were more subdued. Actually, I think most of us were just tired. The bus was waiting where we'd left it. One by one, we climbed onboard gratefully.

"Well," said Allison Redding, grabbing a seat next to me and Faith, "that was loads of fun, wasn't it?"

As Bill and Ginger had settled into a seat across the aisle, I looked over to make sure she wasn't talking to them. Neither her dog nor her husband was paying any attention to her. I took that to mean that the perky comment had been addressed to me.

"Loads," I agreed. I'm afraid my level of excitement didn't quite match hers.

"Come on"—she poked my arm and bounced in her seat—"admit it. It was nice to do something that made Ginger and Faith look like a couple of stars."

There was that.

Allison's voice dropped. "You were watching the others. I know because I was, too. Did you see Brando snarl at that little boy with the catcher's mitt? Ben covered it up pretty well, but I'm pretty sure that Simone noticed. And speaking of Simone, who died and left her queen? The way she was always bossing everyone around and telling them what to do? It was enough to really get on my nerves."

Actually, though I'd seen Simone interacting with the other contestants throughout the day, for the most part, she'd left Faith and me alone. At the time, I hadn't thought much about it, but now I found myself wondering if she'd avoided us on purpose. A signal to the rest of the committee about whom she favored and whom she didn't? Or maybe she'd simply wanted to dodge my propensity for asking questions.

"Now Cindy . . ." Allison was still talking. Apparently I didn't even have to respond to keep the flow of words coming. "She's someone I think I could really be friends with. She loved watching Ginger play with her ball. Did you know she has a Border Collie named Gus that's a disc dog? How cool is that?"

While Allison chattered and bounced beside

me, I was leaning against the back of the seat with my eyes half-closed. Faith had given up any pretense of interest in our surroundings. The front half of her body was draped across my lap and she was sound asleep, her body rising and falling with each rhythmic snore.

"They all have dogs," I said. Adding a small amount of input to the conversation seemed like the polite thing to do.

"All who?"

"The judges. They all have dogs, not just Cindy."

"I guess that makes sense, doesn't it? I mean, why work for a dog food company if you don't like dogs? That would be counter-intuitive. Simone, let's see, I could picture her with a Maltese."

"Pomeranian," I said.

Allison giggled. "That fits. Now Doug, he ought to have something sleek and kind of sexy. Maybe a German Shorthaired Pointer."

I tipped my head her way. "Sleek and sexy?"

"Don't you think so?"

"I hadn't really thought about it."

"What's to think? Just use your eyes, for Pete's sake."

If I opened my eyes fully, I thought, they'd be staring at Allison's husband who, just for the record, was not very sleek and sexy. More like rumpled and comfortable.

"I'm a newlywed," I said. "I've stopped looking."

Allison reached over and patted my arm. "Time passes," she said. "You'll get over that."

I hoped not.

"Doug has a chocolate Lab," I said. "His kids named it Hershey."

"Doug is married?"

Allison sounded surprised, and maybe a tad disappointed. Which made me think that maybe we shouldn't be having this conversation almost within earshot of her husband.

"I believe he's divorced."

"Ahh, that makes more sense."

That comment got my attention. I actually opened my eyes. "Why?"

"Because, well . . . you know."

No, I didn't. I hate it when that happens.

"I know what?"

Allison leaned closer. Her voice, already low, dropped to a whisper. "Don't you get the impression that he might have something going on with Simone?"

Doug and Simone? I hadn't picked up on that at all.

My gaze went reflexively to the front of the bus. The pair in question were seated on opposite sides of the aisle. Simone was working on her BlackBerry. Doug was talking on his cell phone. Whatever Allison thought she knew, I still wasn't seeing it.

"Really?"

"Really." Allison nodded. "They've got vibes."

"Vibes," Bill snorted from across the aisle. I guessed he had been listening in. Maybe this was his retaliation for the "sleek and sexy" comment. "Don't pay any attention to her. She loves all that psychic, woo-woo, mumbo jumbo stuff. She won't even get out of bed in the morning until she's consulted her horoscope."

"It's a valuable forecast of what the day contains," Allison said primly.

"It's a crock," her husband replied.

I was more inclined to his way of thinking. Horoscopes were fun to read, but I wouldn't plan my life around them.

"You just don't get it," said Allison.

"Wouldn't be the first time," Bill agreed equitably.

"That leaves Chris," Allison said thoughtfully. The advertising director was sitting with the other judges up front. Allison gazed at the back of his head with a small frown. "I'm not sure I see him with a dog at all. Maybe a cat or a gerbil."

"A ferret," said Bill. "Or possibly a hamster."

Trust me, coming from ardent dog people, these were insults.

"What's wrong with Chris?" I asked.

Bill shrugged. "Don't ask me. Miss Woo-Woo over there is the one with all the answers."

Miss Woo-Woo, surprisingly, didn't seem offended by the title. I was guessing she'd heard it before.

"Don't you think Chris is just the tiniest bit . . . strange?" she asked.

"In what way?"

"For one thing, he skulks."

"He's a skulker," Bill agreed with a nod.

"What does that mean?" I directed the question to Allison, since she was the one with the answers.

"He's sneaky," she whispered. "Always kind of popping up where you least expect him. And he doesn't like Ginger."

"That's the main problem, isn't it?" said Bill. "He's been like that all along. Even the first time we met. It was like he never gave her a fair shot. Now I ask you, how can you like someone who doesn't like your dog? What would be the point?"

Words to live by, there.

"I think Chris likes small dogs," I said.

"Like that's an excuse," Allison sniffed. "I'm telling you, there's something the matter with him."

Could be they were right. At any rate, I wasn't about to argue. I was too tired for that. Besides, all available evidence pointed to the fact that there had to be something wrong with *somebody* in our group. Considering how little I'd accomplished thus far in narrowing down the list, Chris seemed as likely a suspect as anybody.

On that happy thought, I leaned back, followed my Poodle's example, and let the motion of the bus lull me to sleep.

19

Summer has always been my time to kick back, take things easy, and enjoy life for a while. This annual vacation from most responsibilities allows me to recharge my internal batteries. It prepares me to tear into the upcoming school year with the enthusiasm and direction that my students might be lacking. As a side benefit, I also get to indulge in one of my favorite luxuries: sleeping late in the morning.

At least that's the way things are supposed to work.

But this summer something had gone horribly wrong. The demands that the Chow Down contest had placed on my time and energy were much more wide-reaching than I'd bargained for. When Faith and I arrived home that night from the day's jaunt into the city on behalf of Champions Dog Food, I was tired, I was cranky, and I needed a break.

I pulled into the garage, opened the door to the house, and Faith went bounding on ahead. The Poodle, predictably, had recovered her high spirits after snoozing in the bus on the way back. She couldn't wait to see what sort of new excitement might be waiting for us at home.

I could hear the other dogs racing to come and greet us. They barked in welcome, and I picked out Faith's distinctive voice as she replied. I dragged myself into the kitchen, tossed purse, keys, and cell phone onto the counter, and sank into the nearest chair.

"Long day?" asked Sam. He'd followed in the Poodles' wake. Who needs good ears when you have a canine security system?

"Very."

I rested my arms on the table, put my head down, and closed my eyes. After a minute, I realized that Sam hadn't responded to my comment.

"Did I say that out loud or did I just imagine it?" I asked, voice muffled by my arms.

"No, I heard you." Sam was smiling; I could hear it in his voice. "I was waiting for details."

"Don't hold your breath."

"That bad?"

"That long, anyway. Remind me again why I want Faith to be the face of Chow Down dog food."

Sam pulled out a chair at the table and sat down. "Because it's important to your son?"

"Oh, right. I knew there was something."

"I have an idea."

"Perfect," I mumbled into my sleeve. "One of us should be using his brain."

"Why don't you go upstairs and take a bubble

bath? Meanwhile, I'll get some coals started in the hibachi. By the time they're ready to cook, I bet you'll feel much better."

Sam had had a gas grill until a few months earlier when I'd given it away to my ex-husband in a sudden fit of inspiration. Long story there. Suffice it to say that we were now making do with a more primitive arrangement.

"That doesn't sound half bad. Are you sure you don't mind?"

"Nope."

"I'm leaving you with all the work."

"I think I can cope. Davey'll help." Sam got up, placed his hands on my arms and pulled me to my feet. He turned me in the direction of the hallway that led to the stairs and gave me a gentle push. "Go."

"Yes sir."

He watched me walk away. "You're cute when you're submissive."

"Don't get too used to it," I said.

Davey's and my former house, an older abode in a busy family neighborhood, sported plumbing and fixtures that had been built in the middle of the previous century. He and I shared a bathroom with a small, no-frills bathtub that doubled as a shower. Hot water was supplied by an economy water heater that worked well enough for brief showers but was unpredictable when it came to long, luxurious baths.

Consequently, moving to the new house with its state-of-the-art master bathroom and spa had been a revelation. Now I had a separate, glassed-in shower stall and a spacious tub with a whirlpool that could comfortably seat three. There were ledges for plants and candles, and all the hot water I could possibly want. The only thing lacking in my life was the time to relax and enjoy it all.

When I reached the top of the staircase, a turn to the right would have taken me toward Sam's and my room. To the left lay Davey's bedroom. Aside from a few minutes over breakfast, I hadn't seen my son all day. It didn't take me two seconds to decide which way I wanted to go.

Davey's door was open but he wasn't there. Furnished when the house had belonged to Bob, the room had bunk beds, a ceiling fan painted like an airplane propeller, and posters of the hottest cars Davey could find. Two dresser drawers hung partly open, and a pair of dirty socks had been kicked under the night table. The wooden train set we'd erected in one corner seemed to have been involved in a catastrophic collision with a fleet of matchbox cars. In short, everything about the space made it clear that there was a growing boy in residence.

I backed out of the doorway and wandered into the bedroom next door. By contrast, it was nearly empty and mostly serene. The walls were painted a sunny shade of yellow. Eyelet curtains framed the windows. Sam and I had pictured this room as a nursery. Since the need had yet to arise, we hadn't purchased any furniture.

The only two things the room currently held were a Shaker rocking chair, with a well-worn cushion, and a wooden toy chest, hand-painted with scenes of small white bunnies playing in a meadow. Both pieces were left over from when Davey had been a baby. Both had been a cherished part of his earliest routines.

Looking at them brought back a flood of happy

memories of those long, quiet hours spent in my son's company. I sighed softly and hoped that soon there'd be another child with whom to continue the tradition.

Without stopping to think, as if the need was as natural as breathing itself, I walked across the room and sat down in the rocking chair. My toe pushed against the polished floor and the rocker began to move gently back and forth. The sway and the rhythm were enormously comforting.

My shoulders relaxed. My neck unknotted. A half-formed smiled curled drowsily across my lips.

"Hey, Mom!"

Davey came barreling into the room like a runner rounding third base. His sandals slid on the hardwood floor; his legs shot out from under him. His hip hit the boards hard enough to make me wince, but Davey came up smiling.

"Hey what?" I asked.

"Sam-Dad said you were taking a bath. What are you doing in here?"

"Thinking."

"Ugh. Thinking is for school."

"No," I said, "thinking is for whenever you want to feel smart."

"School," Davey repeated. "Definitely. Sam wanted me to ask you if lamb chops were okay for dinner?"

"Fine by me," I said. Anything I didn't have to cook myself tended to be fine by me.

"And he asked me to bring you a glass of wine. Something yellow."

"White," I corrected, noting that his hands were empty. "Chardonnay?"

Davey nodded. "But it looks yellow. I'm not sure you're going to like it."

"I bet I will." Sam was pretty well briefed on my preferences when it came to white wines. "Where did you put it?"

"Next to the bathtub. That's where you were supposed to be." The clear-cut logic of an eight-year-old on a mission.

Davey got up, stepped over to the toy chest, and lifted the lid. He peered inside. "It's empty."

"You knew that. It's been empty for years."

"Yeah, well." Davey shrugged. He was ever hopeful when it came to the magical appearance of new toys.

"That's a baby chest. Your toys are in your closet and your desk and your shelves. You have too many to fit in there."

"We need another baby."

"I know," I agreed.

He closed the lid and sat down on the box, settling in for a chat. "How long does it take?"

"That depends." Too bad he hadn't brought my wine into the nursery, I thought. It was beginning to look like we might be there a while.

"On what?"

"On whether you're asking about the length of the pregnancy itself or how long it might take before that to get pregnant."

"Both."

My son. Ever curious. What could I say? I supposed he took after me.

"Women are pregnant for nine months, give or take a little."

"Wow." Davey's eyes widened. "That's a long time. Are you sure?"

"Pretty sure," I said with a smile. "I had you, remember?"

"Yeah, but that was a while ago. Maybe you forgot. Faith was only pregnant for two months when she had Eve."

"Dogs are different. Their gestation is sixty-three days."

"And she had a whole litter, not just one."

"Yes, but human babies take more time to develop. Were any of those puppies as smart as you are?"

Davey thought about that. I knew he was debating Eve's mental acuity. Sad to say, I'd known people who weren't as smart as that dog.

"Maybe," he decided finally.

"Maybe not."

I reached over and gave him a nudge between the ribs. Davey dodged away, laughing. He's terribly ticklish if you know the right spots. He rolled off the edge of the toy box, a stunt accompanied by more dramatics than were strictly necessary, and landed on the floor beside my feet.

"Rock," he said, grabbing the chair's runner and pushing it down.

"Want to join me? You used to love this chair when you were little."

"Nah. I'm too big to sit in your lap now."

He shook his head firmly and I gathered we were talking age rather than actual size. It seemed like such a short time ago that Davey had been happy to nestle in my arms. It was sad to think those days were over.

"Nine months," he said. "So if it's July now"—he ticked off the months on his fingers—"that means I have to wait all the way until *next March*?"

"Maybe longer," I admitted. "You can't start counting until I get pregnant."

"Well, why don't you?" Davey asked. From where he was sitting, it all looked easy.

"Sometimes things don't happen just because you want them to."

"Yeah, but you and Sam-Dad are married now."

"That helps."

Sam and I had been together for several years, but we hadn't started trying to have a baby until just recently. Now it seemed as though everyone expected overnight results.

Getting pregnant with Davey had been a breeze. It hadn't required effort, or planning, or even much forethought at all. But I'd been nearly a decade younger and at a totally different place in my life. I was trying hard to be patient, but it was difficult when both Sam and I wanted it to happen so badly.

"In the meantime, you've got Maggie to play with."

"Maggie's pretty cool," Davey agreed. "But she needs more hair."

I sputtered a laugh. "It'll come."

"And when she grows up, she'll be a girl."

"That happens."

"I think I'd rather have a little brother."

I reached down and ruffled his sandy hair. "I think when the time comes, you'll take what you get."

Davey slithered out from beneath my hand. He's reached the age where displays of affection mostly just embarrass him. "Can I pick the name?"

"You can help."

"Cool. I'll start thinking up some good choices."

"You do that. Girls' names, too. Just in case."

"Okay." Davey braced a hand against the toy chest and stood up. "Are you ever going to take a bath?"

"Probably not." We'd been talking so long that I'd missed my chance. "But that's okay." I reached over and gathered my son into my arms for a quick hug. "I feel much better now."

"You do?"

"Nearly perfect."

"Not me," Davey, wriggling away. "I'm hungry."

"Why don't you go check on dinner? It smells like it might be almost ready."

Davey, never one to do things by half measures, dashed from the room. I stood up and followed, retrieving my wine from the bathroom before heading down to the kitchen.

When I got there, the back door was standing open and everyone was out on the terrace. Sam was bending over the hibachi. Davey was setting the picnic table. The swarm of Poodles was supervising.

It was the perfect start to a perfect evening. The weather was warm with a light breeze. The lamb chops were excellent. The company was sublime. I finally got to drink my glass of Chardonnay.

In fact everything came together so well that I thought nothing could spoil my feeling of well-being. That is, until the phone rang later that night just before we went to bed. I picked up and found Bertie.

"Here's a news flash," she said.

"What?"

"Lisa Kim has disappeared."

"No she hasn't. I saw her earlier today. We went into New York for the Chow Down contest."

"And nobody's seen her since."

"How do you know that?"

"Since she was going to be gone most of the day she asked a mutual friend to dog-sit for her. Sue expected Lisa and Yoda to be back by five or maybe six. When she didn't show up and didn't answer her cell phone, Sue started calling around. Finally she remembered that I had a connection to one of the contestants and tried me. I told her I'd check with you."

It was nearly eleven now. The bus had arrived back at the Champions Company in Norwalk at around four o'clock. I hadn't been paying any attention to her but I assumed that Lisa had gotten in her car and left, just as the rest of us had.

So where had she been for the last seven hours?

20

"Is Sue still at Lisa's place?" I asked.

"She's been there all day," Bertie confirmed. "Lisa and Larry don't have a huge kennel, but still, you can't just go out and leave ten dogs to fend for themselves. Sue was trying to be helpful . . . you know, because of what happened to Larry. She told Lisa to call her if she needed anything and Lisa did."

"And she hasn't heard anything since Lisa left this morning?"

"Not a peep. Lisa's cell phone goes straight to voice mail, and she hasn't answered any of the messages Sue's been leaving. What were you guys doing in New York anyway?"

I sighed and sat down on the edge of the bed. It was late, but I had time to talk. Davey had already been asleep for a while; I'd just checked on him and found him curled up under his sheet. Faith had been in her customary place at the foot of his bed and I'd sent her downstairs with Sam, who was putting the Poodles outside one last time. It would be at least five minutes before that whole crew reappeared.

"It was another competition for the contest. The judges wanted to see how the dog food–buying public would respond to each of the finalists so they stuck us all in a bus and drove us down to Central Park. Sort of like a free-form focus group, I guess."

"*That* sounds like fun," Bertie muttered. Her sarcasm wasn't lost on me.

"It took up most of the day," I grumbled. "This must be why parents used to believe that children should be seen and not heard. I'm beginning to come around to that way of thinking myself."

Bertie barked out a laugh. Clearly she didn't believe me. That was all right; I didn't really believe myself.

"Listen," she said. "Sue's really worried. According to her, Lisa is one of the most responsible people she knows. It's not like her to disappear and not tell anyone where she's going."

"Has Sue contacted the police?"

"She tried to do that earlier. But they won't file a missing persons report on an adult until three days have passed. She checked with the local hospitals, too. They didn't have any info, either."

"I wonder if the police would pay more attention if they knew that Lisa is the wife of a man who died under suspicious circumstances last week."

Bertie thought about that for a minute. "Maybe you should call the police and tell them."

Her confidence in my abilities was touching, if misplaced.

"Bertie, pretty much every policeman I've ever

spoken with has thought he knew exactly what he was doing. I've tried taking them information before. They never listen to a word I say."

"Well they should," my sister-in-law replied stoutly.

"I'm with you there."

I heard the scramble of feet coming up the steps, twenty-two feet, to be precise. It was like listening to a herd of buffalo approach. Luckily my son can sleep through almost anything.

Faith sheared off and went into Davey's room. Tar, as had recently become his habit, went with her. That left Eve, Raven, and Casey to keep Sam and me company. Eve got comfortable inside her open crate. Raven chose a spot beneath the window where the sun would hit her first thing in the morning. Casey eyed the king-sized bed hopefully.

I pretended not to notice. Sam, following along behind, wasn't so lenient. "You know better," he said in a low voice. The Poodle dipped her head in acknowledgment. She went and lay down next to Raven.

The man loves his dogs, but he enjoys snuggling with his wife more. You can't fault him for that.

Sam looked at me and lifted a brow.

"Bertie," I mouthed silently.

He looked down at his watch and then up again. We don't get many late-night phone calls. "Everything okay?"

He was asking about family—checking on Maggie and Bertie and Frank—so I nodded.

"Are you talking to Sam?" Bertie asked.

"No."

"You are, too. I can always tell. Tell him I said hi."

"Bertie sends her love," I said to Sam.

"Me too," he replied and went to brush his teeth. Just one big, happy family here.

"So what are we going to do about Lisa?" asked Bertie. "I told Sue I'd get back to her tonight. I have to tell her something."

"Let me think," I said. Like that would help. I'd been thinking since we'd first started talking and nothing brilliant had occurred to me yet.

"When did you last see Lisa?"

"Four," I said. "Maybe four-thirty. The bus dropped us off back in the Champions parking lot. I got in my car and came home. Until hearing differently from you, I figured she did the same."

"Huh," said Bertie. "That's no help. How was Lisa acting earlier? Was she happy? Sad? Unusually distracted?"

Was it just me or had Bertie assumed the role that I usually played? How unexpected was that? Maybe spending day after day in the company of a child under the age of one had fried my sister-in-law's brain. But no matter what the reason was, I was happy to play along. When it comes to figuring things out, I've found that two heads are almost always better than one.

"Aloof," I said.

"Pardon me? Did you just sneeze?"

"No, I said that Lisa and Yoda were keeping their distance from the rest of us. Not that, from what I've seen so far, there's anything unusual in that. Lisa isn't very chatty. She hasn't warmed up to any of us. And of course, under the circumstances, no one would dream of pushing her.

"Lisa sat by herself on the bus both ways. There was an open seat beside her, but she has that way of angling her body that lets you know you're not welcome. The only person I saw her talking to for any length of time in the park was Simone."

"She's one of the judges?"

"Right. The PR director. Lisa was looking kind of stressed and Simone went over to see if she could help."

"Stressed by what?"

Bertie was relentless. Was this how people felt when I backed them into a corner and grilled them for information? I hoped not.

Sam emerged from the bathroom. His teeth were brushed and he was mostly naked. And I was stuck on the phone, reliving my day.

Not a perfect state of affairs.

"Stressed by what?" Bertie repeated, then paused. "Sam's back, isn't he?"

"Um-hmm."

"Ready for bed? Dressed in his jammies?"

"Yes to the first. No to the second."

"Oh." A wealth of meaning permeated that small syllable. "I guess I'd better go then."

But now she had me thinking. "Maybe Simone—" I said.

"Maybe tomorrow," Bertie replied. "Have fun." The phone clicked off.

I sat there frowning, and wondering if maybe Simone knew something useful. Considering how careful Lisa was to keep the rest of us at bay, the two of them had seemed surprisingly close earlier.

Sam reached out and took the receiver from my hand. He listened, heard the dial tone, and replaced it in the cradle.

"Time for bed," he said.

It wasn't like he had to ask me twice.

* * *

With the advent of cell phones it seems like we've become a society that's constantly in touch. People chat while they drive, while they work, while they're shopping in the supermarket. Sometimes I think people don't even care who they're talking to anymore, as long as they're connected to someone.

Even I, who regard my cell phone as a necessary evil, seemed to be spending a lot more time on the phone these days. So of course when I got up the next morning, the first thing I did was make another call. Well, let's not jump ahead. As anyone with dogs knows, the first thing I really did was let the Poodles outside for a run.

Then I poured myself a cup of coffee, pulled out an old dog show catalogue and looked up the Kims' address in the back. They lived in Southport, a town too far away to be covered by my phone book; but thanks to the wonders of technology, I was able to get the number off the internet.

After what Bertie had told me the evening before, I didn't actually expect anyone to answer when I dialed. But I hadn't even heard one ring before the phone was snatched up.

"Hello?" The voice sounded breathless and eager. What it didn't sound like was Lisa.

"Hi . . ." I thought fast. "Is this Sue?"

"Who's this?"

"Melanie Travis. I'm Bertie Kennedy's sister-in-law? We haven't met but she called me last night—"

"You're the one who's in that contest with Lisa."

"Yes."

Sue expelled a breath. "Have you seen her? Do you know where she is?"

"No, that was why I was calling you. To see if there'd been any further news."

"Nothing," Sue said flatly. "The last information I got was when Bertie called me after she spoke with you. I ended up staying here and spending the night on the couch. I guess I half-expected Lisa to come wandering in at three AM but no such luck. Now I don't know what to do. It's not like I can just put my entire life on hold until I hear something. But I can't pack up ten dogs and take them home with me either."

"What about calling a professional pet-sitter?"

"Yeah, I was thinking about maybe doing something like that. I know Lisa is going through a bad patch right now, but let me tell you, this is one hell of a way to treat a friend."

"It sounds like you're more pissed off than worried," I said.

"I guess I don't know how to feel. Or what to think. Maybe I jumped the gun, contacting the police and all. For all I know, this could be like one of those crazy college things. You know, where you go out and get wasted and don't make it home at night?"

"Have you known Lisa since college?" I asked.

"No, but come on. Everyone's experience is more or less the same, isn't it?"

Not mine, I thought. But then I'd had to take on responsibilities young. I couldn't recall a single time in my life that I'd ever been too inebriated to at least call and check in with someone who might have been worried about me.

"Lisa does have some old sorority friend around here. I think maybe they were roomies or something. If I could remember her name, I'd give her a call. I bet she might be able to shed some light on this whole thing."

"Maybe."

I didn't sound convinced, and I wasn't. Lisa was too old for shenanigans like that. Plus when I'd seen her last, she'd had Yoda with her. It was a stretch to imagine the elegantly groomed Asian woman out barhopping to the point of incapacity, all the while holding a little Yorkie in her arms.

"Instead I had to call her boss," Sue said, sounding annoyed. "It's not like he was any help."

"Her boss? Lisa has a job?" That was news to me.

"No, sorry, not her actual boss. Lisa doesn't work. Larry was the one who took care of earning the money. I meant that guy who's running the contest."

"Doug Allen?"

"That's the one. I talked to him earlier this morning. He didn't have a clue. Said pretty much the same thing you did. That you all got off the bus in Norwalk yesterday afternoon and went your own separate ways. He had no idea where Lisa might be."

It was only eight o'clock now. How early had she called Doug? I wondered.

"Maybe half an hour, forty-five minutes ago," Sue said when I asked. "I woke up with a crick in my neck from sleeping on the freakin' couch and I was in a mood to get some answers. Since the last people who had seen Lisa were the ones associated with the contest, that seemed like a good place to start."

"Doug was at work at seven-fifteen?" I was only thinking out loud, but Sue answered the question anyway.

"No, Lisa's address book had Doug's home number in it, so that's the one I called. But like I said, it didn't do me the slightest bit of good. He said if I was worried that I should report her missing to the police. Like I couldn't have come up with that idea myself."

"Wait a minute," I said. "Back up."

Sue sighed. "I told this to Bertie, I just assumed she passed it on. Adults have to be missing for—"

"No, not that. The other part, about Lisa's address book."

"It was just sitting there on top of her desk. It wasn't as though I had to go digging around in her drawers to find it. All I did was open it up and look—"

"I don't care where you got it from," I said impatiently. After all, it wasn't as though I was above snooping around in other people's things. "Lisa had a listing for Doug Allen in her address book?"

"Yup. Office. Cell. Home. I called the home number because it was early and that's where I got him."

I thought back to the first time I'd gone to the Champions Company. Each of the finalists had been given a goody bag of products on their way out. Doug's business card had been attached to the top. The card had listings for Doug's office, cell phone, and fax numbers. There hadn't been a home number on there, I was sure of it.

So what was that phone number doing in Lisa Kim's address book?

21

Lisa Kim's disappearance was a concern, but it wasn't the only thing I was worried about. There was another, even more pressing item on my agenda. Despite repeated attempts, I had yet to come up with the slightest clue about what was going on with Crawford. It was time to kick that investigation into high gear and take my queries straight to the source.

Well, the next best thing, anyway.

Terry—that indefatigable supplier of information, gossip, and innuendo—was clearly the person I needed to talk to. And considering that in the current humid summer weather my hair was hanging around my shoulders like a Puli's straggly mop, it wasn't hard to come up with the perfect excuse.

Terry had been cutting my hair—and, if the truth be known, consulting on my wardrobe—since shortly after we'd first met. I wasn't the only exhibitor currently exploiting his extracurricular talents, though I probably was the only one prone to showing up at Bedford Kennel at odd hours, plopping myself down on a kitchen stool, and telling him to snip away.

Under normal circumstances, I would have called ahead and asked if it was a convenient time for a visit. But since I was half-afraid I'd be told that it wasn't, I decided instead to simply show up.

Sam and Davey were once again occupied with the ongoing construction of the tree house. The Poodles, lying in the shade in the backyard, were happy to keep them company. That left me in the Volvo by myself, heading north into Westchester County.

Crawford's tenure in the dog show world rivaled Aunt Peg's. But while she had dedicated her efforts to producing and maintaining a family of Standard Poodles whose quality was unparalleled, Crawford's life had been devoted to winning in the show ring. In a career that had by now spanned several decades, he had quickly found his way to the top, and a number of the most celebrated Non-Sporting dogs in history had come from Bedford Kennel.

Approaching the residence, which was on a quiet, rural road lined with stone walls and mature trees, I felt a small pang. I counted Terry and Crawford among my good friends, but I'd never before had the temerity to simply drop in without notice. Even now, I wasn't sure it was such a good idea. At least it was Wednesday; that had to count for something.

Professional handlers do the majority of their work on the weekends. Saturdays, Sundays, and sometimes Fridays are devoted to the shows themselves. Thursdays are for grooming dogs and getting ready. Monday is a recovery day. So the two days midweek are about as close as handlers ever come to having a day off.

The good news: Crawford and Terry probably wouldn't be working when I arrived. The bad news: I had no reason to suspect that either one of them was hoping to spend their limited leisure time with me.

In the end I chickened out and called Terry on my cell phone from the road at the end of their driveway.

"Hey doll," he said. "What's up?"

"I need a haircut. Badly."

"Like that's news. If you'd let me maintain that trim every six weeks like I want to, you wouldn't have to go through the oh-so-attractive shaggy dog stage."

Can you tell we'd had this conversation before?

"What's your schedule look like today?" I asked.

"Could be doable. When today?"

"How about now?"

I turned on my blinker, eased past a mailbox marked Bedford Kennels and pulled through a break in the stone walls. Gravel crunched beneath the Volvo's wheels as I headed down the long driveway toward the house. The big white Colonial looked more like a stately country home than a business, in part because the matching kennel building, with its covered runs and spacious paddocks, was hidden out back.

"You're in the neighborhood?"

"I'm virtually at your back door."

I pulled around the house. Dogs—several Poodles, two Dalmatians, and a Chow—that had been snoozing in their runs jumped up and began to bark. Terry's face appeared in the kitchen window.

"You weren't kidding," he said, snapping his phone shut with a flourish.

By the time I got out of the Volvo, Terry had the door open and was standing on the sill waiting for me. Dressed in shorts, a linen shirt, and scuffed topsiders, he still managed to look like every woman's dream. Except for the whole gay thing. And the highly suspicious look on his face.

"Hey there!" I said jauntily.

"Hey yourself." He folded his arms over his chest. "To what do we owe the honor?"

"I told you, I need a haircut."

I swooped in and kissed him firmly on the cheek. Gestures like that make Crawford uncomfortable, but not Terry. He smirked, grabbed my shoulders, and steered me back so he could buss the other cheek, too, European-style.

"Yes, well, you also need to win the lottery and I don't see you standing in line at the gas station."

Terry had snapped out the sarcastic reply without thinking. I looked at him and arched a brow. He stopped and reconsidered. "Oh right, you have Sam, the video game mogul. Strike that last part."

"Consider it stricken." Without waiting for an invitation, I walked past him into the kitchen.

Recently redone, the room was sleek and modern. It had granite counters, polished hardwood floors, and appliances that were large enough to prepare food for an army. Left to his own devices, Crawford mostly used the microwave. Lately, however, Terry had been taking cooking classes. It looked as though the shiny pots and pans that hung from a rack above the center island were finally beginning to get some use.

"Coffee?" asked Terry. His own mug was already sitting on a counter.

"Please." I pulled out a stool and hopped up onto it.

He opened a glass fronted cabinet, got out another mug, and filled it almost to the top. Then he carried it over to the Sub-Zero fridge. "Just milk, right?"

I nodded.

If I'd made coffee for Terry, I'd have added two sweeteners, no milk. We were close enough to be that conversant with each other's personal habits; how had I ever imagined that he wouldn't realize why I had come?

"Where's Crawford?" I asked casually.

"Out." He sloshed milk into the mug, then slid it toward me across the counter. "Running errands."

"Supermarket, dry cleaners?" I smiled as I asked the question. Crawford wasn't the domestic type.

"Something like that."

Terry slid onto a stool opposite and I sipped at my coffee. The flavor was deep and rich, with just the slightest hint of almond.

"You like?" he asked.

"I like."

"Good. Now tell me why you're really here. And make it entertaining, if you don't mind. I could use a little distraction."

"I have questions," I said slowly, wondering what sorts of things Terry might be wanting distraction from.

"So what else is new?"

"You may not like these."

"Oh, *please*. Has that ever stopped you before?"

No, I thought. Not really.

"I want to know what's wrong with Crawford," I said.

Terry's expression was bland. "What makes you think anything is?"

"Because I pay attention to details and I'm not stupid. I've seen him taking it easy with his entries and leaving shows early. He isn't acting like himself. He hasn't been for the last month."

"What if I told you that nothing was going on, that everything was fine?"

"I wouldn't believe you."

"You think I would lie to you?"

Terry sounded genuinely offended, and I realized that if I persisted I might be pushing the boundaries of our friendship.

"I think you would do anything you felt was necessary to protect Crawford." Partly to mollify him, partly because it was true, I added, "It's one of your better qualities."

Terry shook his head. He wasn't appeased. "And yet you're sitting in my kitchen asking me to betray a trust."

My stomach went hollow. "So there is something wrong."

"Crawford's a very private person. You know that as well as anyone. He doesn't talk about his personal problems and he certainly wouldn't want me to. There may be an issue or two. Tests are being run, things are being looked at; that's all I'm going to say. Crawford doesn't want this to be a subject for discussion."

"Not even with friends?"

"Not even." Terry was firm. "In my place, you know you'd respect his wishes. How can I not do the same?"

"You can't," I said softly. Even I could see that. "Is there anything I can do to help?"

"No."

"You'll let me know if that changes?"

"I will."

"I'm holding you to that."

Terry laughed. "I never expected any differently." He tipped back his head to finish the last of his coffee. "Well, now that that's out of the way, do you still want your hair cut or was that just a clever ruse to get you in the door?"

"Of course I want my hair cut. Can't you tell?"

I'd given him an opening the size of a barn door and I thought Terry would go for the easy insult. Instead he stared at me, narrowing his eyes. After thirty seconds or so, I began to get nervous.

"What?"

"Shush, I'm thinking."

He stood up, walked around the island, and placed his hands on either side of my head. His fingers tunneled gently back through my hair. Terry was so close that I could smell the faintly musky aroma of his aftershave and see the smooth muscles of his chest through the sheer linen. Coming from another man, the touch would have felt intimate, maybe even erotic.

But this was Terry we were talking about. As he lifted his hands and let the hair fall back into place, I glanced up. His eyes were focused not on me, the woman seated in front of him, but on some thought process that had to do with scissoring, or styling, or setting a trim.

The sad fact of the matter was, as far as Terry was concerned, I might as well have been an ungroomed Poodle.

"I'm thinking it's time for a change," he said.

"Easy for you to say."

I liked my hair long. I'd been wearing it down around my shoulders for years. Or, to be honest, forever. On previous occasions, Terry had added shape, and layers, and wispy bangs. And I'd learned to give him free rein because when it came to hair, he had good instincts.

But now it sounded like Terry was talking something momentous. I wasn't sure I was ready for that.

"Have you ever thought about going blond?"

I reared back in my seat. "You must be joking!"

"Why?"

"Because . . ." I sputtered automatically. Then I stopped and thought. "Brown is a good color, a fine color. Maybe not exciting, but certainly perfectly decent. It matches my eyes."

"Your eyes are hazel. Hazel goes with blond."

I shook my head as my thoughts on the subject began to define themselves. "Blond isn't me, it's somebody else. Someone who wants to be noticed, someone with bigger boobs, someone who has a whole lot more time than I do to spend worrying about how they look."

"I see," Terry said thoughtfully. "So it's a maintenance issue." Notice how he ignored the whole bigger boobs part.

"Mostly, I guess."

"Then I have another idea."

The fingers were back, lifting, parting, rearranging. Terry could see what he was doing; all I could do was feel. The touch of his fingers brushing through the strands of my hair was hypnotic. I had to keep reminding myself that the man caressing my scalp had an ulterior motive.

"Short and shaggy," he said, his fingertips pressing gently now and moving in a circular motion. "I'm picturing a Meg Ryan look."

"Meg Ryan is a blonde," I said suspiciously.

"Ignore that part and focus on the cut. All wisps and layers, kind of a gamin thing. It'll be fabulous on you. And just think how easy it will be to take care of. Just wash your hair, shake your head, and go."

"The blond thing was a ruse, wasn't it?" I grumbled. "You were setting me up."

"So sue me. It doesn't mean I'm not right."

"I like my long hair."

"It's boring. It never changes."

Unlike Terry's hair, which shifted shades and styles regularly. No doubt he was the darling of whichever hair salon he frequented. At the moment Terry was blond again, his hair long enough to curl down over his ears. He looked like a charming cherub. One who was itching to get a pair of scissors into my hair.

"Sam likes my hair long," I said. It was beginning to feel like I might lose this battle.

"Sam likes *you*." Terry was digging around in drawers and cabinets. He laid out a towel on the countertop and began setting out the tools of his trade. "He wouldn't care if you wore a bag over your head."

Terry might be right. I hoped he was. Because I was beginning to imagine what it might feel like not to have to blow my hair dry after I showered.

Not to have anything clinging to the back of my neck in the heat of summer.

"You're not thinking too short," I said cautiously.

"Here." His fingers brushed my chin, then the lobe of my ear. "And along here. Maybe a bit longer in the back. But it will have body, and swing. It'll move when you move. It will give Sam a good excuse to buy you a new pair of diamond earrings."

"I don't need new earrings."

I was arguing for the sake of arguing now. The decision had already been made and I suspected we both knew it. Certainly Terry, who now had a spray bottle of water in his left hand and a comb in his right, looked ready to rock and roll. Trust a man who showed Poodles for a living to be ready to start snipping at a moment's notice.

"Last chance to say no," he said, spritzing away.

I shook my head, letting my hair slap back and forth across my shoulders for the last time. "I trust you."

Terry leaned toward me, his voice lowering intimately. "That's a dangerous thing to say, doll."

"Haven't you heard? Danger is my middle name."

Terry laughed. Then he picked up his scissors and went to work.

22

The first cut sent a long skein of hair slithering down my shoulder. I shifted on the stool and hoped my trust hadn't been misplaced. There was no turning back now.

"Stop fidgeting." Terry poked me with the tip of the scissors. "If you want me to get this right, you have to sit still."

"Yes sir."

I couldn't see him but I knew he was grinning. That made me feel better and I began to relax.

"Talk to me," Terry said as he worked. "How's your summer going? Tell me what you've been up to."

"You know perfectly well what I've been up to. Faith and I are engaged in an epic battle to become the new face of Chow Down dog food. Whether we want to be or not."

"Of course I know that, but I want details, the newest scoop. What's going on behind the scenes?"

The scissors continued to flash open and shut,

nicking off bits and pieces of hair. I watched them go without regret.

"For one thing, Lisa Kim has disappeared—"

"Wow." He uttered the word with no inflection at all. I'd led with my biggest news and Terry sounded almost bored.

I turned my head slightly to look at him. Firmly but gently, Terry turned it back. I sighed and faced the far wall.

"That doesn't surprise you?" I asked.

"Should it?"

"Yes." I might have sounded a little huffy. "Every time someone disappears it surprises me. I like people to stay where they're supposed to be."

"Well then," said Terry, "there's your problem. What makes you think that *you* know where people are supposed to be?"

I didn't answer. I imagined that was my way of acknowledging that he might have a point. Hair continued to fall to the floor around the legs of the stool. My head began to feel lighter.

"Lisa left a whole bunch of dogs behind," I mentioned after a minute. "Ten Yorkies, to be precise. Don't you think she would have cared about what happened to them? If she'd left of her own volition, wouldn't she have made provisions for their care?"

"Larumph mookie," Terry mumbled.

I swiveled in my seat. He was holding a comb between his lips. Considering all the time he spent doing exactly that at dog shows, you'd think he would be better at talking around an obstacle. I reached up and took the comb from him.

Terry wet his lips and pursed his mouth. "Sit still," he said. "I'm trying to work here."

"You always talk when you work. Why should today be any different?"

"It isn't." Less gentle than he'd been the time before, Terry repositioned me. "I can talk to your back perfectly well."

"Fine," I said. "Where were we? Oh, I remember, you were muttering something about Lisa."

Terry reached around and retrieved the comb. He used it to feather through the hair over my ears. "No, I was muttering about Larry. The dogs were his passion, not hers. Didn't you ever notice that? He was the one who babied them, fussed over them, took them in the ring. Lisa was just along for the ride. You know, the good wife supporting her hubby's hobby and trying to make it look like she wanted to be involved, when she really couldn't have cared less."

"Interesting," I said. Terry's observation expanded on what Bertie had told me. Not only that, but his assessments were usually pretty astute. "I never saw either of the Kims at any shows. The first time I met the two of them was at the opening reception in Norwalk."

"Then you're probably assuming Lisa's a dog person."

I nodded.

Terry growled a correction. My twitching and fidgeting was definitely trying his patience. "I wouldn't jump to that conclusion if I were you. Maybe Lisa met up with some sort of foul play, maybe she didn't. But I could see her taking off and leaving those dogs behind. I don't think she would have worried about it the way you or I would have. Did Yoda get dumped too?"

"No." I was careful not to shake my head.

"Wherever Lisa's gone, Yoda seems to have disappeared right along with her."

"There you go, then."

"There I go . . . what?"

"She took the potential moneymaker with her. I rest my case."

"I didn't know we were making cases. Since you know so much about it, where did Lisa go?"

"Oh please. I haven't the slightest idea. I never said I knew *everything*."

Maybe not, but he'd been guilty of implying it a time or two. I decided to switch tacks. "How's it coming? Can I look in a mirror?"

"Your hair looks faboo. And no, you can't look yet. Not until I'm finished."

"But—"

"Think of your head as a soufflé. If you open the oven door too soon the whole thing falls flat."

"That's a really terrible analogy," I said. At least I was hoping it was.

"Tell me something else." As hair continued to fall to the floor, Terry was determined to distract me from the matter at hand. "How are the other contestants doing? Who seems to be winning?"

I spent the next fifteen minutes regaling him with the story of our trip to Central Park. Terry listened with rapt attention, humming softly under his breath as he worked.

"So?" he asked at the end. "You still didn't answer my second question. Now that you're most of the way through the process, who's going to win?"

"I wish I knew," I said fervently. "I really hope it isn't me."

"You mean Faith."

"Yes, but I also mean me. Because much as it's

supposed to be our dogs that are competing to represent Chow Down, it's been obvious that the owners are part of the selection process. When we participate in these events, it feels like we're on trial, too."

"Maybe you're overidentifying."

I couldn't entirely rule that out. Certainly I'd seen it happen at dog shows often enough: owners who treated their dogs like their children or siblings. Who took every loss personally and celebrated each win as if their own merits had been on the line. But I was pretty sure that wasn't the case here.

"I don't think so," I said. "The judges seem to spend as much time interviewing the owners as they do observing the dogs. Doug Allen even admitted as much the other day. I guess they need to make sure that whoever they pick will be up to the task."

Terry nodded absently. His hands were moving through my hair more slowly now. The bulk of the work had already been done. Now he was adding the finishing touches. I hoped he liked what he was seeing.

"If you wanted to win I'd be in your corner all the way," he said. "But since you don't, I'm rooting for the Reddings and Ginger."

I pondered that for a minute and decided that the couple and their Brittany would probably be my choice, too. Nevertheless, I was curious to hear his reasoning. "How come?"

"Process of elimination, I guess. Dorothy's only in it to gratify her own ego—"

I laughed. "We all seem to be in it for that."

Terry kept going without missing a beat. "Mac-

Duff's getting older. He needs a rest more than he needs a new job. Lisa doesn't have the right temperament. Being named spokesdog is going to be a lot of work, and she'd never be able to offer Yoda the support she'd need. Ben? He wants the win badly, but if he doesn't get it, he'll find something else. Trust me, he's the kind of guy who always lands on his feet."

"So by default that leaves you with Bill and Allison."

"Plus, of course . . . They really need the money."

"They do?"

I spun around. Luckily Terry had seen that coming and he held his hand away from my head, scissors angled outward. Otherwise I might have lost an ear.

"How do you know that?"

"Everybody knows that, doll."

"I don't."

"Okay, make that everyone who's been paying the slightest bit of attention. It's not cheap to put championships on a dog in three different disciplines. Think about it."

He was right, of course. Up until now, I'd considered only how the Brittany's varied accomplishments would affect her standing in the contest. I hadn't stopped to think about the amount of time and effort, not to mention the financial commitment, that had gone into producing a record like hers.

I was mostly conversant with the cost of showing a dog in conformation. Depending on the breed, the quality of the dog, and whether the owners handled themselves or hired a professional to do the job for them, the cost of procuring a championship could easily run into the thousands. Exhibiting week after week wasn't cheap, no matter how you looked at it.

"Who showed Ginger in breed?" I asked.

"I think Allison started her, but the two of them didn't get very far."

I remembered the conversation I'd had earlier with the couple. "I'll bet she got too nervous taking her in the ring."

"Something like that. Anyway, Ginger went to Todd to get finished."

Todd was Todd Wickham, a top professional handler so well known among dog show aficionados that he went by just one name, like Madonna or Bono or Sting.

"That must have cost plenty."

"Even more so because Ginger, for all her glowing attributes, doesn't happen to be a particularly good Brittany. She was originally bought as a family pet, and for Bill to play around with in obedience. But once the Reddings started going to shows, Allison was seduced by the glamour of the conformation ring and decided that she wanted Ginger to finish there, too.

"You know Todd. He could walk a pot-bellied pig in the ring and convince the judge it was a French Bulldog. And even he had a hard time getting that last major on her."

I supposed that showed what little I knew about Brittanys. I'd always thought that Ginger was a perfectly fine specimen of the breed. Certainly she was a pretty dog to look at. Then again, I'd learned enough from Aunt Peg to know that the fact that a dog was attractive didn't necessarily mean that it had correct structure or breed type.

"It all adds up," Terry was saying. "Even when you do part of it yourself, there are entries, gas, and hotels. Not to mention time off from work. Which, by the way, neither Bill nor Allison is doing at the moment. Right now their idea of gainful employment seems to consist of promoting Ginger."

"Are you sure? First time we met over at Champions, Bill was wearing a suit and tie. I thought he looked like he'd left work to come to the reception."

Terry shook his head. "The way I heard it, Bill was in the habit of cutting out on work whenever something that looked like more fun came up. He got laid off about six weeks ago. Maybe he had an interview the morning you saw him. Or could be he was thinking of the contest as his potential new job. One hundred thousand bucks would take care of a lot of bills."

It would indeed.

While we'd been speaking, Terry had finally stopped working. He'd laid the comb and scissors down on the counter. He studied me carefully, then reached up to nudge a few errant strands of hair into place with his fingers.

My hair had been damp when he'd started cutting it. Usually Terry would blow it dry when he was done. But now it was so much shorter, it felt as though it had dried already. I slid off the stool and lifted a tentative hand to touch the results.

"No touching." Terry slapped my hand away. "Look first."

He led the way to a powder room off the kitchen, flipped the light switch, then stood back so I could slip past him and see the mirror.

I was almost afraid to look. What if I hated it? I'd seen the mound of hair on the floor beneath the stool. I'd never done anything this drastic before. If it was awful, it would take years to grow back. Sam had married a woman with long hair. What if he hated it . . . ?

"Would you stop agonizing and look already!"

So I did.

Slowly I turned to face the mirror. My eyes widened. For a moment, I didn't even recognize the face I saw there. Now framed by a cap of loose, tousled curls, it looked like it belonged to a totally different person.

"It turns out your hair has a lot of body when it's not weighted down by all that length," Terry said.

I was still staring at my reflection. I'd had long hair all my life. Long *straight* hair. I would never have imagined that lopping off seven or eight inches would make this big a difference.

"Wow." I exhaled.

That didn't seem to be the response Terry was hoping for. He squeezed into the small room next to me. Our faces swam side by side in the mirror. Mine still looked like I'd been poleaxed. His looked unsure.

"Is that wow good, or wow bad?"

"I think I love you," I said.

Terry grinned. "I'll take that as a compliment."

I shook my head, gently at first, and then harder. The curls bobbed and spun, then settled back into place. "Upkeep?"

"Wash, finger comb, maybe add a little gel if you feel like it. That's all there is to it."

After years of hassling with a blow dryer and hot

rollers, that routine sounded like heaven. "Will you marry me?"

"You're already married."

"Damn."

"But I'll do your hair forever."

"Will you?" I turned to face him. An image of Crawford flashed before my eyes. Suddenly the moment felt serious. So many things were perfect in my life right now; I didn't want any of it to change. "Promise?"

"Promise," Terry affirmed. "Scout's honor."

Neither of us could control the future. He knew that as well as I did. But just for that moment, I wanted to believe.

"Scout's honor," I echoed softly. It came out sounding like a prayer.

23

That weekend it was my turn to go to a dog show in support of Sam and Tar. While I was there I'd also be helping Bertie with the three Poodles she was going to be handling. Nobody gets a free ride around here.

The show was outdoors, held on the polo grounds in Farmington, Connecticut. Luckily we got perfect weather for the event: warm, sunny, and not too humid. One thing about dog shows; nothing short of an oncoming tornado will shut one down. Over the years, I've shown through high winds, unexpected sleet, and near-flood conditions. A perfect dog show day is a rarity, and it was more than enough to put all of us in a good mood.

"All" referred to Sam and me, Aunt Peg, Bertie, and Maggie. Davey was with his father for the weekend, and Frank was tending to business at The Bean Counter. There was no way, however, that Bertie could give a string of a dozen dogs the professional handling job they deserved and take care of a six-month-old baby at the same time. That was where Aunt Peg came in. She had volunteered to baby-sit.

Even if I hadn't had other reasons for being at the show, I'd have come just to watch that. At the best of times, Aunt Peg can be a dubious influence on those around her. When it comes to managing children, any parents in the vicinity had better sit up and pay attention.

When Davey had been in my aunt's care, she'd been known to feed him mountains of sweets and encourage him to disregard any inconvenient rules. Most of the time, she treated him like he was simply a height-challenged adult. Of course Davey adored her all the more for it. Which was a constant reminder that I probably don't know as much about parenting as I'd like to think I do.

When we arrived at the show, Bertie, Maggie, and Aunt Peg had already been there for several hours. I knew Bertie had had a pair of English Cockers to show at nine AM, but Poodles weren't scheduled until after lunch. I figured I'd allowed plenty of time to make myself useful on Bertie's behalf.

Aunt Peg didn't agree.

"You two must have slept late this morning," she said when Sam backed his SUV up to the side of the grooming tent and we began unloading our gear. Bertie was nowhere in sight but she'd left Aunt Peg in charge.

"We did," Sam replied with a cheerful wink. Nothing Peg says ever ruffles his feathers. "That's the beauty of having only one dog to show."

"I'm not showing *any* and I still managed to get here bright and early."

"That's because you had a job to do . . ." My voice trailed away. Aunt Peg was staring at me rather rudely. I couldn't decide whether she looked fascinated or horrified.

"What on earth happened to you?" she asked.

"Nothing."

Sam was stacking crates. He looked over, reached up, and patted his head. I still didn't get it. He fingered his hair and lifted a brow. The lightbulb went off. I pirouetted with a smile and showed off my new hairdo.

"Terry happened to me," I said. "Do you like it?"

"I don't know. It's a big change. I might have to think about it."

"I didn't have to think about it," said Sam. Passing by on his way back to the car, he tousled my hair with his hand. "I loved it right away."

"You're supposed to," Peg informed him. "That's your job."

Maybe in a parallel universe, I thought. When it came to marriage Aunt Peg was clearly an optimist.

"Speaking of jobs . . ." I cast a quick glance around the jumble of tables and crates. "You haven't lost Maggie, have you?"

"Certainly not. I know precisely where my namesake is. She's taking her midday nap."

Between the generators that powered blow dryers and radios, and the constant babble of conversation, you might have thought that the noise level alone would have precluded napping under the grooming tent. But I'd seen my niece in action.

When Maggie wanted to sleep she was oblivious to all outside influences.

Sam paused in the act of unfolding the legs on his portable grooming table. "Where?" he asked, which saved me the trouble of doing the same.

Aunt Peg gestured toward a medium-sized wooden crate in a lower row. "Bertie was hoping to set up a playpen but there wasn't room under the tent and she didn't want Maggie out in the sun, so we had to make do."

I stooped down and peered into the crate through the mesh doorway. Blissfully asleep within, Maggie wasn't at all perturbed by her unusual surroundings. She was snuggled contentedly in her baby seat, with her eyes closed and her blond head tipped to one side. One small hand was curled into a fist beneath her chin, the other clutched her favorite toy, a pink stuffed dog with a button nose and floppy ears.

"She's such a little doll," I said softly.

"When she's asleep," Aunt Peg muttered. "When she's awake, that child has an opinion about everything."

Sam ducked his head and didn't say a thing. I suspected he was thinking the same thing I was. Maggie came by that trait honestly.

"Where's Bertie?" I asked.

"Showing a Bouvier over in ring eight. I expect she'll be back shortly."

Table and crate in place, Sam was unloading Tar from the car. The big Poodle threaded his way down the narrow aisle and hopped up onto the grooming table. Turning a tight circle on the rubber-matted top, he lay down and placed his head between his paws.

"I'll go park the car," I said. We'd been in place beside the tent for only a few minutes, but already there was a line of other vehicles waiting for our space in the unloading zone.

"Thanks," said Sam. "I'll get to work on Tar."

"And keep me company," said Peg. "So far, my job has proven to be rather boring."

Just wait, I thought. When Mags awoke from her nap she would be raring to go again and Aunt Peg would have her hands full just trying to keep up.

Following instructions from the parking crew, I left Sam's SUV on the other side of the polo grounds at the end of a long line of cars. From there, I cut back across the freshly mown field. This time I approached the show from the other side, where the rings were set up in a tent-covered double row and the judging in several different breeds was in progress.

Ring eight was on the corner. I headed that way and scanned the crowd for Bertie, but it looked as though Bouviers had already finished. A group of exhibitors with Boxers was clustered by the in-gate. Several others were beginning to file into the ring for a class.

My steps slowed as I watched the dogs in the ring and mentally compared them with Brando. Boxers were a popular breed with spectators, and they usually drew a large audience. They weren't a breed I'd had much exposure to, however, and I wasn't expecting to see anyone I knew. Which was why it came as such a surprise when I recognized Cindy Burrows standing next to the ring.

What, I wondered, could have brought the Chow Down product manager to a dog show all the way up in the middle of Connecticut?

Boxer fans were packed in tight at ringside. I maneuvered my way toward the front of the crowd, keeping Cindy in sight. The other times I'd seen her she'd been dressed for work. Today, Cindy looked young and fresh and pretty in a flower-sprigged sundress and low-heeled sandals. Her hair wasn't confined to its usual French braid; instead she wore it loose and curling down around her shoulders. Briefly, I felt a pang of regret. Then I realized how much cooler I felt with my new short hair and the feeling passed.

I got as close as I could, then leaned around a couple still separating us and said, "Hello."

Cindy jumped slightly and cast a startled glance my way. "Melanie . . . !" She didn't exactly sound pleased to see me. "What a surprise. What are you doing here?"

As one, the couple between us shifted forward, like they were afraid we might try to talk across in front of them and block their view. I could hardly blame them; much as I had no stake in the Boxer judging, I felt the same way when Poodles were in the ring. I drew back several steps, giving up my ringside spot. Cindy did the same. The couple, still staring fixedly into the ring, looked relieved by our departure.

"My husband is showing one of Faith's relatives," I said. "What about you? I thought Gus was a fris-bee dog. I didn't know you were into dog shows, too."

"I'm not really. This is my first one. I'm just learning how things work and what it's all about."

Cindy was smiling but she looked uneasy. She sent a furtive glance skirting past me and into the ring. I turned and looked, too. Open Bitch was being judged. None of the exhibitors appeared familiar to me and I wondered who we were looking for. I knew only one person who owned a Boxer.

"Where's Faith?" Cindy asked brightly. "Is she showing, too?"

"No, she's retired from breed competition. Poodles are required to be "in hair" if you want to show them, and a trim like that takes a huge amount of upkeep. I cut Faith's hair off when she finished her championship, so now she's just a pet."

Just a pet. In the eyes of some people who showed dogs, those words were about the biggest insult you could offer. I'd never been able to understand why. I'd enjoyed Faith's show career. I loved the fact that she'd been well-bred enough and well made enough to finish her championship in style. But now I adored not having to worry about her coat all the time. Truth be told, I was enjoying the "just a pet" stage of our relationship more than the ones that had preceded it.

"You're not giving Faith enough credit," Cindy said. "All of the finalists are highly accomplished canines. None of them could be labeled as *just* an anything."

I nodded in agreement but my thoughts were elsewhere. If I'd had a catalogue, I would have checked to see if Brando was entered. Since I didn't, I went with my gut and said casually, "So . . . Is Ben showing today?"

Cindy hesitated. I got the distinct impression that I'd posed a question she'd rather not have to answer. But since we were standing beside the Boxer ring, she must have realized that I would see for myself sooner or later.

"Yes, he is," she said after a moment. "Actually,

that's why I'm here. He asked me to come and watch him show Brando. You know . . . so I could see the dog in his element?"

Not to mention the dog owner, I thought. No wonder Cindy hadn't been happy to see me. I was betting there had to be some sort of rule against contest judges fraternizing with the finalists. And yet she'd put on a pretty dress and come to the dog show anyway.

Ben was more than a decade older than Cindy was, possibly closer to two. But he was handsome and charming and I could see how he might have been able to turn her head. I could also imagine him using that connection to his advantage.

"Ben and Brando are in the Best of Breed class," said Cindy. "Those are the dogs they call specials."

"Yes, I know," I said.

Standing there gazing into the ring, I remembered what Terry had said about Brando's faults. Competition in Boxers, especially among the champions, was usually pretty fierce. Ben wasn't stupid and he didn't strike me as the kind of person who liked to lose, so I sincerely doubted that he made a habit of specialing the dog.

But Boxers, unlike Poodles, don't require a lot of upkeep to be made show-ready. As long as a dog is kept in fairly good weight and muscle, they can be exhibited on a whim. Like in the event that an owner felt a sudden need to try and impress someone.

I looked back at Cindy. The judging was moving right along. The Open class was over. Winners Bitch had come and gone. The champions were now entering into the ring. And Cindy looked ready to be impressed.

"Doesn't he look handsome?" she said as the pair took their place in line.

"Brando?" I asked. "Or Ben?"

She colored slightly. "Brando, of course."

"He looks great," I agreed. And to my untrained eye, he did. Which was probably why nobody had ever asked me to judge Boxers.

"Ben doesn't look bad either," I commented.

Cindy slid a glance my way, probably checking for ulterior motives. Which of course I had. Nevertheless, as the judge asked the exhibitors to take the dogs around for the first time, I trained my gaze on the entries in the ring and kept my expression perfectly bland.

"There's nothing going on between us," she said firmly.

"Good to know."

"We're just friends."

The two denials didn't have the effect Cindy must have been hoping for. In fact, they made me even more suspicious. Besides, even if that was the extent of their relationship, that hardly made everything all right. Even friends might feel pressured to help one another out when it came to winning a contest. Especially one that boasted such a lucrative prize.

And when it came to choosing the finalists, I remembered, Cindy had been the one who happened to like big dogs.

"Did you and Ben know one another before the contest started?" I asked.

"No." Her tone was sharp. "We met for the first time at the reception."

In the ring, the judge was performing her individual examinations. Though we were speaking to one another, Cindy and I were both facing forward; the dog person's version of multitasking. Neither one of us wanted to miss a thing.

"Even though you'd been the one to promote the big dogs?"

Cindy gave her head a quick, emphatic shake. "That was just a coincidence. I didn't know a thing about Ben or Brando when I first read their application. They reached the final five through their own merits."

"And you became 'just friends' after that."

"That's right. Ben's a nice guy. I admit I was kind of surprised when he first called me, but I was flattered, too. I mean, he's pretty famous and all . . ."

Cindy was blushing again. I felt almost sorry for her. Call me a skeptic, but I sincerely doubted that Ben would have pursued the young woman if she hadn't been in a position to further his chances in the contest. Surely that thought must have occurred to her.

"So Ben was the one who approached you?"

"Well, *yeah* . . . It wasn't like I would have called him. Ben said he really wanted to get to know me better. But right away we both agreed we needed to keep things low-key until after the contest was over. You won't—"

"Spread the news around?"

Cindy nodded. "I'd really appreciate it if you kept things to yourself. People might take things the wrong way, you know?"

Of course I knew. I was taking it the wrong way myself.

"Weren't you afraid that people would see the two of you together here?"

"I didn't even think about that. Coming all the

way up here to Farmington seemed safe enough. It didn't even occur to me that we might run into someone we knew."

That was because Cindy wasn't a dog show person. Exhibitors routinely traveled all over in search of good judges and facilities. A ninety-minute drive was nothing compared to some of the trips I'd gone on.

"Oh!" she said. "The judge is going back for another look at Brando. That must be good, right?"

I could have told her that it was probably too little, too late, but I knew she'd find that out in a minute when the judge made her final selections. Suddenly I had no desire to stay and watch Cindy watch Ben lose.

"I hope you have a good time today," I said.

"Thanks, I'm sure I will. Ben promised to show me the insider's view of the dog show world. I know I'm going to be fascinated."

Cindy wasn't that much younger than me but suddenly I felt eons older. She looked as though she had stars in her eyes; I wasn't sure I'd ever been that naive. It would have been nice to believe that Ben wasn't just using her as Brando's ticket to fame and fortune but that seemed like a long shot to me. I really hoped that when the contest was over, and his use for her had ended, that he let her down gently.

Heading back to the grooming tent, I pondered this new information. A secret relationship between a judge and one of the finalists? If I was in that situation I would want to keep things quiet, too. Cindy said that she and Ben had met for the first time at the reception, but I wasn't sure that I believed her.

Could Larry Kim have discovered something he wasn't supposed to know? Had he threatened to make a fuss? Was Ben the person I'd heard arguing with him in the stairwell just before he fell? And what, if anything, did this have to do with Lisa Kim's disappearance?

I blew out a windy sigh. That was my problem. I was always good at coming up with questions. It was the answers that gave me headaches.

24

"There you are, finally," Aunt Peg said when I got back to the setup. "We were wondering what kept you. Sam thought perhaps you'd gotten lost."

Sam slipped me a quick wink. He was busy line brushing Tar and didn't look like my extended absence had caused him the slightest bit of concern.

It was Peg who'd apparently grown bored while waiting for Maggie to wake up. In my absence, she'd taken it upon herself to remove Bertie's Standard Poodle from his crate and begin brushing out the dog's mane coat. That was supposed to be my job, but I wasn't complaining. It was good for Aunt Peg to have something to do.

Some people cherish peace and quiet, but not Aunt Peg. She sees such times as opportunities to stir things up. And trust me, we've all been there. It's not a pretty sight.

Today, thankfully, it looked as though Aunt Peg

had used her powers for the sake of good rather than evil.

Bertie was back at the setup, too, and she had her Toy Poodle out on a tabletop. "Excellent hair," she said. "Terry?"

"Of course. I'd never trust anybody else to make such a drastic change."

Bertie's third Poodle entry was a Mini. I leaned down, opened a crate, and let the medium-sized black bitch hop out into my arms.

"He did a great job." Bertie stopped brushing. She reached over and poked my shoulder until I turned around and she could consider the cut from all angles. "I've been thinking about going shorter myself. Ever since Maggie was born, I just don't have the time—"

Aunt Peg yelped. We all turned to look at her. Even the Standard Poodle, who'd been snoozing on the grooming table, opened his eyes and lifted his head.

"Is *that* why?" she asked.

It took me a minute to figure out what she was talking about. Then I sighed. "No."

"No what?" asked Sam.

"No, we're not pregnant."

"Oh." He looked nonplussed by the sudden switch in topic. "Good to know . . . I guess."

"Trust me." I patted his arm. "When there's news, you'll be the first to hear."

"And I'll be second," Aunt Peg said firmly.

I might have been tempted to make a rude reply. Fortunately for the sake of family harmony, Sam answered first. "I think Davey might be the second person we tell. But you can be third."

Aunt Peg looked ready to argue. Quickly I

turned to Bertie and changed the subject again. "Have you heard anything more from Sue about Lisa's whereabouts?"

"All I know is that as of last night, she's still among the missing. Since it's been three days, Sue was finally able to file a police report. I don't think it's going to help much though."

"The police still don't think that Lisa's disappearance might be related to Larry's murder?"

Bertie shook her head. "Not that they've let on. The detective Sue dealt with told her it seemed likely that Lisa might have gone home for a while to stay with her family."

"Leaving ten dogs behind in her basement?" No matter what Terry had said, that still sounded crazy to me.

"Technically she arranged for their care," said Bertie. "She left them with Sue."

"But only for one day," said Aunt Peg. She'd been following the saga from the start.

"I know. I'm not saying I think they're right, I'm just repeating what I was told. And by the way, the Yorkies are no longer in Lisa's basement."

"Where are they now?" asked Sam.

"Sue was at her wit's end so I told her I'd help out. As of Wednesday afternoon, Lisa's dogs have been sitting in my kennel. So now I guess we're all waiting to see what happens next."

"I hope you're charging board," I said.

"In theory, yes. But that only helps if Lisa shows up to claim them. Otherwise I'm going to be the one who's stuck finding ten new homes."

"If Lisa *did* go off somewhere to be with her family," said Aunt Peg, "does anybody know where that might be?"

"Sue thought maybe Florida. Apparently there was an address book that had some information. She took it with her and left it with the Southport police when she filed the report."

"I hope they're following up," I said but, based on my past experiences with the police, I tended to doubt it.

If the authorities didn't believe that Lisa had met with foul play, they probably weren't concerned about where she was. Of course they weren't the only ones. Terry hadn't been worried either. Even Sue had seemed more upset about the inconvenience Lisa's unexpected absence was causing her than about any dire possibilities.

So maybe I was the one who was overreacting. That seemed like a shame considering that I barely knew the woman. If I ever dropped off the face of the earth, I hoped people would pay more attention than this.

I looked over at Sam. "If I disappeared, would you look for me?"

His hands went still. His expression was pained. "Am I on *Candid Camera* or is this just my day for really weird questions?"

"I'm serious."

"Yes, I would look for you. Forever, if that's what it took."

"That's so sweet," said Bertie.

"A husband ought to know where his wife is," Aunt Peg said crisply. "The main problem with Lisa's disappearance is that her husband is gone, too. For all we know, this might be nothing unusual. Lisa might make a habit of disappearing."

"Her husband isn't just gone," I pointed out. "He was murdered. Which is pretty unusual, too."

"Maybe Lisa ran away," said Bertie. "Maybe she was frightened."

"Of what?" asked Sam.

"Her husband's murderer?" I guessed.

"But if she knew who that was," said Peg, "why not just turn him into the police? Why run away?"

"Maybe he's blackmailing her," said Bertie. "Maybe he knows some deep, dark secret from her past."

"Maybe you've been watching too many soap operas," Aunt Peg sniffed.

Bertie only laughed. "You're right about that. I have to do something to pass the time while I'm standing in the kennel grooming dogs."

"I guess we'll find out soon enough whether or not Lisa left of her own volition," I said.

"Why do you say that?" asked Sam.

"Because ever since the contest started, our presence has been required at events that take place every couple of days. When the next one occurs, we'll see whether or not Lisa and Yoda show up. I thought she would withdraw when Larry died but she didn't, so either the contest or the prize money must be pretty important to her. I'm betting that's what will flush her out."

"When is your next event?" asked Aunt Peg.

"I don't know, I haven't heard yet. Usually I get an email and a couple days' warning. Maybe there will be a message waiting for me when we get home."

As it happened, I didn't have to wait that long. We finished grooming the four Poodles—Bertie's three plus Tar—and Maggie awoke just in time to accompany us to the ring for the judging. Aunt Peg fed her great-niece a bottle while Bertie won Reserve Winners with her Toy, put two points on the Mini, then placed second in a large Open class with the Standard. In a strong group of specials, Tar was awarded Best of Variety.

As Sam was waiting to have his picture taken with the judge, my cell phone chimed. Bertie was heading back to the setup; she had Maggie in her arms and the Standard Poodle on a leash. I handed the two Poodles I'd been holding to Aunt Peg, then stepped away from the ring so I could hear better. I found myself talking to Doug Allen.

"I'm glad I reached you," he said.

"What's up?"

"Something really exciting. Everything just came together and since it's short notice I wanted to speak to each of you personally and make sure that you were onboard. How would you and Faith like to be on television?"

Several answers sprang immediately to mind. Probably none were what Doug wanted to hear. I'd never sought fame out, but now it looked as though it might be coming to find me anyway. Or at least coming to find my dog.

I gave myself a mental kick. I had to keep reminding myself that this was all about Faith.

"That sounds interesting," I said cautiously.

"Interesting? It's going to be terrific!" Doug was back in cheerleader mode. "The five of you have been booked as a group on *This Is Your Morning Show.* You're going to appear in a segment with their resident pet expert, Darren Abernathy. He'll talk about canine health, proper diet, and the importance of good nutrition. Then he'll plug the contest and introduce each of you to a national audience."

On those rare mornings when I had time to check out a news-and-entertainment show, I'd seen Darren Abernathy at work. Whatever credentials he might possess for calling himself a "pet expert" they weren't evidenced by the advice he dispensed. Much of it was simply common sense, leavened with a dose of good-old-boy humor. Abernathy didn't believe in using crates, his training methods looked dubious, and he'd been known to refer to Poodles as "froufrou dogs." It wouldn't surprise me if we hated each other on sight.

"Great," I said flatly.

"I knew you'd be excited," said Doug. "This is a huge opportunity for everyone involved. Not only that, but it will be our last group event. The committee and I will be making our final selection after the appearance on Monday morning, and we'll be announcing the big winner at a press conference on Tuesday."

Much as I had wanted to be finished with the contest, suddenly it seemed as though everything was moving at warp speed. "Monday morning?" I said. That was only thirty-six hours away.

"That's right," Doug confirmed. "We have a five-minute segment during the last half hour of the show, so we'll be on the air sometime between eight-thirty and nine. The producer wants us all to be at the studio by six thirty."

I gulped. "AM?"

"Of course AM," Doug said with a hearty laugh. "Otherwise it wouldn't be a morning show."

I did the calculations. To be at a television studio in midtown Manhattan at six-thirty, Faith and I would need to leave home shortly after five. Which meant getting up around four-thirty. Oh joy.

"What will we be doing between six-thirty and eight-thirty?"

"Oh, you know, the usual. Having your hair and makeup done. Eating bagels in the green room, chatting with the other stars that are appearing that day . . ."

I guessed I was supposed to be seeing those things as incentives.

"We're talking about live television here, so they can't afford for anything to go wrong. The producers like to get everyone in place early just to make sure that there are no last minute slipups."

I thought about Ben, for whom punctuality didn't seem to be a strong suit. Then I thought about Lisa, who might not appear at all. I wondered what Doug intended to do about that.

"What about Lisa?" I asked.

"What about her?"

"Have you spoken with her?"

There was a pause, as if maybe Doug was wondering why I thought that was any of my business. I waited him out.

"Not yet," he said finally. "I'm still trying to reach her."

"You know she's missing, right?"

"No." His tone was firm. "I don't know that."

He was lying and I wondered why. Was Doug simply trying to put a good face on things, or was he covering up something he didn't want me to know?

"Lisa's friend, Sue, said she spoke to you early in the week right after Lisa disappeared."

"I believe I may have had a brief conversation with someone . . . It seems to me that I understood there had been a mix-up in some arrangements she made with a friend . . . But, uh, nobody told me Lisa was missing . . ."

Another lie, assuming that Sue had been telling me the truth. They were beginning to pile up now. I decided to keep prodding and see where that would lead me.

"After we all returned from New York on the bus last Tuesday, Lisa and Yoda didn't go back home. Nobody has seen them since. When Sue called you, she was hoping you might have some idea where Lisa had gone."

"Nobody has seen them since?" Doug repeated. He was beginning to sound agitated. "Are you sure about that?"

"A friend of mine has been taking care of her dogs. If Lisa had reappeared, she would know about it. I guess this means that the police haven't contacted you?"

"Er . . . no. Something is going to have to be done about this, and quickly."

"I agree," I said. Then Doug continued to speak and I realized we weren't talking about the same thing at all.

"Getting this spot on the morning show is an enormous coup for Champions Dog Food and for Chow Down. This kind of national exposure will be invaluable to our product launch and the subsequent marketing campaign. Now is not the time for Lisa to be playing games."

"If indeed she is," I said quietly.

Doug didn't hear me; he was still talking.

"All I can say is that we've promised five finalists for Monday morning and no matter what it takes, five finalists are going to appear. With or without Lisa, Yoda had better be there or heads are going to roll."

25

Monday morning, four-thirty AM arrived all too soon.

Even that close to the longest day of the year it was fully dark outside when my alarm sounded; the sun wouldn't be rising for at least another hour and a half. As I climbed out of bed, Sam rolled over sleepily, opened one eye, and waved good-bye in my general direction. So much for sympathy.

Even Faith, who normally loves to accompany me on outings, was loathe to drag herself out of bed. Or in her case, off the foot of the bed. Showered and dressed, I called to her quietly from the doorway to Davey's room. Like Sam, the Poodle opened her eyes but didn't stir.

"Come on," I whispered so as not to disturb my sleeping son. "We have things to do."

Since I'd devoted several hours the previous evening to clipping, bathing, and blowing her dry, I knew Faith understood that we had somewhere to go. What she didn't understand apparently was why we needed to leave in the middle of the night.

That made two of us, I thought grumpily.

When I called a second time, Faith rose slowly and stretched. Looking thoroughly put upon, she hopped off the bed and padded to my side. "Nobody ever told you being famous was going to be easy," I muttered, leading the way down the stairs.

Ten minutes later we were on the road. Traffic was light at that hour, or at least not as bad as it would be shortly. The sun rose while we were crossing the Triboro Bridge and the Manhattan skyline looked serene and beautiful bathed in an early morning glow. Faith, still looking faintly disgruntled and snoozing with her nose between her paws on the seat beside me, missed the whole thing. Then again, since dogs score pretty high on the Inner Peace scale, she probably didn't need the lift as much as I did.

I left the Volvo in a parking garage two blocks away from the midtown address I'd been given, and Faith and I presented ourselves to the studio receptionist with a few minutes to spare. The streets and sidewalks below had been mostly quiet, but the tenth floor workplace was a hub of sound and activity. Everyone looked wide awake and incredibly busy. They had probably all been up for hours.

The receptionist signed us in, then turned us over to an efficient looking assistant. That young woman checked off our names—Faith's and mine both, I saw—on a clipboard she was carrying. Then she escorted us down a hallway to the green room which, I noticed immediately, wasn't green at all.

About half the participants in our segment had already arrived. Dorothy, sitting next to a table filled with breakfast items, looked as bleary-eyed as I felt. Bill and Allison, side by side on a couch with Ginger sitting between them, appeared predictably chipper. Chris Hovick, nursing a tall cup of coffee, looked rumpled and glum. Cindy and Doug were conferring quietly about something in one corner of the room. Unfortunately their whispered voices didn't carry.

I waited only long enough for Faith to touch noses with the other dogs, then made a beeline for the coffee. Faith lifted her muzzle, sniffing the air in front of the table and scoping out the food choices. The selection consisted of bagels and muffins. No dog biscuits.

Coffee in hand, I went and sat next to Dorothy. Faith turned a small circle, then lay down at my feet. "What's that about?" I asked under my breath, nodding toward Doug and Cindy.

"I don't know. Simone was in here a few minutes ago. She said something to Doug that didn't make him happy, then she turned around and left again. Doug called Cindy over and they've been talking ever since."

"What about Ben and Brando?"

"I haven't seen them yet. But you know Ben, he's always running late."

"Lisa and Yoda?"

Dorothy chuckled. "No sign of them either. Maybe our little group of five finalists just got reduced to three. The odds are improving every minute, aren't they?"

She reached down and gave MacDuff a cheerful pat. The Scottie gazed up at his owner adoringly. Chris sipped his coffee and regarded them both over the lip of his cup with a stern expression. I guessed I wasn't the only one in the room who wasn't a morning person.

"Chris?" Doug beckoned to the advertising director.

Chris rose slowly from his seat. He looked like he'd prefer to do almost anything rather than join his fellow judges, but he set down his cup and ambled in their direction.

A large monitor on one wall had been showing only a blank screen, but now another assistant ducked into the room and turned it on. The volume came up, and I heard the morning show's theme music begin to play. Rob Dalton and Darlene Minnick were the show's cohosts. Both were poised and perky, with a natural, unaffected manner that went over well at the crack of dawn. The program opened with Rob and Darlene sitting side by side behind a news desk, trading jaunty banter.

The assistant remained standing beside the monitor. He waited a beat until all our eyes turned his way. "Everybody good?" he asked.

Dutifully we all nodded.

"Excellent! Someone will be along shortly to escort each of you upstairs to hair and makeup. In the meantime, just make yourselves comfortable and enjoy the show." He dashed out through the open doorway and disappeared.

"They're going to do our hair and makeup," Dorothy said happily. "Imagine that! I wish I'd remembered to set my VCR this morning before I left home."

"We did," said Bill. "We can make an extra copy for you if you want. This show is going to be Ginger's television debut. There was no way we were going to miss having a tape of that."

"MacDuff has been on TV lots of times," Dorothy replied. "Westminster and the other top shows get plenty of coverage. But still it's exciting . . . And of course I'd love to have a tape of this appearance, seeing as it will most likely be the beginning of our new career."

Oh really? I thought. Bill and Allison looked surprised as well. Chris, who should have been listening to what Doug and Cindy were saying, turned his head and glared in Dorothy's direction.

"I guess it will be a beginning for one of us," Allison said pointedly.

Dorothy looked unruffled by the correction. If she was trying to psych out the competition, her tactics seemed to be having the desired effect. Across the way, Doug was now staring hard at Chris, wondering, no doubt, how he'd lost his subordinate's attention. This room had more undercurrents than a Jacuzzi.

Suddenly I realized that pictures of each of our dogs—the ones we'd submitted with our contest entries—were flashing by on the TV screen. Darlene was speaking and we all went silent to hear what she had to say.

"Coming up in our last half hour is a special treat for all you dog lovers out there," she said in a voice primed with bubbly enthusiasm. "I would say that includes just about everyone, wouldn't you, Rob?"

"I certainly would!" the cohost replied. "I know it includes me, and today we have some really special canines for you to enjoy. Five dogs—Brando,

Ginger, Faith, MacDuff, and Yoda—have been selected from among thousands of entries nationwide
to be the finalists in the 'All Dogs Are Champions'
contest sponsored by Chow Down Dog Food. The
winning entry will be the new spokesdog—" Rob
paused for a well-rehearsed chuckle—"for that excellent product."

"And here's the best part!" Darlene chirped.
"The lucky winner of the contest will be chosen by
you, our discriminating viewers. After watching
the program today and seeing each of the dogs interact with our pet expert, Darren Abernathy, all
you have to do is log on to the Champions web site
and vote for your favorite."

"So be sure to stay tuned for the entire show,"
Rob finished up. "We know you won't want to miss
a thing!"

The screen went dark as the network went to
commercial. It took us all a moment to adjust to
the fact that the introduction to our segment was
over. Then Doug's face creased in a broad grin.

"That went well," he said heartily.

"Top-notch," Cindy agreed.

"They mentioned the name of the product, the
contest, *and* the company," said Chris. "And that
was only the initial promo. This is going to be excellent."

They were so busy congratulating themselves
that they didn't seem to realize that their three
contestants hadn't said a word. Finally I was the
one who broke the silence.

"I thought the judging committee was going to
be picking the winner of the contest," I said.

"Yes, well . . ." Doug slid a wary look our way.
Until right that moment, it hadn't occurred to

him that there might be a problem. He lifted his hands and rubbed them together, playing for time. "Of course. That's right."

"That's not what Darlene said," Bill pointed out.

The three committee members glanced at one another. Like maybe they were trying to formulate an instant plan.

"She must have been reading the wrong copy," Cindy said quickly.

"I don't think so," Dorothy muttered. "She got all our names right."

"But she was mistaken about the other thing," said Chris. "You know how it is with live TV. Sometimes stuff gets mixed up."

Bill and Allison didn't look convinced either. Instead we were all digesting this last-minute change. It added a whole new set of parameters to the game we'd been playing, and we all knew it.

"It'll be easy enough to figure out when we get home," I said. "All we have to do is log on to the Champions site ourselves and see if there's a way to vote."

"Right . . ." Doug said. His voice sounded strained. "About that . . ."

"Yes?" Allison prompted.

Ginger looked up at her owner and cocked an ear. If Dorothy and I had been dogs, we would have done the same.

"I imagine you might see something on the web site about voting for your favorite finalist," Chris said slowly. "But it's not what you think."

"What is it, then?" I asked.

"The popular vote is only going to act as a guideline," said Doug. "It's something we'll take into consideration when we formulate our choice.

It won't be the entire deciding factor, just another facet of the competition."

"After all," Cindy said with a laugh, "if we did that, we'd lose control of the outcome. It's not as though we can let just *anyone* pick our new Chow Down spokesdog for us."

I didn't agree. The judges had already narrowed the choice down to five, presumably deserving, finalists. It didn't look to me as though the public could go very far wrong. But that wasn't how the situation had been presented to us. And it now seemed quite possible that all the energy we'd expended trying to impress the committee over the last several weeks was going to count for nothing.

"It's our decision," Chris said firmly. "Really. We wouldn't have it any other way."

"Then maybe you'd like to make that clear before we appear before a national audience," Bill Redding commented.

"Good idea," said Doug. He looked happy to grab an excuse to make an exit. "I'll go do that."

No sooner had he passed through the doorway than Ben and Brando came walking in. The actor paused to survey the room. His eyes slid over each of us in turn.

"Hey guys! Great morning, isn't it?" he said cheerfully. "It looks like most of the gang's already here. Did I miss anything important?"

The screen lit back up as the morning show continued. One by one we were escorted up to the eleventh floor to have a layer of on-air makeup applied, and to have our hair combed out by the studio's stylist. Even she was impressed with my new haircut. Terry would get a big kick out of that; I made a mental note to tell him about it later.

While I was gone from the green room, Dorothy and the Reddings had filled Ben in on the latest developments. Unlike the other contestants, he relished the idea of leaving his fate up to a popular vote.

"You guys just don't have enough faith in your dogs," he said, dropping a hand down to scratch the top of his Boxer's tight skull. "Brando here, he's a star and he knows it. I don't mind letting America choose. I'm confident that they'll pick the right dog."

Ben's bravado had a certain appeal. Both Chris and Cindy looked impressed with his assessment. That was reason enough to keep the rest of us from arguing with him and we went back to watching the show.

Doug had yet to reappear; I imagined he was probably checking with the producer about our segment. Simone had passed through briefly, greeted each of us, and then left again. There still had been no sign of Lisa and Yoda.

I glanced at my watch. Time was passing rapidly. Our turn would come up shortly. Earlier I'd been enjoying having a behind-the-scenes look at a live TV show, but now my stomach was beginning to quiver with nerves.

Resting beside me, Faith looked composed as always. I knew she'd do a good job. I just hoped I wouldn't fall flat on my face.

"Does anyone know where the ladies' room is?" I asked.

"Down the hall and to the left," said Allison. She looked as though she might be feeling some butterflies, too. "Do you want me to keep an eye on Faith while you're gone?"

"Thanks, that would be great."

I left the Poodle in a down-stay and went and attended to business. Heading back a few minutes later, I decided not to take the direct route. So far, all I'd seen of the television studio was the reception area and the green room. They were interesting but not nearly as exciting as getting a sneak preview of the actual set would be.

There were plenty of people in the hallway but everyone seemed intent on carrying out their duties. Nobody paid any attention as I pushed through the heavy door that led to the area where the show was being telecast. I slipped quietly into the cavernous room and hung back in the shadows against the wall.

Around the cameras and technicians, I could see Darlene sitting on a plump couch, interviewing a rising young tennis player. A kitchen set, currently dark, was off to the right. On the far side of that was a set that had been built to resemble an outdoor park. There were trees, and benches, and an area of open space in the front. Unless I missed my guess, that was where our segment would be taking place.

The interview ended; the show cut away to commercial. The tennis player stood up and stretched. A technician stepped up onto the set and unhooked his microphone.

"Good job!" said Darlene. She made eye contact and patted the tennis player's arm, her hand slim and white against his tanned muscles. "That should bring the fans flocking to your next tournament."

"Right." He gazed past her, looking bored. "Whatever."

I wondered why he was there if he didn't have something he wanted to promote; but I'd been so busy looking around that I'd missed the interview and didn't have a clue. It was time for me to get back to Faith.

I slipped out the nearest door and found myself in a room filled with mostly empty cubicles. That wasn't the way I'd come in. When I went to retrace my steps, however, I found that the heavy door that led back to the set had locked behind me.

Just great, I thought. Now I had no idea how to get back to where I was supposed to be.

An open doorway on the other side of the room led to a corridor that appeared to go in the right direction. I headed that way. I'd almost reached the opening when the sound of a familiar voice stopped me in my tracks.

"I can't believe you let this happen!" Doug Allen was saying.

He sounded furious, and I wondered who he was talking to. The conversation seemed to be coming from the hallway on the other side of the wall. I shrank back into the nearest cubicle and ducked down beneath the partition.

"You've got a lot of nerve blaming me," a woman said, sounding equally irate. It took me a moment to place her voice. But when she spoke again, I realized it was Simone Dorsey, Champions' PR director. "It's not my fault that she isn't here."

They had to be talking about Lisa. I inched a little closer around the partition. I didn't want to miss a thing.

"Try telling that to the producers. They don't care whose fault it is, they just want me to fix things. And that means coming up with the five finalists I promised them."

"I don't know what you expect me to do about that now."

"I expect you to do your job. This contest was your idea, your baby. You were the one who said you knew how to make everything work out. You were supposed to be staying on top of things."

"I *am* on top of things."

"Great," Doug said, his voice heavy with sarcasm. "Then where is our fifth finalist? Even the dumbest member of the audience is going to be able to count high enough to realize that one of the dogs that appears in all our promotional material is missing."

I thought back to the conversation I'd had with Allison on the bus back from New York. She'd told me that Doug and Simone were romantically involved. What I was overhearing didn't sound like a lover's spat, however. This fight was all business and clearly serious.

"You're in charge of public relations," Doug was saying. "Go find the producer and smooth things over. Isn't that what you're supposed to be good at? But for God's sake, whatever you do, don't tell them the truth."

"I'm not stupid," Simone snapped. "I'll think of something."

"Do that. You got us into this mess, now you can get us out."

I heard the sound of their retreating footsteps. One set of heels and another of leather-soled shoes headed off in different directions. After a minute, I popped out of the cubicle and stuck my head into the hallway. The coast was clear.

Even better, I could see the reception area at the end of the corridor, which meant that I knew where I was. And how to get back to where I belonged.

As I hurried to return to the green room before the producers came to get us for our segment, I thought about what I'd heard. Doug had criticized Simone's behavior with regard to Lisa's absence. Was he simply lashing out and looking for someone to blame? Or did he actually believe that Simone had had something to do with Lisa's disappearance?

Then I turned onto the hallway that led to the green room and saw that we'd already been summoned. All other thoughts fled as I hurried to catch up with the other finalists. Allison was walking at the back of the group with my Poodle by her side. Both of them were looking for me anxiously.

"Thank God," she said, when I caught up. She pressed Faith's leash into my hand. "You just made it. It's time to go be on TV."

26

Well, not quite.

It turned out that live television operated like much of the rest of the world. Hurry up and wait was the order of the day.

Our group was escorted back to the large room I'd just come from. Standing in the wings, I saw that the show was currently off the air; the network had cut away to local affiliates for morning news and weather. Darlene, Rob, and members of the crew were standing around chatting, drinking coffee, and relaxing for a few minutes until it was their turn again.

While the rest of the finalists were staring wide-eyed at the set, I took a moment to reconnect with Faith. I scratched under her chin and rubbed her ears and let her know that everything was all right. That was the problem with having a dog who was so attuned to my every mood; I knew she was picking up on my nervousness and wondering what was up.

As we waited, a couple of sound technicians scurried in and out among us, affixing small microphones to our clothing and asking each of us to speak in turn. One by one, we giggled and mumbled our way through the sound check. Then came Ben's turn.

He sighed and rolled his eyes, letting everyone know that he found the whole exercise incredibly boring and said, clearly and distinctly, "Now is the winter of our discontent, made glorious summer by this sun of York."

Richard the Third, I realized. What a show-off.

"I'm guessing you've done that before," Darlene Minnick said with a smile. She'd come over to introduce herself and been stopped in her tracks by Ben's minisoliloquy.

"Many, many times." The actor inclined his head with studied grace as he reached out and took her hand in his. Up close, Darlene was smaller than she appeared on television, almost tiny, in fact. Ben leaned down to minimize the distance between them. "I'm Ben O'Donnell."

"I knew that name sounded familiar when I saw it in my notes," Darlene replied. "You were on that soap opera *Moments in the Sun*, weren't you?"

"Yes, I was. Thank you for remembering."

"You were very good, and I was really hooked. I tried never to miss an episode. I used to run home from high school every afternoon to watch it."

Ouch, I thought. That had to have hurt.

But Ben didn't let it faze him. "It's always a pleasure to meet a fan," he said. His voice had dropped to a deeper octave and I realized that he hadn't released the woman's hand. "Especially one who's in the business and understands the rigors of our profession."

"Have I seen you in anything lately?" asked Darlene. "Please don't tell me you've retired. Talent like yours shouldn't go to waste."

"At the moment, you might say that I'm between opportunities. I'm reading scripts and looking for that next important role. In the meantime, I'm amusing myself by letting my champion Boxer, Brando, participate in this worthwhile endeavor."

Really, it was hard not to laugh. Listening to Ben's version, it sounded as though Brando had submitted his own contest entry and that all of us were engaged in doing some sort of charity work.

Darlene, however, was nodding in agreement. Maybe that had something to do with the fact that Ben was *still* holding her hand. On only a minute's acquaintance, the two of them looked pretty chummy.

Chris stepped aside as Cindy elbowed her way through the group to stand beside the pair. She didn't bother to mask her annoyance. I wondered if it had ever occurred to her that Ben looked like the kind of man who would flirt with a lamppost if he thought it would advance his opportunities.

"Darlene," she said sharply. "Maybe you'd like to move on and meet our other finalists?"

"Of course." With one last look at Ben, the show's cohost slowly withdrew her hand. When Darlene turned to the rest of us, her professional demeanor was firmly in place. "Welcome to *This Is Your Morning Show.* I can't tell you how pleased Rob and I are that all of you have dragged yourselves out of bed so early in the morning to come and join us."

We all smiled appreciatively, as we were meant

to. It was easy to see why the show was so popular with viewers. Darlene exuded a warmth and sincerity that came across as well in person as it did on television.

"Segments with dogs are my favorites," she said. "I always say it's no fair that Darren gets to be the one who has all the fun. Have you met Darren yet?" She turned around and scanned the room. "I'm sure he'll be here any minute. He likes to have a few words with the dog owners before they're on the air. Everyone feeling okay?"

Dutifully, we all nodded.

"Anyone nervous?"

Most of us nodded again.

Darlene laughed. "Don't worry about that. Trust me, you'll all look great on camera and most of the focus will be on your dogs anyway. Take a few deep breaths and remember to just act natural. Once it starts, the segment will be over before you know it. Oh good, here comes our pet expert now."

Once again, introductions were made. Darren Abernathy was carrying several index cards. He thumbed through the stack as we were presented, staring at each handler-and-dog team as if trying to commit facts and faces to memory. I wondered what he had written in advance about Faith and me. Considering his bias against Poodles, I wasn't feeling terribly optimistic.

Then Darren reached the end of the line and began to frown. He held up his last card and looked around the set. "We go on in two minutes. Where's the Yorkie?"

Doug gulped.

Darlene went slightly pale. "I sent Jerry up to

your room with a note twenty minutes ago," she said. "Didn't you get it?"

"No, I didn't get it. Don't tell me there's been a change. You know I don't like change. What did it say? I'm prepped for these five breeds. There better not be any last-minute substitutions."

Darren's mood was suddenly thunderous. Our judging committee began to look worried. Was I the only one who found it astounding that the show's renowned *dog expert* was incapable of ad-libbing about a breed he hadn't prepped for? Even Aunt Peg could have pulled that off creditably.

"No subs," Darlene said soothingly. "But the Yorkie's out."

"Out? What do you mean, *out?*" He waved the last index card in the air, like maybe he thought he was a magician and that would cause the missing dog to appear.

"The dog and owner aren't here," Simone said.

Darren swung his gaze her way. "Who are you?"

They'd been introduced only a minute earlier, but clearly Darren hadn't been paying attention. Simone looked a little taken aback by the man's rudeness. It was obvious she wasn't accustomed to being overlooked.

"Simone Dorsey, director of public relations for Champions Dog Food."

"You're the one who was responsible for bringing me five dogs for my weekly segment. Five finalists from your 'All Dogs Are Champions' contest. A Brittany, a Poodle, a Scottie, a Boxer, and a Yorkie." He ticked off the breeds on his fingers. "That's five. Why do I only see four here?"

"There was a bit of a problem—"

"No shit, Sherlock."

"Our fifth dog-and-handler pair became indisposed."

"Indisposed?" Darren's eyes narrowed. "What does that mean?"

I glanced discreetly at the other finalists. We were all wondering the answer to that, too.

"Lisa became ill and she couldn't make it. None of us had any warning. It was a last-minute thing."

"How ill?" asked Darren.

"Violently," Simone confirmed. Standing beside her, Chris made retching noises.

"I see. And there was no one else who could have brought the dog . . ." He looked down and consulted his notes. "This Yorkie . . . Yoda?"

"No, there wasn't." Doug stepped in to continue the story. "Each of our five finalist dogs is a cherished family pet. They work together with their owners as a team. Once Lisa became ill"—he shrugged helplessly—"there really wasn't anything we could do."

Darren turned back to Darlene. "This is a fine mess. I hope you realize that changing from five dogs to four will upset the symmetry of my entire presentation. I'll have to eliminate some things I meant to say and pad others. My delivery will undoubtedly suffer."

The cohost patted his arm, just as I'd seen her do earlier with the tennis player. "You're a professional," she said earnestly. "I have every faith in your ability to cope. I'm sure you'll do just fine."

Darren blinked several times. He seemed to be considering whether Darlene was being sincere or simply humoring him. "Just make sure I'm not the one who gets blamed if things don't go as planned," he said finally. Then he spun around and walked away.

"Don't mind Darren," Darlene said when the pet expert was out of earshot. "He's always a little cranky first thing in the morning. He'll come around."

It seemed to me that if Darren had problems dealing with dogs and early mornings, then he had the wrong job. But nobody was asking for my opinion and I wouldn't have dreamt of offering it. No doubt Aunt Peg would have been impressed by my restraint.

After all the drama that preceded it, amazingly our five-minute segment went off almost without a hitch. Much of the piece was devoted to a lead-in about dog food choices. Darren talked about the importance of good nutrition and of feeding your dog a balanced diet. Then he introduced Doug and the two of them discussed the lengthy research-and-development process that Champions went through before introducing a new dog food to the public.

After that Simone was brought out to speak about the company's commitment to providing the best possible canine products to the dog owners of America. She gushed about the exciting contest that Champions had decided to sponsor, mentioning that it had drawn thousands of worthy entries from all over the country. I thought Simone's performance was a bit over the top, but Darren, Darlene, and Rob were all smiling so I guessed it played well.

Then came our turn. Darren introduced each of the finalists. He spoke briefly about the attributes of each featured breed. Then, one by one, we were pushed out of the wings to join the others under the hot lights. I might have been trembling slightly, but Faith was perfect.

Brando and Ginger had preceded us onto the set. Ben, Bill, and Allison had had their turns and were now seated at opposite ends of the park bench. Doug and Simone were standing behind them, looking like a pair of proud parents. When Darren beckoned me out to join him, it was Faith who responded to the hand signal. I just followed along in her wake.

"And here we have our third finalist, Standard Poodle, Faith, and her owner, Melanie Travis," Darren was saying. "Melanie, most Poodles I know have names like Fifi and Pierre in honor of their French heritage. How did you come to name your Poodle Faith?"

Good grief, I thought. With all the wonderful things there were to say about the Poodle breed, *that* was all he could come up with to ask me? Not only that, but the expert had his facts wrong.

"Actually, Darren," I said with a bright smile, "Standard Poodles originated in Germany, where they were bred to be used as hunting dogs, so names like Adolf or Heidi might have been better choices. But Faith comes from a long line of American champions and she was given to me by someone who wanted to demonstrate her faith in my abilities."

"Isn't that interesting?" Darren said, sounding as though he thought my answer had been anything but.

The other finalists had been asked a second question at that point. They'd been given the opportunity to explain why they thought their particular dog was best suited to be named winner of the contest.

Darren didn't bother to do that with us. Instead he merely leaned down and gave Faith a dismissive pat on the head, then waved us back to a seat on the bench. Obviously it didn't pay to contradict the man in charge, even when he didn't know what he was talking about.

Dorothy and MacDuff were up last. Dorothy strode confidently out into the spotlight but the Scottie hung back. His feet simply stopped moving. When he hit the end of his short leash, Dorothy gave the leather strip a snap.

"Come along," she said briskly.

"Yes, please." Darren crouched down and tapped the floor in front of himself, drawing the Scottie forward. "What a dignified little dog you are."

MacDuff didn't look much impressed by the flattery but Dorothy was beaming. "He really *is* special, isn't he? MacDuff has known what a star he was from the time he was a tiny puppy. Now we're fortunate that the good people at Champions Dog Food are going to let the whole world know how wonderful my boy is. 'All Dogs Are Champions' is the perfect name for this contest and MacDuff will be the perfect winner. Really, when you look at all that he's accomplished, there's nobody else here that can hold a candle to his record—"

"Very good," Darren interrupted, shutting her down. He liked to hear himself speak entirely too much to listen to a long-winded monologue from someone else during his air time. "He certainly looks like he ought to be a little trooper. Now that we've seen all of our wonderful finalists—"

Abruptly he stopped speaking. Darren was staring off into the wings and I turned to see why.

Having grown accustomed to the bright lights, it took a moment for my eyes to adjust. Then it took another for me to believe what I was seeing. The segment producer was waving frantically, trying to cue Darren that he had more to do, that the piece wasn't finished yet.

Standing beside the producer was Lisa Kim. Yoda was cradled in her arms.

"Holy crap," Ben said under his breath. "Where did she come from?"

Lisa smiled uncertainly as if she wasn't sure of her welcome. But the producer had already placed his hand between her shoulder blades and was pushing her forward, out in front of the cameras.

Live TV, I thought. You had to love it.

27

"What have we here?" Darren said smoothly, "It looks as if there's one more dog to add to our lineup."

When the camera shifted to pick up Lisa and Yoda, the pet expert glared daggers at the producer, who ignored his fit of pique and pointed to his watch. Good thing Darren had recovered quickly; I had a feeling the rest of us looked like we were in shock.

Simone's hands, resting on the back of the bench near my shoulder, had tightened their grip until her knuckles turned white.

Dorothy was shaking her head. "No way," she muttered. "No way . . ."

I just stared, listening while Darren introduced our late arrival. Lisa's posture was stiff and her smile looked strained. The cameraman pulled in for a close-up shot of Yoda, then simply stayed there. At least the Yorkie, with her topknot tied up with a jaunty blue bow, looked cute.

Darren had rearranged his copy before the segment started and now with the unexpected addition, he found himself running short of time. He showcased the Yorkie briefly, threw in a quick wrap-up, then cued Darlene and Rob. A minute later the show cut to commercial. Our first television appearance was history.

As soon as the lights dimmed and the cameras focused elsewhere, Lisa strode off the set and into the wings. Doug immediately went hurrying after her.

Simone looked as though she wanted to follow, then thought better of it. Instead she went the other way; I watched as she thanked the cohosts and the producer for their help with our appearance.

A technician slipped in behind me and unhooked my microphone. When that was done, I stood up and stretched, then gave Faith a pat. I was happy our part was over; and happier still that we hadn't acquitted ourselves too badly.

Bill, looking bemused, was gazing in the direction that Lisa and Doug had disappeared. "*What* is going on around here?" he asked.

"Beats me," said Ben. He yanked off his own mic and handed it back. "Lisa certainly stole our thunder, showing up at the last moment like that, didn't she?"

She had indeed. It wasn't hard to imagine that our earlier contributions would have been all but eclipsed by the adorable image of the little Yorkie that had stayed onscreen throughout the last sixty seconds of the piece.

"She can't do that," Dorothy said firmly. "I'm going to file a protest."

"Can't do what?" I asked.

"She can't just drop out of the contest and then drop back in again. It ought to be against the rules."

"Technically, I don't think she ever dropped out. And thanks to her eleventh-hour arrival today, Yoda hasn't missed any of our appearances."

"We'll just see about that," said Dorothy.

She started to stalk away but Chris materialized from somewhere behind the cameras and grabbed her. Arm around her shoulder, he herded the older woman toward the exit door.

Lisa and Doug hadn't returned. And by now Simone and Cindy had disappeared as well. It was time for us to leave.

Preappearance, we'd had people with us every minute, telling us where to go and what to do. Now suddenly everyone had lost interest in us. The staff and the producers were moving on to upcoming topics, and we were on our own.

Bill and Allison found a spot in the wings from which to watch the remainder of the show. Ginger lay down quietly at their feet. Ben took Brando and went hurrying back to the green room. I wondered if he was looking to smooth things over with Cindy. Faith and I rode the elevator down to the ground floor by ourselves.

I figured we'd go get our car, drive home to Connecticut, and that would be that. But of course, in my life, nothing is ever that simple. Come to think of it, I'd probably be disappointed if it was.

Instead Faith and I exited the building and ran right into Lisa, Doug, Simone, and Cindy. The four of them, plus Yoda, were standing in a tight little cluster in the middle of the sidewalk. All of them looked angry, and it sounded as though they were all trying to talk at once.

I could only catch snatches of what was being said. Doug and Cindy were berating Lisa. She was attacking them right back. Simone was placing blame on anyone and everyone.

Smokers, gathered in the shade of the building, were listening in avidly. Even jaded New Yorkers didn't get to see a live show this entertaining every day. It was enough to make me want to walk past the whole bunch and pretend that I didn't know any of them.

Instead sympathy slowed my pace. Well . . . maybe that and a little curiosity. Faith sensed my ambivalence and used that as an excuse to detour over toward the group and touch noses with Yoda. For once the Toy dog was on the ground rather than in her owner's arms.

In that brief moment of hesitation on my part, Lisa felt the slight tug on her leash, glanced over to see what was causing it, and caught my eye. She looked stressed, unhappy, and desperately in need of rescuing.

I didn't even stop to think. I simply veered in, linked my arm through hers, and said firmly, "Come on. Let's get out of here."

For a second, I didn't think she'd come. But Lisa wanted an escape and I'd conveniently offered her one. She swooped down, grabbed Yoda up off the sidewalk, and away we went.

It all happened so fast that Doug was still speaking as we made our getaway. I was pretty sure I heard Simone gasp.

"Hey!" Cindy cried in protest.

Lisa and I didn't stop. We didn't look back either. Our pace didn't slow down until we'd turned the corner. Then I took a deep breath and checked to make sure that no one was following us.

Fortunately the coast was clear. It would have been a little embarrassing if we'd had to start to run. Faith probably would have enjoyed herself though.

"Where are we going?" Lisa asked after a minute had passed. She sounded perfectly content to follow my lead.

"Home." I steered her toward the parking garage where I'd left the Volvo. "Back to Connecticut. How did you get here?"

"By train. Metro-North."

"With Yoda?"

Lisa nodded. "She's small enough to fit inside my bag and she knows enough to keep quiet. The conductors never notice and the other passengers think it's cute."

"Well, unless you have an objection, you can drive back out with me and Faith. I'll drop you off at the train station where you left your car."

Doing so would take me out of my way but under the circumstances that hardly seemed to matter. Fate had just handed me a golden opportunity to find out what the heck was going on, and I wasn't about to pass it up.

"Sounds good," said Lisa.

After the verbal pummeling I'd just witnessed, I got the impression that anything that put distance between her and the Champions crew would have sounded good.

I retrieved the Volvo and we pulled out into city traffic, which had grown exponentially in the last several hours. Lisa sat in silence, which was fine by me; I needed to concentrate on not missing any turns or hitting any double-parked cars.

By the time we'd crossed the bridge back out of Manhattan and were zipping along the highway, however, I was ready to hear some answers. Faith, who'd given up her shotgun position to Lisa, was curled up on the backseat. Yoda was tucked in beside her. I turned off the radio and set the stage. No distractions, no excuses.

With luck, Lisa would chalk up my intrusiveness to the cost of being rescued. The woman owed me something, didn't she?

"You caused quite a sensation showing up like you did back there," I said.

"Ummm."

She might have been agreeing with me. Then again, she might just have been stretching her lips. It was hard to tell.

Lisa folded her hands in her lap and stared determinedly out the windshield. Like she was afraid that if she took her eyes off the road, we might hit something. It wasn't the most promising start to a conversation.

"So what's up?"

"Up?" Her gaze flickered my way.

"You know . . . Everyone's been looking for you. Where have you been?"

"Looking for me?" Lisa sounded amazed. As if this was the first she'd heard of that.

"That's what happens when people disappear." Up until this point I'd had very little interaction with Lisa. Maybe I'd overlooked the fact that she was mentally challenged. "Other people look for them."

This time she actually turned and looked at me. "I didn't disappear."

"When we got back from Central Park last week, you and Yoda left Champions but never arrived home. Nobody knew where you were."

"Oh that."

Yes that! I wanted to scream. But I'm a teacher, I've had practice holding my tongue.

"That was no big deal. I just needed . . ." She stopped and thought. "I guess I needed a little time off."

Though I was tempted, I refrained from drumming my fingers on the steering wheel. Instead I reminded myself that patience was a virtue to be cultivated, even under trying circumstances.

"I can see that," I said. "There's been a fair amount of upheaval in your life recently."

A grimace twisted Lisa's mouth. "You can say it, you know. My husband died. It's amazing how many different ways people find to dance around the reality. It's like everybody thinks that if they come up with a suitable euphemism, it will make all of us feel better. Well, maybe it works for them, but it doesn't for me."

All righty then. Since we were done trying to put a nice face on things, she wasn't the only one who could be blunt.

"Larry died under suspicious circumstances," I said.

"Another reason why I felt I needed to get away."

Fortunately most of the traffic on the highway was heading into the city. I could take my eyes off the road without fear of causing a major pileup. "Were you afraid? Did you feel threatened?"

"No . . . Yes . . . No." She didn't sound sure of either answer. I put that aside for the time being.

"There must have been something that made you run away. After all, you left all your dogs behind."

"Not Yoda. And besides, a friend was looking after the others."

Judging by her dismissive tone, she seemed to think that the fact that she'd left first Sue, and now Bertie, holding the bag was unimportant.

"Only for one day. Sue expected you to be back that afternoon."

"What can I say? I had a change of plans."

"Caused by what?"

Lisa turned and leveled a look my way. "Is that really any of your business?"

Well . . . No. But I wasn't about to admit that. Instead I zigzagged the conversation in another direction.

"Would you like to know where your Yorkies are now?"

"I assume they're right where I left them."

"No, they're not. Sue had other things to do. She took the dogs and boarded them at a nearby kennel."

Lisa swore under her breath. I wondered if she was picturing the size of her board bill. Good. That meant that Bertie stood a chance of being paid for her time and trouble.

"If you'd given your friend the courtesy of letting her know your plans, you could have had a say in what happened to your dogs," I pointed out. The fact that Lisa was annoyed didn't slow me down. If anything, it made me want to push her harder. "Sue had no idea when you'd be coming back. She called around to all your friends. She contacted the local police."

"Then she overreacted."

"You left behind your entire family of dogs. They were sitting in pens in your basement. Who would do something like that if they had a choice? Sue was worried about you. She thought maybe something terrible had happened."

"The Yorkies weren't my family," Lisa said shortly. "They were Larry's. His dream, his mission, his accomplishment. It's not that I don't care about what happens to them, but I'm not about to let them run my whole life anymore. You know what showing can be like . . ."

She looked at me and I nodded.

"It takes over everything if you let it. People get obsessed with competing, with winning. I've spent my life doing exactly what was expected of me. I've always been the good girl who did what other people wanted. And where did all that good behavior get me? Nowhere that I wanted to be. It was time I did something for myself for a change."

I pondered that as we zipped across the New York–Connecticut border. It sounded as though Lisa's problems had started long before her husband's death.

"Was Larry one of those people who was obsessed with winning?" I asked.

"Yes. Of course, I never could have admitted that before. Larry would have found my words unseemly and disloyal. Even now, it's hard for me to realize that he's really gone and I can speak my mind as I choose."

"Your marriage wasn't a happy one."

"It had its happy moments. More in the begin-

ning than later. I thought I married for love. Afterward I found out that my husband saw me as little
more than another prize that had been worth pur-
suing and winning."

"So," I said, probing carefully, "I guess you're
not sorry he's dead."

"Of course I'm sorry he's dead!" Lisa snapped.
"I only wanted to be free of him. I didn't want him
to die."

So she said. I wondered if a lie detector would
turn up a different answer.

"Why didn't you get a divorce?"

"I was working my way toward that. That was the
whole point."

Huh?

"The point of what?" I asked.

"Of entering Yoda in the contest. In order to
win my freedom, I had to have a plan, a place to
go, a source of income. Of all our dogs, only Yoda
was mine and mine alone. She was the one who
would provide me with what I needed to make my
escape."

"By winning the contest and the spokesdog contract."

"Exactly. There would have been poetic justice
in that, don't you think?"

"If it happened. But you might not have won."

"I wasn't worried about that."

"Maybe you should have been."

"I don't think so. Before everything fell apart,
Yoda was a shoo-in to take home the prize."

I'd heard Dorothy make similarly assured pre-
dictions about MacDuff's chances. And the Reddings seemed to feel Ginger was invincible. Where
did all their confidence come from? It was de-

pressing to think that I might be the only finalist who actually thought her dog could lose. Didn't Faith deserve better of me? And how had I managed to get myself so tied in knots over a contest that I didn't even want to win?

"Here," Lisa said suddenly, pointing at the EXIT sign. "This is where you need to get off."

"But this is Darien."

"Right."

"I thought you lived in Southport."

"My car is here," she insisted. "At the train station in Darien."

I put on my blinker and eased the Volvo off onto the exit ramp. "So you didn't run very far. You've been staying in Darien."

Lisa nodded. As the car slowed, the two dogs in the backseat stood up. Faith shook out her hair. Yoda hopped her front feet onto the armrest and looked out the window.

The train station wasn't far from the exit. I didn't have much more time now. "Where have you been, Lisa?"

"With an old friend."

"Who?"

"Someone whose support I could count on. Someone who let me think for myself and didn't try to tell me what to do."

I thought back quickly. Just recently someone had mentioned Lisa having a friend from the past in the area. After a moment, it came to me. It had been Sue. She'd said that Lisa's college roommate lived nearby.

"Your roommate from college," I said.

Lisa's head whipped around. Her eyes widened in surprise. "Simone told you about that?"

So help me, I nearly hit a tree. Good thing the Volvo responded quickly when I jerked the wheel back on course.

Simone? I couldn't believe it. The company's PR director was Lisa's old friend from college?

That put an interesting spin on things, didn't it?

28

"You've been staying with Simone?"
I tried to sound like I'd had that piece of information all along, but some of the incredulity I was feeling must have crept into my voice because Lisa clamped her lips shut.

"She's an old friend of yours," I said.

Grudgingly Lisa nodded.

"I saw the two of you talking last week in the park. I suppose I should have put two and two together."

"I just needed to get away for a little while, okay?" She stared out at the street in front of us, as if she was willing me to drive faster. Fortunately there were plenty of traffic lights along that stretch of the Post Road. "That's not a crime."

"No, of course not." Though it had been a big inconvenience for everyone around her. Including Simone, who'd protected her old friend's privacy and taken the heat from Doug for it. "What made you decide to come back?"

Lisa sighed. "For one thing, hiding out began to feel a little childish. For another, Simone made a better roomie in college than she does now. She said something that made a lot of sense though. She told me that Yoda and I needed to go on and compete. That if we gave up and let someone else win the contest, Larry would have died for nothing."

I could see the railroad bridge approaching. The station was on the near side. Another minute or two and Lisa would be gone.

"Does that mean you think your husband's death had something to do with the competition?"

"It happened at the dog food company. What else could it have been?"

"You told me that Larry suffered from vertigo," I said. "Earlier you said that you thought he might have tripped and fallen."

"The police have indicated to me that such a scenario is highly unlikely. So now I have to wonder what really happened. The authorities tell me they have many suspects, but no evidence against any one particular person."

Welcome to the club, I thought. I put on my turn signal, pulled through a break in the oncoming traffic, and drove up into the parking lot. There was time for just one more question.

"Why Larry?" I asked.

"Pardon me?"

"If the murder *was* related to the contest, if it was meant to influence its outcome, why was Larry the finalist who was targeted? All five of us have a shot at winning. So why would someone go after only Yoda? What made the murderer believe that she was the strongest contestant?"

For a minute I didn't think Lisa was going to answer. We'd reached the train station, after all. I half-expected Lisa to retrieve Yoda from the backseat and scramble from the car. But she didn't.

I slid the Volvo into an empty parking space, and turned off the ignition. Then we both sat in silence.

"I'm not proud of this," she said finally. "But you have to understand the desperation I felt. It led me to make some decisions I might not otherwise have made."

"Go on."

"It was also Simone's idea, though I'm not blaming her for a minute. I agreed to go along."

It occurred to me I might have gray hair before I found out what we were talking about. "With what?"

"Chow Down has been in development for more than a year, and during that time Simone was the one who came up with a brilliant idea to promote the new product launch. Champions would hold a contest that would draw entries and attention from all over the country. The publicity it would generate would be well worth the hundred-thousand–dollar prize. She took the idea to Doug and it was approved."

Lisa's voice faltered briefly. When she spoke again, it was with renewed determination. "Then Simone came to me, her oldest friend, and also a woman who was struggling with a husband she no longer loved and a marriage she didn't know how to get out of."

"Simone recommended that you enter the contest."

"She did more than that."

The lightbulb went on. I should have seen this sooner.

"She promised you that Yoda would win, didn't she?"

"There didn't seem to be any harm in the idea." Lisa's words came tumbling out in a rush. "After all, the contest was going to be a boon to the company. And Yoda would make an excellent spokesdog for the product. So we weren't stealing anything, we were just manipulating some results. It wasn't as if anybody would be hurt by what we were doing."

Nobody except the thousands of other hopeful contestants who had written essays and taken pictures, and entered the contest in good faith. And maybe me . . . who'd apparently devoted half my summer to a competition that had been rigged right from the start.

"Did Larry know about that?" I asked.

"No, of course not. I certainly couldn't explain what I needed the money for. I told him about the contest after I'd already entered it. He thought Yoda was chosen to be a finalist in the same way all the others were."

But someone must have known that the little Yorkie was slated to win. Someone who had lured Larry into the stairwell for a clandestine meeting.

"Who else did Simone tell?" I asked.

"I don't know. I never had any idea how she made the arrangements. Simone just told me that everything was all set and that ensuring the correct outcome would not be a problem."

Except that, as things turned out, she couldn't have been more wrong.

"So what happens now?" I asked.

Lisa shrugged. "We go to the press conference tomorrow. The judges announce the winner. And Chow Down has a new spokesdog."

"Yoda?"

"I have no idea anymore," Lisa said. She sounded unbearably weary. "At this point, I just want it all to be over."

Lisa wasn't the only one who wanted the whole thing to be finished. I was tired of running around participating in events that I now knew had been all but meaningless. The summer was slipping by, and I'd hardly had a chance to stop and enjoy any of it.

When Faith and I arrived home, I discovered that Sam and Davey had been making plans. They'd decided to hold a cookout and they'd invited Aunt Peg, Bob, Frank, Bertie, and Maggie to join us.

I should have been elated at the prospect of a family gathering. And I would have been, if only I hadn't felt so thoroughly enervated.

That was what getting up and starting the day before dawn did to a person, I told myself. But secretly I was hoping there was another reason for my lack of energy. It had been so long since I'd been pregnant with Davey that I didn't remember what I'd felt like then. Nor did I have any idea whether I should expect to feel the same now. On the other hand, there was also the distinct possibility that it was all just wishful thinking on my part.

But whatever malaise was dragging me down, it was enough to make me spend much of the evening in a lounge chair on the deck, watching the bulk of the festivities from the sidelines. After a while,

Sam came over and sat down on the end of the chaise.

I moved my legs to make room for him. His hand drifted down onto my knee, fingers moving over the warm skin absently. I loved that part about being married: the touching that was just that easy and comfortable.

"You okay?" he asked.

"I'm just a little tired, that's all."

"Want me to bring you something to eat?"

I'd nibbled around the edges of a hamburger earlier, but passed up corn on the cob and potato salad. Now Frank and Bertie were serving up a watermelon. It looked cool, and pink, and juicy, but I couldn't seem to work up any desire to have a slice.

"No thanks, I'm fine. Really."

"You're sure? You didn't eat much dinner."

I hadn't realized he'd been watching. Another benefit to being married: when it came to my well-being, Sam didn't miss much. After years of looking out for myself and Davey, it was nice to have someone looking after me for a change.

"I'm just not hungry."

"You? Not hungry? That must be . . ." He started to grin, then abruptly the words died in his throat and his expression shifted. His eyes dropped to the region of my stomach, then came back up. "Anything you want to tell me?"

"Not yet," I said softly. "At the moment, I'm still in the hopeful stage. As soon as I know for sure . . ."

"When?" Sam tried not to sound impatient; he didn't entirely succeed.

I'd already read the instructions on the pregnancy kit and done the calculations. "Soon. Just give me a couple more days."

"Anything you want." His hand was still resting on my knee. He squeezed gently before pulling it away.

"A girl," I said, "with your eyes and your smile."

He stood and looked down at me. "I'll do my best."

Sam went back to our guests who were, for once, on their best behavior. By some unspoken agreement, no one tried to make me eat dessert or help clean up. They didn't drag me over to join in the games of croquet or frisbee football that sprang up after dinner.

Even Aunt Peg refrained from badgering me about the latest scoop on the contest. Sam must have filled her in and she'd decided that getting her information secondhand was good enough.

Faith never left my side all night. And when the rest of the Poodles grew tired of running around the yard, they came and flopped in a semicircle around my chair. It was a little like having my own canine honor guard and I appreciated their quiet company.

The sun finally began to dip low in the sky. Bertie lit the scented candles we had scattered around the deck. Frank turned on the bug-zapper. Clutching her stuffed dog to her chest, Maggie fell asleep in her baby seat. Davey was looking ready for bed himself.

As Sam helped Frank and Bertie load a mound of baby essentials and leftover food into their car, Davey scrambled up into the tree house. Aunt Peg had brought an American flag to decorate his new outdoor abode. Now as she supervised from the ground, the two of them debated where it could be hung to best effect.

While that was going on, Bob strolled over to say good-night.

Over the previous decade, Bob's and my relationship had been as tumultuous as a roller-coaster ride. We'd been in love, and we'd been close to hating one another. We'd lived together for several years, then been apart and not speaking for more time than that.

Recently we'd finally reached a stage of equanimity. Bob wasn't just my ex-husband and Davey's father. He was a real friend now, and the relationship that had evolved had come as a bit of a surprise to both of us.

Like Sam, he sat down on the end of the lounger. Unlike my husband, Bob was careful not to sit too close. His expression when he looked at me was equal parts gratified and wistful.

"Congratulations," he said softly. "I know how much you've wanted this."

I pushed myself forward and sat up straight. "Wanted what?"

"A new baby. A little brother or sister for Davey."

"Not so fast," I said. "We're trying, that's all. Nobody's sure that anything's been accomplished yet."

"It has."

The certainty in his tone made me pause. I tipped my head to one side thoughtfully. "What makes you say that?"

"I was there the first time, remember? You have just the same look . . . the same glow."

I shook my head in automatic denial even as I felt my heart leap with hope. Might Bob know something I didn't? Could he possibly be right?

My hand lifted to my face. I touched my cheek, half-expecting to feel heat. When I didn't, I felt silly.

"I'm not glowing," I said.

"You are." Again the same certain tone. Bob's gaze drifted past me to the people in the yard. The sound of Davey's laughter floated to us on the breeze. "You did a great job first time around. You'll be a wonderful mother now too."

"How would you know? You weren't there."

The words, motivated by the fear that he might be getting my hopes up for nothing, came out before I could stop them. They were unworthy of both of us.

"My loss," said Bob. I was happy he hadn't taken offense. "Sam won't make the same mistake."

No, he wouldn't, I thought. Our child would be surrounded by all the love and security that two adoring parents and an older brother could provide.

"Does he know yet?" asked Bob.

I smiled at that. "*I* don't even know yet."

"Trust me." Bob's hand found mine. He held my fingers firmly. "If you ever need anything . . ."

"An uncle? A baby-sitter? A godfather?"

"Name it," he said. "I'm your man."

"Funny thing about that," said Sam, coming up beside us. "I thought I was her man."

Bob stood. He held up both hands, palms out. "You won't get any argument from me. I was just telling Melanie how lucky she is."

I gazed up at Sam. My eyes found his in the dim light. "And I was telling him I knew that."

I rose to join them and my stomach flipped. All at once I felt light-headed. Sam reached out a steadying hand but I didn't notice. Right at that moment, my thoughts focused inward, I didn't see a thing.

Holy moley, I thought with a sudden, incandescent rush of pure joy. Bob *was* right.

29

Not that I was about to say a word to anyone until I was absolutely sure. Like scientifically, medical evidence sure. Pee-on-a-stick sure. It was one thing for me to get my hopes up. But if I was wrong, I didn't want Sam and Davey doing the same thing.

So I got on with my life as though nothing had changed. For the first time, I was actually happy to have a contest-related event to attend. At least it would serve as a distraction until enough time had passed and I could get the answer I was dying to have.

Better still, tomorrow's press conference would be the end of the line as far as my finalist duties were concerned. When that final appearance was over, the competition would be, too. One lucky dog and owner would continue on to fame and fortune and my life could go back to normal. The prospect was almost enough to make me giddy.

Would Yoda's name be the one announced as previously planned? Like Lisa, I wasn't sure. So many elements of the contest had gotten derailed since the five finalists had been brought together for the opening reception, it wasn't hard to imagine that the outcome might take an unexpected turn, too.

Before the final decision was announced to the press, however, I needed to corner Simone Dorsey and get some answers. Surely she had to realize that her manipulation of the results might have played a part in Larry Kim's death.

I sincerely doubted that she would have passed information like that along to the police. Now, however, I was armed with enough knowledge to bluff her into opening up. That gave me an unexpected advantage and I intended to make use of it.

The press conference was scheduled to take place at the Champions Dog Food headquarters at four o'clock that afternoon. I imagined that that time had been chosen to draw news teams from the local affiliates so that they could report on the story live at five. I put in a call to Simone's secretary and told her that Faith and I needed an appointment at three.

"I'll have to see if she's available," the woman replied.

"Make her available. She won't want to miss what I have to say."

All right, so maybe that wasn't strictly true. But the implication that I might have some vital information related to the contest was enough to get me a spot on Simone's calendar. The fact that the information was more vital to my interests than hers was something we could discuss when I got there.

Since this was to be Faith's last contest appearance, I went all out with her grooming. She'd looked good when we'd appeared on TV the day before, but now I was aiming for perfect. I didn't expect my Poodle to win, but I did want the judging committee to experience at least a small pang of regret at passing her by.

I reclipped Faith's face, her feet, and the base of her tail. I bathed her in the tub, then devoted two hours to blowing her hair dry, section by section, so that when I was done, her entire coat was straight and plush and full. Scissoring in the lines, I emphasized the length of the Poodle's legs, the crest of her neck, and rounded off her topknot and the pom pon on her tail.

Sam and Davey had borrowed Aunt Peg's beach card and gone to Todd's Point for the afternoon, so when Faith and I headed out, only the other Poodles were home to escort us to the door. Having spent more time on Faith's appearance than I had on my own, I paused in front of the hallway mirror and took a quick look to make sure that my hair was combed and my shirt was clean. The reflection I saw in the mirror looked pretty much as I expected.

Nope, I thought critically as I examined myself from several perspectives, if anything was glowing, I didn't see it.

Faith and I arrived at Champions with time to spare. My Poodle would have preferred that we take the stairs, but I wasn't ready to face them again just yet. Instead, we rode the elevator up to the third floor.

Even though we were a few minutes early, Simone didn't keep us waiting long. Promptly at three, the PR director opened her office door and stood expectantly in the doorway. I wondered whether she'd actually been working or whether she'd been sitting inside watching the clock until it was time.

"You wanted to see me?" she said.

I filed that under "R" for rhetorical and walked past her into the small room. Simone outranked Cindy Burrows and probably Chris Hovick, too, but her office wasn't any more impressive in size or decor. Idly I wondered if that rankled. If it was one of the reasons that she might not have seen anything wrong in diverting company funds in a friend's direction.

"Well?" Simone said, in her best get-on-with-it tone. "What's this all about?"

I helped myself to a seat. The chair looked like it had been designed by Le Corbusier. It was small and uncomfortable, but at least it made me sit up straight.

"I drove Lisa home from New York yesterday," I said.

"So I gathered." Simone didn't sound pleased. She walked around behind her desk and sat down. "I'd have been happy to bring her back myself, but once you swooped in like the Lone Ranger and spirited her away, I figured she'd made other arrangements."

"She did. We had a long talk on the way."

Simone lifted a brow disdainfully. Obviously she didn't feel threatened by anything her friend might have told me. I wondered if she'd spoken with Lisa since. I was betting no. Judging by her past behavior,

Yoda's owner seemed to want to avoid confrontation.

"Lisa told me how you had set up the contest so that she and Yoda would win."

"That's ridiculous. I don't have any idea what you're talking about."

"I think you do. I know that you and Lisa are old friends. That the two of you went to college together."

Simone looked briefly startled, then her expression turned bland again. I'd managed to get her attention though. Good.

"So?" she said.

"So she needed to find a way out of an unhappy marriage and you offered to help."

"Naturally I offered emotional support. A bit of advice, a shoulder to cry on. That's what friends are for."

"You offered more than that. You offered a contest, specially engineered with her in mind. Nationwide publicity, thousands of entries, good PR out the wazoo, all of that controlled by a small committee of handpicked people who would select the winner. Yoda would end up being the spokesdog for Champions' newest product and Lisa would gain a new direction in life, not to mention the financial security she needed to leave her husband."

"That's an interesting story," Simone said evenly. "But that's all it is, a piece of fiction. It's not what happened."

Time was passing and we weren't getting anywhere. I needed to shock Simone out of her complacency.

"What happened next was all your fault," I said.

"The plan that you and Lisa made resulted in Larry Kim's death. What went wrong, Simone? Did you begin to get nervous when he nearly took his dog and walked out of that first meeting? That would have ruined everything, wouldn't it? Were you the one I heard arguing with him that day in the stairwell? Did he make you so angry that you reached out and gave him a shove?"

"No, of course not!" Simone had picked up a paper clip from her blotter. She twisted and untwisted the small piece of metal between her fingers. "I wasn't anywhere near Larry when he fell. It was up to Lisa to make sure that Yoda remained a contestant. I didn't have anything to do with that."

"But you admit that you and she had cooked up a scheme—"

"I'm not admitting anything. Why should I?"

"Well, for one thing," I said, "if you don't, I'll take my information to the police. I hear they're having a hard time narrowing down their list of suspects. This ought to help them sort things out, don't you think?"

"Wait!"

I'd started to rise, but now I paused. Faith, who'd stood when I did, stopped, too. Faster than most humans at picking up on nuances, she looked back and forth between us, waiting to see who was going to cave in first. Thankfully, the answer was Simone.

"I don't think that's necessary," she said. "Especially now, when we're just about to announce the winner of the contest. That's the last kind of publicity Champions needs. I'm sure you and I can discuss this between ourselves and come up with an equitable solution."

"Like what?" I asked. Just my luck, she was probably thinking of offering Faith the top prize in exchange for my silence.

"Let me think," Simone said. "And in the meantime, you should do some thinking too. I hope you realize that you have nothing to gain by exposing the contest to undue scrutiny."

"I disagree. Exposing irregularities in the contest judging will help the police find Larry's murderer."

"Oh please. Surely you don't want me to believe you're doing this to be *helpful*." She stared at me across the width of her desk. "Did you even know Larry Kim?"

"No. We met for the first time at the opening reception."

"You wouldn't have liked him."

As if that made it all right that he'd been murdered?

"Does that matter?" I asked.

"Of course it matters," Simone snapped. "Lisa never should have married Larry. He was all wrong for her. I told her at the time but she wouldn't listen. She thought she knew better."

"It was *her* life. Right or wrong, Lisa had a right to make her own decisions."

"Not when she was going to come running to me after the fact to clean up the mess she'd made of things. It was just pure luck that Chris had already come to me with the idea—"

Simone stopped speaking so abruptly that it was like putting an exclamation point on what she'd left unsaid. I sank back down slowly into my seat.

"*Chris* came up with the idea for the contest?" Quickly I filled in some blanks and rearranged the pieces of the puzzle to fit. "That's interesting. I was sure I'd heard that you were the one who deserved the credit for that."

"Not entirely." Simone gave a careless shrug. She couldn't quite pull it off. "It was more of a joint effort. You know, colleagues brainstorming for the good of the company."

"Except that Chris thought of it first."

Simone, I noted, didn't refute the assertion a second time.

"There were four of you on the judging committee," I said after a minute. "Lisa had your vote, we know that. Who else had you gotten to agree to your plan?"

"Yoda was the best candidate for the position. He'd have drawn votes from the other judges even without my support."

"Maybe, maybe not. After all, Cindy prefers big dogs and lately she's been spending her own downtime hanging around with Ben O'Donnell. Then there's Chris, who got his pet Scottie from Dorothy Foyle. So I'm assuming that Doug must have been your ace in the hole."

"Doug's my boss. Why would he do anything just because I asked him to . . . ?" Abruptly Simone went still. "Wait a minute! *Cindy's been seeing Ben?*"

"Yup."

"That stupid girl. What the hell is she thinking?"

"Maybe the same thing you're thinking when you're with Doug."

Simone started to speak. Then she stopped and sighed. "Shit. Is there anything you don't know?"

Plenty, but I started by stating the obvious. "I don't know who murdered Larry Kim."

"It wasn't me."

"That's what everybody says. But Lisa thinks her

husband's death was related to the contest, and I have to agree. Someone saw Yoda as a threat. The killer must have known that the Yorkie was supposed to win. He thought he saw a way to eliminate her from the competition and he took it. So this is important, Simone. Who else was in on your plan?"

For once, the PR director didn't argue. Finally she seemed to have found my logic compelling enough to try and help me work things through.

"Lisa and I came up with the idea," she said slowly. "And once Doug had seen Yoda and realized what a great spokesdog she would make, he agreed to go along."

"So it was just the three of you?"

That would have been enough to decide the outcome in their favor. Yoda would have had two votes out of four, including Doug's, which Cindy had told me earlier counted for more than the others.

"And Chris," said Simone.

"Chris?" I repeated. That was the second time his involvement had surprised me. "How did he find out what was going on?"

"It was during a meeting we had about the direction we wanted the contest to go. Upper management only."

I assumed that meant just the vice president and the two directors, excluding Cindy, who was only a product manager.

"Chris felt that his input wasn't being given the weight it deserved. He thought we were ignoring his contributions. Oh, let's be frank. He threw a hissy fit. He wanted MacDuff to win the contest, and if MacDuff wasn't going to win he wanted to know the reason why. Finally, just to shut Chris up, Doug told him that Yoda was our pick and there was nothing he could do to change that."

"I wonder where Chris was when Larry was killed?" I asked. I'd been thinking out loud and didn't really expect an answer, but it turned out that Simone's thoughts had mirrored mine.

"He'd already left the conference room. He said he was going upstairs. Chris's office is on the fourth floor. He said there was someone he needed to see."

Bingo, I thought.

30

The door to Simone's office opened. Her secretary stuck her head in. "Everybody's going down to the lobby for the press conference. And Mr. Allen just called. He wants to see all the finalists in the conference room for a quick briefing before they head downstairs."

"You'd better go." Simone rose quickly. I got the impression that she didn't mind having an excuse to get rid of me. "Doug hates to be kept waiting."

"What are we being briefed on?" I asked. Surely Doug wasn't planning to spill the beans about the winner. More likely, we'd be receiving a lecture on how to conduct ourselves in front of the press when we lost.

Simone just shrugged. Now that our meeting was over, her thoughts had clearly moved on.

"Go," she said, making shooing motions with her hand. "Tell Doug I'll see him downstairs."

Faith and I left the office and headed in the direction of the conference room. Walking down the hall, my feet were dragging. Faith kept scampering on ahead, then having to stop and wait for me to catch up.

The truth was, now that my association with Champions Dog Food was about to come to an end, I wanted more time. As soon as the contest winner had been announced, the finalists would disperse and the committee members would move on to new tasks. And I'd be out of excuses for hanging around and asking questions. I might be forced to concede that I hadn't been able to figure out who killed Larry Kim.

Faith and I hadn't gone very far when I heard the door to Simone's office open behind us. I paused and took a peek back.

Though nearly everyone on the third floor was gathering by the elevator to head down to the lobby, the PR director was striding purposefully in the other direction. As I watched, she reached the door to the fire stairs, shoved it open, and ducked inside.

Briefly, I gazed back in the direction of the conference room. The other finalists were probably already there with Doug. No doubt they were waiting for me and Faith to show up.

Duty warred with curiosity. Sad to say, it was a brief battle. I wanted to know where Simone was in such a hurry to get to and there was only one way to find out.

"What the heck," I said to Faith, chucking her under the chin and alerting her to the fact that we were about to go the other way. "It's not like we were going to win anyway."

We reached the stairwell just in time to hear the heavy fire door shut on the landing above us. Together, Faith and I went running up the steps to the fourth floor. I eased the door open slowly.

Simone's heels were beating a brisk tattoo on the shiny floor. Thankfully, they covered any noise I might have made. I watched Simone detour right when she reached Chris's office. She shoved open the door and marched inside without knocking. Faith and I slipped out of the stairwell and followed.

The fourth floor, like the one below, was now mostly deserted. The majority of the Champions employees were down in the lobby, waiting to share in the excitement of the press conference and the big announcement. Nobody noticed what Faith and I were doing as we crept quietly along the corridor.

I'd expected that we would have to be right beside the doorway to hear what was going on, but Simone must have been counting on nobody being around. Either that, or she was simply too angry to moderate her voice. Even though we were still two doors away, I was able to hear the first words she addressed to Chris.

"Are you crazy? What the hell did you think you were doing?"

"Calm down, okay?" Chris's voice was pitched much lower than Simone's, but it didn't matter. Faith and I were close enough now. I could hear just fine. "What's the matter? What's going on?"

"I'll tell you what's going on," she snapped. "The deal we made is off!"

"No, it's not. You can't do that."

"I can and I am."

"It's too late," Chris said. He sounded triumphant. "The announcement's about to be made."

"There's still time. Doug won't start the press conference until I get there. All I have to do is pull him aside and tell him I've reconsidered."

"You'll just end up making yourself look like an idiot. You already told him you thought MacDuff should win."

What? I shrank back, shocked. Where had *that* come from? Wasn't Simone supposed to be Yoda's most ardent supporter?

"Only because you blackmailed me into changing my vote when Lisa went AWOL," said Simone.

"Hey man, Larry was dead and she was gone. Nobody had any idea when she was coming back. You've got a lot of influence around here, but even you couldn't convince Doug to name a missing finalist as the winner."

I leaned forward again, hand cupped around Faith's muzzle to ensure her silence. This was getting more interesting by the moment. Simone had thought she was doing the right thing by keeping Lisa's whereabouts a secret and it looked as though it had ended up costing them both.

"Besides," Chris countered. "Blackmail is a pretty strong word coming from someone who stole my idea and passed it off as her own."

"I told you at the time that that was an accident. It wasn't supposed to happen. Doug and I were going through a rough patch when you approached me with the proposal for the contest. I was going to give you credit when I took the idea to him. Honestly, I was. But next thing I knew he was calling me clever and innovative—"

"Words he would have applied to me, if he'd known the truth."

I maneuvered until I could see Simone through

the crack between the door and the jamb. She had her arms crossed over her chest.

"You could have told him," she said.

"Yeah, right. Like he'd have taken my word over yours. Especially after you'd already gotten to him first."

"You know what they say about the early bird . . ."

"Oh, stuff it," Chris said impatiently. "This discussion is over. Nothing is changing. We're both going downstairs to stand and smile for the press while Doug announces that MacDuff is the very deserving winner of the 'All Dogs Are Champions' contest."

"No way," Simone replied. "Trust me, that is not happening. Now that I've been made privy to *additional information,* I'm going back to my original plan, and you won't dare to try and stop me."

"What additional information?"

"Are you sure you want me to spell this out for you, Chris? Because you don't come off looking very good. You were the one who was in the stairwell with Larry Kim when he fell, weren't you?"

Chris shook his head in denial, but Simone ignored him and kept speaking. "I guess you thought that if you could eliminate Yoda, MacDuff would have a clear path to winning the contest. Is that why you pushed Larry down the stairs? Were you hoping to injure Yoda so badly that she couldn't continue to compete? You ended up with more than you bargained for, didn't you?"

The phone on Chris's desk rang. Looking murderously at Simone, he reached over and picked up the receiver.

"I'm on my way," he said. "Yes, she's here, too. We'll be coming right down." There was a pause, then he added, "No I haven't seen Faith or Melanie. I don't know where they are."

"They went to the conference room," Simone said. "That was at least ten minutes ago."

"No, we didn't."

Faith by my side, I stepped through the doorway. I've never been very good at skulking around, and besides, I wanted to hear Chris's reply, too. Simone might let him get away without answering her questions, but I wasn't about to.

"Oh, fu—" Chris looked up. Then he turned back to the phone and said, "No, nothing's wrong. Melanie's just shown up. We're all on our way."

"How much did you hear?" Simone asked.

Chris hung up the phone and walked out from behind his desk.

"Everything. Except the answer to your last question."

Chris turned his back on Simone and looked at me. "Seriously. You didn't believe all that garbage she was saying, did you?"

"Most of it."

"You think *I* killed Larry Kim?"

"Someone did. Why not you?"

"What would I have stood to gain?"

"I don't know yet. But I do know that you really wanted MacDuff to win the contest. Just like Simone really wanted Yoda to win. Maybe you had some sort of deal going with Dorothy."

"Goddamn deals." Chris snorted out an exasperated sigh. "I've heard enough of that crap to last me a lifetime. I'll tell you what the *deal* was that I had going with Dorothy. If I could get MacDuff to win the contest, my mother would get off my back. How's that for an incentive?"

"Your mother?" Simone looked just as puzzled as I felt. "What does she have to do with anything?"

"Dorothy Foyle is my aunt. She's my mother's dotty sister, excuse the pun. When she was busy traveling all over the place showing MacDuff, my parents never saw her, which suited them just fine. Then MacDuff got old and got retired and suddenly Dorothy had time on her hands. For the past several months she's been calling every day, dropping by my parents' house to chat, and basically driving my mother nuts. And when my mother's unhappy, everyone else around her had better watch out."

Every once in a while it was nice to be reminded that I wasn't the only one with problem relatives.

"Next thing I know, Dorothy comes up with this big plan. Or maybe it was my mother's plan. Who even cares anymore?" Chris reached up and raked his fingers back through the sparse hair at his crown. His frustration with his family was so palpable that I couldn't help but feel sorry for him.

"Wouldn't it be nice if MacDuff could be on television? Wouldn't that be a wonderful outlet for his talents instead of just letting them go to waste? As if a dog his age has any ambition left. For Pete's sake, he's nearly fifty in human years. Let's see who we know who has connections . . . What about Chris? Surely he could be useful somehow. He works for a major dog food company . . ."

Chris was rambling on, almost talking to himself now. Simone was staring pointedly at her watch. She was probably wondering how much longer Doug could continue to hold up the press conference. As for me, I was waiting for Chris to get to the point.

"So my aunt and my mother sit me down at the kitchen table and feed me cake and tell me all about this supposedly brilliant idea they've cooked up between them to hold a contest—"

"Wait a minute!" Simone cried. "You mean you had the nerve to put me through the wringer for taking credit for your idea and it wasn't even yours to begin with?"

"Yeah, something like that." Chris's watery blue eyes blinked behind his wire-rimmed glasses. "Ironic, huh?"

Sheesh, I thought. These two deserved each other.

"And then what?" I asked impatiently.

"And then," Chris said, "Simone grabbed the idea for the contest and ran with it. Next thing I know, not only was I not getting any credit but Dorothy and MacDuff weren't winning either. Talk about your basic lose-lose situation."

"And that was worth committing murder over?"

"How many times do I have to tell you? I'm not a murderer and I didn't kill anyone. If I'd thought that was a plausible way out, don't you think it would have occurred to me that it was simpler to fix the problem at the source and just strangle my Aunt Dorothy? The only thing I did was talk to Larry and try to make another deal."

My head was spinning from all these backroom machinations. Were Faith and I the only ones who hadn't been approached? I wondered. I supposed that said something, probably unflattering, about how seriously we'd been taken as contestants.

"Fine," Simone snapped. "We'll have to finish this later. We're holding everything up downstairs. Let's go."

The four of us filed out of the office. Later, my
ass, I thought. We could all walk and talk at the
same time. Simone and Chris headed for the elevator. Faith and I followed. I wasn't about to let the
two of them out of my sight.

"So you didn't intend to kill Larry," I said to
Chris. "You only wanted to make a deal with him."

"That's what I'm trying to tell you. By that time,
I'd pretty much figured out that Simone was back-
ing Yoda because Larry and Lisa needed the money
from the advertising contract. Well, Dorothy didn't
care about the money. What she wanted was the
fame and the excitement. The chance to see Mac-
Duff back in the spotlight again. So after the opening reception, I pulled Larry aside—"

"In the stairwell," I said, just to make sure that I
was keeping things straight.

"Right. It's not like I wanted anyone to overhear
what I was saying. I told him that since the fix had
already been put in once, if he'd agree to work
with me, I was sure we could make a mutually ben-
eficial business arrangement. All he had to do was
withdraw Yoda from the contest and let MacDuff
win and I'd make sure that he and Lisa got the
money they needed."

"Oh . . . my . . . God," Simone said softly as the
elevator doors opened and the four of us stepped
inside.

Chris hit the button that would take us to the
lobby. "What's the matter? It's not as if I was doing
anything worse than what you'd already done
yourself."

"You idiot!' she said. "Larry didn't know about
the arrangement I'd made with Lisa. He wasn't
supposed to know anything about that. The Kims

didn't need money, Lisa did. She was going to use it to buy her freedom. From him."

Chris gulped. "I guess that explains his reaction."

"Which was?"

So help me, I half-expected him to say that Larry Kim had thrown *himself* down the steps. At that point, I was almost ready to believe it.

"He turned kind of pale and got this funny look on his face like someone had just punched him in the gut. I remember wondering what he was so upset about. He'd already made one deal, so it wasn't like he could say he didn't know how the game was played."

"And then?" I asked.

"And then nothing," said Chris. "Larry reached out and pushed me away from him, like he found me repulsive or something. So I left. Last time I saw him, he was standing in the stairwell, holding Yoda and staring off into space. I don't have any idea what happened after that."

31

Well, *somebody* had to know, I thought, as the elevator bumped to a gentle stop and the doors whooshed open.

I supposed I should have been prepared for the scene before us, but my mind had been on other matters. It was chaos. Bright lights seared my eyes. My ears were assaulted by a cacophony of sound. Cables snaked across the floor. People were everywhere.

Faith took one look at all the commotion and pressed up hard against my thigh. As the two of us stood and stared, I dropped a hand down to steady her. Between the Champions employees and news teams from several local stations, the press conference had drawn a huge crowd. Simone must have been superb at her job to have garnered coverage like this.

Chris and Simone both recovered faster than I did. They moved past me into the lobby and immediately began to work the crowd. Meanwhile

Faith and I had to scramble to beat the closing elevator doors.

"Where have you been?" Doug demanded, materializing at my side. He wrapped his fingers around my upper arm and closed them like a vise, as if he was afraid Faith and I might disappear again if he didn't hold on to us.

"I was upstairs with Chris and Simone. We were having a very enlightening discussion."

Doug steered me toward an alcove on the side of the lobby. The other four finalists were waiting there, bunched together in a tight little group. Nervousness emanated from them like a palpable wave.

Doug growled under his breath. He was clearly not amused by my excuse. "Now is not the time for enlightenment."

"On the contrary, it may be the only time. Or the last chance we're going to get."

"For what?"

"To figure out who murdered Larry Kim."

We'd almost reached the alcove. Abruptly Doug stopped walking. Since he was still holding my arm, I got yanked to a halt, too.

"That's not why we're here."

"It should be."

"What is the matter with you?" He jerked his hand back and forth, giving me a rude little shake. "Don't you understand what's at stake here? This is a huge PR opportunity for everyone involved. Champions Dog Food is about to award someone an advertising contract worth one hundred thousand dollars. Think about that for a minute. And think about what you might be jeopardizing if you continue on with this crazy behavior."

"I have thought about it." I stepped away and

pulled my arm free. I'd had just about enough of
Doug's bullying. "And I'm not the one who's acting crazy. Nor am I jeopardizing anything, because
I already know what my chances are of winning
this contest. They're zero, nada, zip. And you know
how I know that? Because the outcome was fixed
from the start."

Somebody gasped. I didn't see who it was, but
the small sound was enough to let me know that
the other contestants were listening to our conversation.

Ben stepped forward from the group. Brando
was at his side. "What are you talking about?"

"Nothing," Doug said quickly. "Melanie doesn't
know what she's saying."

"I know exactly what I'm saying. This contest is a
sham, it has been all along." I turned and addressed the other finalists. "All the events we've attended, the competitions we've participated in, they
were just a waste of time. Chow Down's spokesdog
was hand-picked before the other four of us were
even selected to be finalists."

Dorothy looked shocked. Lisa was shaking her
head vehemently. Allison and Bill were paying
attention though.

"Who is it?" asked Allison. "Who's the winner?"

"Good God!" Doug roared. "You're about to
ruin everything."

His hand raised. For a moment I wasn't sure
whether Doug meant to hit me or clap his palm
over my mouth to shut me up. It all happened so
fast that I didn't have time to move to defend myself.

It turned out that I didn't have to. Ever attuned

to the mood of the humans around her, Faith took care of that for me.

As Doug's hand came up, she leapt toward it. Her teeth closed over his wrist and dragged his arm back down. Only when his hand was back at his side did she let go. The Poodle's dark eyes fastened intently on his and their message was clear. *Don't try that again.*

The other finalists were all dog people. They didn't even blink when Faith leapt to my defense. Besides, they had bigger things to worry about.

"The contest couldn't have been decided that early," said Ben. "Cindy told me just last week that she'd been able to sway a couple of votes in my direction."

"Cindy wanted to date a television star," I said. "She'd have said anything she thought would keep you happy."

"*You* were seeing Cindy?" asked Bill.

"What of it?" Ben turned on the other man. "It's not like the rest of you wouldn't have used something to your advantage if you could. Take Dorothy, for instance. She sold Chris Hovick a Scottie puppy. His pet dog is related to MacDuff."

I remembered that Ben had been sitting near Dorothy and me that day on the bus. He must have been eavesdropping on our conversation.

"They're not the only ones that are related," I said. "Dorothy is Chris's aunt."

Doug spun around to face her. "Is that true?"

Dorothy glared at me, then reluctantly nodded.

"That's against the rules," said Lisa.

"Don't tell me about rules," Dorothy snapped. "I should have been the one to make up the rules.

After all, I'm the one who came up with the idea for the contest in the first place."

"No, you didn't." Doug sounded a little desperate. He looked like a man who knew he was losing control of a situation and had no idea how to regain order. "The contest was Simone's idea."

"That's what Simone told you," I said. "But she stole the idea from Chris and passed it off as her own."

Doug shook his head. "Why would she do something like that?"

"Because she needed a way to channel money to her old friend, Lisa. I think you know about that part—"

"I knew it would be about the money," Bill broke in. "It always is, isn't it? Well, if that's the deciding factor, we need money, too."

Suddenly everyone was speaking at once.

"Like I don't?" said Ben. "If we're talking about need—"

Lisa looked across at the Reddings. The couple was standing side by side with Ginger between them. "At least you two have each other," she said softly. "You have no idea how important that is."

"Wait!" Dorothy cried. "Hold the phone. What did you mean"—this was addressed to me—"when you said Doug knew about Simone needing to get money to Lisa?"

"Lisa wanted to leave Larry," I said. "The contest was set up to give her the means to do so."

"No, you have it all wrong," Dorothy replied. "The contest was supposed to put MacDuff on television."

"Cindy told me the contest would revive my career," said Ben.

Nobody paid any attention to him.

"Chris was trying to do what you wanted," I told Dorothy, "but he lost control of the process. When he realized that the prize that was supposed to go to MacDuff would be going to Yoda instead, he tried to make a deal. He talked to Larry Kim in the stairwell after the opening reception. He offered him money to withdraw his dog from the contest."

"Larry was a very proud man," said Lisa. "He would have been hugely insulted by such an offer. He would never have withdrawn for money. He never backed down from anything where he felt that his honor was at stake."

And there it was, I thought, the answer I'd been looking for. Right that moment, I knew who the other person in the stairwell had been.

"It was you, wasn't it?" I said to Lisa. "Larry would never have voluntarily ended your marriage. That was why you needed the money. It was the only way you could escape."

"Everything would have been all right." She shifted her eyes downward, gazing at the little Yorkie she held cradled in her arms. "Not easy, but I would have been able to make things work. Then Chris got in the middle and messed it all up."

"Chris was trying to help," I said. "He offered Larry money he thought the two of you needed."

"Larry was outraged," said Lisa. "We didn't need any money and he was greatly offended. He felt as though someone had offered him a handout. But then he stopped and began to think about it. He began to wonder what I might need the money for."

"You were with him in the stairwell after Chris

left," I said. "Your voice is so soft, that's why I only heard one person arguing."

"Larry had sent me outside to cool off the car but I came back in to see what was keeping him. I must have entered the stairwell on the third floor as Chris was leaving on the fourth. By then the damage was already done. Larry had realized that the money was meant for me. He wouldn't listen to reason. No matter what I said, it didn't make any difference. He told me that unless I changed my mind he would make me very, very sorry. He said I would never see Yoda again."

While Lisa and I had been speaking, everyone else was, too. Clustered around us, the other finalists had continued to bicker among themselves. Doug was alternately playing referee and trying unsuccessfully to keep them quiet.

Now, however, the audience in the lobby was primed and waiting for our appearance. Simone came striding over to see what was causing the delay.

The other contestants saw her coming. One by one they fell silent. Only Lisa and I continued to speak.

"You pushed Larry down the steps, didn't you?" I said into the sudden silence.

Lisa nodded imperceptibly. She clutched Yoda tightly to her chest. "He wouldn't listen. He never listened. Larry made me so mad that I reached out and shoved him. One of us had to go. If he wouldn't let it be me, then it had to be him."

A quick thinking reporter from a local affiliate caught the confession on tape. When it aired that evening, the station was inundated with phone calls. At least half of them came from lawyers offering to take Lisa's case and represent her in court.

Last I heard, she'd chosen a sympathetic woman attorney who was planning to plead temporary insanity—a defense that probably could have been applied to just about everyone who'd gotten involved in the Chow Down contest. I got that news from Bertie, who had delivered ten Yorkies to Lisa's doorstep as soon as the woman was released on bail. I don't think the board bill's been paid yet. I doubt that Bertie's holding her breath.

After all the commotion finally died down, Ginger was named winner of the contest and the new spokesdog for Chow Down. Coming on the heels of a murderer's confession, the announcement seemed rather anticlimactic. But the Reddings were thrilled and I was delighted for them. Mostly I think I was just relieved that Faith's and my part in the whole circus was finally over.

A few days after the press conference, Terry threw a birthday party for Crawford. He wouldn't tell any of us which birthday we were celebrating, but Davey pointed out that there were enough candles on the triple-layer chocolate cake to send up smoke signals.

Crawford was looking well. He was delighted to be the man of the hour, surrounded by family and friends. Shortly after we arrived, he sought me out. Davey had gone off to toss a ball with some other kids his age; Sam was helping Terry at the grill.

Crawford pulled me aside and said, "I hear you've been asking about me."

I knew how much he valued his privacy. I hoped

he hadn't been offended by my snooping. "I was worried about you," I said. "I wanted to help."

"You *always* want to help. Trouble is, sometimes people would rather handle things on their own." The words sounded harsh, but his smile softened them. Crawford reached out and patted my arm awkwardly. "I appreciate the concern."

"Is everything okay?"

"Getting better all the time, now that the doctors know what to treat." He shook his head. "Lyme Disease. Living in Connecticut, you'd think they'd have come up with that idea sooner. But at my age they test for everything else in the book first. And the symptoms can seem pretty dire when you don't have any idea what's causing them."

Amen to that, I thought. Just about everyone I knew had had a bout with Lyme Disease. The diagnosis came as a relief. With proper treatment, chances were that Crawford would be back to normal shortly.

"The medication's helping?" I asked.

"Doing its job, just like it's supposed to, so you can stop worrying now."

"I'm a mother. We never stop worrying."

"Speaking of which"—Crawford drew back and looked me up and down—"rumor has it, you might be about ready to share some news on that front."

He'd caught me by surprise. "What rumor? Who have you been talking to?"

"Never you mind," Crawford said with a chuckle. "But now you know what it feels like to have other people messing around in your business for a change."

I wondered who'd let the cat out of the bag.

Sam and I had found out for sure only the day before. We'd told Davey, who'd leaped and yelled and twirled around the kitchen.

Davey was supposed to be keeping the news a secret for the time being. We didn't want to make an announcement until the pregnancy was further along. But now I was betting that Davey had emailed Aunt Peg. No wonder she'd been casting me such fond looks all afternoon.

"I hope it's true, Melanie," Crawford said. "You look happy."

"I *am* happy. Sometimes I think I must have landed in the middle of a fairy tale. I look around and realize I have everything I ever wanted."

"Not too many people can say that."

"Only the really lucky ones," I said.

I looped an arm around Crawford's shoulders and we strolled back to join the party.

When her Aunt Peg lands a gig as judge at a Kentucky dog show, Melanie Travis welcomes the opportunity for a road trip. Too bad a killer has planned a deadly detour . . .

For a dog lover like Melanie, the opportunity to attend the Kentuckiana Dog Show Cluster is not to be missed. Fortunately, the timing coincides with her spring break from teaching, so she heads for central Kentucky with her sister-in-law Bertie and Aunt Peg, who's accepted a week-long judging assignment. Once there, Aunt Peg reconnects with an old friend, Ellie Gates Wanamaker, a former Standard Poodle exhibitor and a member of a well-heeled Kentucky family. Miss Ellie has been out of the dog show world for more than a decade, but when Melanie invites her to spectate at the Louisville Kennel Club dog show, she's eager to accompany her.

Miss Ellie's presence at the expo center, however, provokes mixed reactions from exhibitors she hasn't seen in years, including some outright animosity. The following day Melanie learns that Miss Ellie has suffered a fatal accident while exercising her dogs. Aunt Peg, however, suspects foul play. Wishing to avoid any scandal, Miss Ellie's pedigreed family prefers to let sleeping dogs lie, but as Melanie begins to sniff around, she discovers Miss Ellie had many secrets, both in the dog show world and amongst her Kentucky kin . . .

1

I was moving fast.

The ground below me was little more than a blur. Scenery flew by with astonishing speed. I was running. . . .

No, not running . . . riding. I was on the back of a horse. I could feel the smooth motion of the muscular body beneath me. I could hear the creak of the leather saddle, and the steady, rhythmic sound of hoofbeats striking the turf.

Their pounding cadence pulsed through me. It drew me in and made me one with the motion. It propelled me onward, as if this heady race was the only thing in the world that mattered.

Where was I? I wondered. What was happening? Was I racing toward something—or was I running away?

I had no answers. All I knew was that I could feel the sharp bite of the wind on my face and a sensation of freedom humming deep inside my bones.

The feeling was heavenly.

It was addictive.

One thing I was sure of—I wanted more.

All at once a pale mist rose on the path ahead of us. Its silvery tendrils lifted and swirled, obscuring all view of what was to come. I found myself leaning forward in the saddle. I gazed in vain between the tips of two dark, pointed ears.

I could see nothing. The vista before me was still blank . . . and suddenly forbidding. In the space of a second, the breakneck speed at which we were traveling lost its appeal.

Frantically I reached for reins, but couldn't find them. My fingers felt thick and stiff. Useless. I screamed into the wind. I told the horse to stop but my words had no effect.

Then the mists shifted and drew apart and I saw that behind them lay only darkness. A void of nothingness. It looked as though my steed and I were racing toward the edge of the world.

Abruptly my stomach plummeted as the ground disappeared from beneath us. My hands flew upward, groping in the air, grasping desperately for purchase that wasn't there. My heart pounded with the sudden knowledge that I couldn't save myself. And then I was falling, helpless as I plunged downward and tumbled into the unknown below . . .

I awoke with a gasp and bolted upright in bed.

My heart was beating wildly in my chest. Mouth open, I was desperate for air. Fire clawed at my lungs. My insides still churned with the sensation of falling. Though my eyes were open wide I couldn't see a thing. Everything around me was black: inky and impenetrable.

I still had no idea where I was.

Clutching the bedcovers in frantic fingers, I

swiveled my head from side to side. A moment later, my gaze alighted on the amber numbers of the bedside clock. Three-oh-two, it read.

Slowly my mind processed the number. With effort I made the connection to what it meant. Compared to my recent speed, I felt dull and sluggish as I worked to reorient myself. I gulped in a breath of cool air and shifted my shoulders, trying to ease their tension.

There was no horse. There was no wind. There was no yawning crater waiting to suck me down into its gruesome depths.

I'd been having a nightmare. That was all.

I gazed around again. My eyes had adjusted to the darkness now. I could see the familiar bedroom surrounding me. I could feel the slight dip in the mattress caused by the weight of my husband, Sam, who was sound asleep beside me.

Relief washed though me and I blew out a long breath. I was safe. I was home in my own house, with my husband, my two sons, and my six dogs.

I heard a soft creak and turned to see the bedroom door nudged slightly ajar by a long black muzzle. My Standard Poodle, Faith, the dog who understood everything about me and who knew my thoughts almost before I did, was standing silently in the doorway.

Faith always sleeps on my older son, Davey's, bed. But now in the middle of the night, something had called her to me. The big Poodle was so attuned to my emotions that she had sensed something was amiss. As I glanced in her direction, Faith tipped her head to one side inquiringly. Even in the murky darkness, I could see the gentle gleam in her eye.

As our gazes met, Faith padded silently across the room. She stepped beside the bed and pressed her nose into my hand, offering her own special brand of comfort. As the Poodle's warm breath filled my palm, I finally felt my heart rate begin to slow. I cupped Faith's muzzle between my fingers and rubbed my thumb over her lips and cheek.

"It's all right, sweetie," I said softly. "You can go back to sleep."

Faith acknowledged the comment with a low swish of her tail but she didn't look convinced.

"Really," I told her. "Everything is fine. It was just a dream."

Faith lifted one front paw delicately and placed it on the bed in silent inquiry. I glanced over my shoulder at Sam. Covers pulled up to his chin, head burrowed deep in his pillow, he was too deeply asleep to realize that his sleeping arrangement was about to become even cozier.

I scootched over toward Sam and patted the space beside me. "Come on up," I whispered. "There's plenty of room."

Faith leapt up lightly. She aligned her body next to mine, lay down on the quilt, and pressed in close. As I settled down beside her, the Poodle's warmth enveloped me.

I closed my eyes and finally slept.

"I had the strangest dream last night," I said the next evening.

The comment was delivered to a full house. It was our son Kevin's third birthday. In honor of the occasion, I had invited some of our relatives to dinner.

In most families a gathering like that would lead to convivial celebration. Not mine, however. My relatives are equally as likely to set the house ablaze as they are to coexist in peace. There's nothing boring about the extended Travis/Turnbull clan, especially when my provocative and ever-entertaining Aunt Peg is part of the assembly.

So far we'd managed to make our way through most of the meal without incident. Minutes earlier, Kevin's birthday cake, alight with festive candles, had been presented to the room with great fanfare. Kev had shrieked and clapped his hands, bouncing up and down in his seat with glee when it appeared.

My younger son was a little hazy about what the concept of three years meant, but he knew all about chocolate cake. When I set the dessert down in front of him, Kev's first impulse was to reach for it with both hands. Luckily his older brother, Davey—a gangly twelve-year-old, teetering on the cusp between childhood and adolescence—was there to quickly intercede. Cupping Kevin's small hands in his own much larger ones, Davey helped his little brother blow out the candles.

The layer cake was cut and served and everyone dug in happily. If I were to be honest I would admit that most of the evening's success was undoubtedly due to Sam's calming influence. When it comes to my relatives, my husband is smart enough and affable enough not to sweat the small stuff. Things that cause me to roll my eyes and rail about the general state of insanity just make him shrug his shoulders and chuckle under his breath.

Lucky man. I wish I knew how he did it.

Sam was seated at the head of the table. On his

right was my Aunt Peg. Now in the middle of her seventh decade, Margaret Turnbull is living proof that age is merely a state of mind. The woman possesses more than enough energy, ambition, and wit to run circles around me effortlessly. Unfortunately it's a circumstance she's not above exploiting to further her own ends. On the other hand, if it weren't for Aunt Peg I would never have discovered the intriguing appeal of the dog show world. Nor would I have Faith, or the other five Standard Poodles that currently grace and enrich our lives.

Completing the group seated around the table was my younger brother, Frank, and his family. For years Frank had been the feckless, thoughtless bane of my existence. But now in his thirties, my little brother was finally grown up and married to one of my best friends, Bertie Kennedy. Their young daughter, Maggie, was seated between them. The child was keeping a beady eye on Kevin, seemingly determined to ensure that the birthday boy didn't get so much as a smidge more cake than she did.

Any minute now the sugar high was going to kick in, I thought as I gazed around the room. And then we'd really be off to the races.

And just like that I remembered my dream.

"I had the strangest dream last night," I said.

"Oh?" Aunt Peg looked up from her cake. "I read a book about that."

"About dreams?" Bertie asked. Her dark green eyes twinkled with amusement. "Or strange things?"

"Dreams, of course. Did you know that they're the way your subconscious works through problems while you're asleep?" Peg peered at me across the table. "Do you have any problems that need working out?"

She would ask that. There's nothing Aunt Peg enjoys more than involving herself in other people's troubles.

"Not that I'm aware of," I replied. "And certainly none that involve a horse."

"A *horse?*" Sam sounded surprised. I couldn't blame him. I felt the same way.

From across the table, Aunt Peg glanced at me sharply. I wondered what that look meant.

"That was what was so odd about it," I said. "In the dream, I was riding a horse. I've never done that in my life. The horse was galloping, we were racing like the wind. It's amazing how real it all felt."

"Real indeed," Aunt Peg muttered under her breath. I waited for her to continue but instead she resumed eating. Nothing could distract Aunt Peg from cake for long.

"Where were you going?" Bertie asked curiously.

"I have no idea. Everything ahead was foggy. I couldn't see a thing. We were just running."

"Maybe you were being chased by a zombie," said Frank.

"No." I laughed. "I don't think so."

"Was it a flying horse?" Kev asked. He has a book about Pegasus.

"No, just a regular horse. A very fast one."

"Maybe it was Willow!" said Davey.

Five years earlier, his father, my ex-husband, Bob, had surprised Davey with a palomino pony named Willow. Even though at the time Davey and I were living in a small house on a tiny plot of land, Bob apparently hadn't foreseen any difficulties with the care and management of Davey's new pet. As ponies went, Willow was lovely, but she hadn't lasted long.

"A pony," Kevin said with sudden interest. He had heard the story from his brother. "I want a pony!"

"Don't be silly." Aunt Peg sniffed. "Why would anyone want a pony when they can have Poodles instead?"

Poodles indeed. We not only had Standard Poodles, we were literally surrounded by them. And as Aunt Peg would have said, what was wrong with that?

Poodles come in three different sizes, but all share the same superb temperament. They're smart, they're endearing, and they have a superior sense of humor. Best of all, Poodles are people dogs. Wherever their family is, that's where they want to be.

Since the birthday celebration was taking place in the dining room, that meant that aside from the eight people sitting at the table, we also had six black Standard Poodles lying in attendance on the floor around us. Five of the six were even wearing party hats. The Poodles didn't look nearly as delighted about that development as Kevin did. In fact, judging by the expressions on their faces, they were feeling rather silly.

In my defense, the hats hadn't been my idea. Sam and Davey had snuck away and done the honors while I'd been busy greeting our arriving guests. But Aunt Peg's horrified gasp when she rounded the corner and saw the assembled crew—she being of the firm belief that Poodles are entirely too dignified to be treated frivolously—was gratifying enough to make me wish that I'd been a coconspirator.

All our Poodles are the Standard variety, the biggest of the three sizes. The top of Faith's head is nearly level with my waist, which positions her entire body within easy reach whenever she and I want to hold a conversation. That comes up more frequently than you might think.

Aunt Peg is Faith's breeder. Indeed she was connected in some way to nearly every dog in the room, her Cedar Crest line having set the standard for excellence in the Poodle breed since before I was born. A dedicated owner-handler in the show ring for decades, Peg had now scaled back her breeding and exhibiting commitments to concentrate on her burgeoning career as a dog show judge. As is true with many of Aunt Peg's decisions, that change in course has had the effect of keeping us all on our toes.

Faith's daughter, Eve, now lying beneath Kevin's chair in the hope there'd be spillage, was the second Standard Poodle I had brought to my marriage to Sam. He'd joined the union with two bitches of his own, Casey and Raven, both of whom were—like Faith and Eve—retired show champions. Sam was also the owner of GCH Cedar Crest Scimitar, also known as Tar.

Formerly an accomplished "specials dog," Tar had numerous Non-Sporting Group and Best in Show wins to his credit. Now, however, like the bitches, he was retired from the show ring and his long, plush, black coat had been clipped off. He, too, wore the attractive and easy-to-care-for sporting trim, with a short blanket of dense dark curls covering his entire body.

Tar was a love. He was the sweetest, most well-meaning dog of the entire pack. But he was also the only dumb Poodle I'd ever met. Somehow, no matter what was going on, Tar always managed to be a beat behind the rest. Punch lines, along with other of life's intricacies, simply went right over his head.

Our newest addition and the only dog currently "in hair" was Davey's Standard Poodle, Augie. Davey was responsible for Augie's care; and with Sam's help, he was also managing the young dog's show career. The collaboration was a successful one as Augie was already halfway toward the goal of accumulating the fifteen points he would need to be named a champion.

In deference to his long and oh-so-valuable top-knot hair, Augie was the only Poodle not wearing a party hat. He didn't appear to be upset about the omission. In fact, I was pretty sure I'd seen Augie sniff derisively in Tar's direction when he thought no one was looking.

Having heard Aunt Peg reference their breed, several dark heads lifted as the Poodle pack turned into the conversation at the table. Ears pricked as they waited to see what would happen next.

"Don't care," Kevin replied firmly to Aunt Peg. "Have Poodles. Want a pony."

"Ponies are too big," I told him mildly. "Besides, you already have fish."

Kev's aquarium, a cherished Christmas present, was visible through the doorway in the living room. My son refused to be mollified. He thrust out his lower lip and started to shake his head. Despite the date on the calendar, we clearly hadn't yet left the Terrible Twos behind just yet.

"And you have cake," I added.

"Cake," Kevin echoed. His expression brightened as Sam reached over and slid another sliver onto his plate. "I like cake!"

"Don't we all," Frank said heartily. He reached over and helped himself to a second piece. "That's why I came tonight."

"And also because it's Kevin's birthday." Bertie leveled a glare at her husband. "Right?"

"Sure," Frank agreed easily. "That, too."

"Has it occurred to you," Sam said to me, "that maybe the reason you were thinking about horses is because of Peg's judging assignment at the Kentuckiana Cluster next week?"

"No," I replied. That thought hadn't crossed my mind at all.

Aunt Peg's upcoming trip to Kentucky had nothing to do with me. Bertie, who was a professional handler, was also making the trip to the Midwest. With four back-to-back dog shows scheduled to take place in Louisville, and several clients whose dogs were looking for majors, she had entered a sizeable string to show. But with spring break starting in just two days—two whole weeks of vacation from my job as a special needs tutor at private Howard Academy—I was looking forward to nothing more strenuous than sleeping late and reading several good books.

"Speaking of which," said Aunt Peg, "while we're on the subject, I have an announcement to make. . . ." She paused and looked around, waiting until she had our full attention.

"Which subject is that?" asked Sam. "Kentucky?"

"Judging," Bertie guessed.

"Cake," Frank contributed, speaking with his mouth full.

"Fish!" cried Kevin.

"Horses?" I teased.

"Bingo!" Aunt Peg turned and favored me with a small nod.

Horses? That was a surprise.

Clearly I wasn't the only one who felt that way. The whole table fell silent with nervous anticipation. With Aunt Peg, you never knew which way the dice were going to roll. She might have wonderful news or it could be something truly alarming. I'd long since resigned myself to the fact that life with Aunt Peg meant existing in a semiperpetual state of suspense.

"As it turns out, my trip to Kentucky has come along at a rather fortuitous time," she informed us.

"Why is that?" I asked.

"I have an asset in central Kentucky that I need to take a closer look at." Aunt Peg beamed at us all happily. "You are looking at the new owner of a Thoroughbred racehorse."